...ian's mouth curled disdainfully. ...try to look a little happier, Grace, ...en I am about to ask your guardians ...your hand in marriage.'

...ce stared at him dazedly, sure that she could ...have heard him correctly. He could not ...ously think—could not imagine—

...t I have no wish to marry you!'

...sh?' He arched scathing brows. 'Wishes, ...ce, either yours or my own, do not enter ...the situation we now find ourselves in,' he ...ured her scornfully. 'We have broken the ...written law of Society.'

...ce was well aware that she should not have ...wed this man the liberty of kissing her—and ...no idea how she was going to face her aunt ...in—but surely that did not mean they had to ...ually marry each other?

The Notorious St Claires

launched with
THE DUKE'S CINDERELLA BRIDE

Look out for Carole's next instalment
in her mini-series.
Coming soon
in Mills & Boon® Historical Romance™

Meanwhile, you can read Carole's latest
Modern™ Romance

THE VIRGIN SECRETARY'S IMPOSSIBLE BOSS

part of the *International Billionaires* collection,
out next month!

THE RAKE'S
WICKED PROPOSAL

Carole Mortimer

MILLS & BOON

First published in Great Britain 2009
Harlequin Mills & Boon Limited,
Eton House, 18-24 Paradise Road, Richmond, Surrey TW9 1SR

© Carole Mortimer 2009

ISBN: 978 0 263 86792 3

Set in Times Roman 10½ on 12½ pt
04-0809-70193

Harlequin Mills & Boon policy is to use papers that are natural, renewable and recyclable products and made from wood grown in sustainable forests. The logging and manufacturing process conform to the legal environmental regulations of the country of origin.

Printed and bound in Spain
by Litografia Rosés, S.A., Barcelona

THE RAKE'S
WICKED PROPOSAL

Carole Mortimer was born in England, the youngest of three children. She began writing in 1978, and has now published over one hundred and forty books with Harlequin Mills & Boon. Carole has four sons, Matthew, Joshua, Timothy and Peter, and a bearded collie called Merlyn. She says, 'I'm happily married to Peter senior; we're best friends as well as lovers, which is probably the best recipe for a successful relationship. We live in a lovely part of England.'

Chapter One

'Good gad! Is that you, St Claire?'

Lucian St Claire, having entered the coaching inn only seconds earlier, and feeling much relieved to at last be out of the relentless rain he had suffered for the last two hours, felt that relief replaced by a sinking dread as he easily recognised the boomingly jovial voice of the Duke of Carlyne.

'It is you!' The Duke strode forcefully down the hallway of the inn to where Lucian stood, removing his extremely wet greatcoat, a smile of pleasure lighting the older man's features as he thrust a hand out in greeting. 'Well met, m'boy!'

'Your Grace,' Lucian murmured softly, giving an abrupt inclination of his head even as he shook the proffered hand, his gaze dark and unreadable.

Deliberately so. He and the Duke had not met for almost two years, but Lucian knew that very shortly the Duke would remember the circumstances of that meeting, and the pleasure would fade from the older man's face. It was a face that had aged considerably in the intervening years, making the Duke appear much older than the late fifties Lucian knew him to be.

Ah, there it was, Lucian recognised heavily. The frown. The flicker of pained remembrance in the eyes. Quickly followed by a forced return of the other man's earlier pleasure in this chance meeting.

Lucian had suffered many such encounters since he had resigned his commission from the army almost two years ago. Too many. And neither time nor frequency had dulled the feeling of guilt he suffered at each such meeting.

For Lucian had survived five years in the army, only resigning his commission after that last bloody battle at Waterloo. A battle that had ensued after many Englishmen and women had thought Napoleon finished, routed, and incarcerated on the Isle of Elba. Only to have him escape that island to rouse his soldiers anew, renewing hostilities in a battle that had robbed Lucian of far too many brothers-in-arms. Most especially three fellow officers, his closest friends.

Including Simon Wynter, Marquess of Richfield, the Duke of Carlyne's beloved only son and heir…

Lucian forced down the memories of his unhappy journey almost two years ago to the Duke's estate in Worcestershire, where he had felt compelled to go in order to offer the Duke and Duchess his condolences on Simon's death.

He had made similar journeys to several of the families of his slain friends, each of them harder than the last as, once his condolences had been expressed a certain look of resentment appeared on the faces of those families at their realisation that he, Major Lord Lucian St Claire, the second of the three sons of the deceased Ninth Duke of Stourbridge, had somehow survived whilst their beloved husband, son or brother had perished.

Lucian had felt no animosity towards those people for the emotion; how could he when he had so often been plagued with nightmares that made him, too, wish that he had not survived!

He decided it was time to take pity on the Duke of Carlyne's confused expression. 'You are visiting friends in the area, sir?'

'Just come from spending a few days at m'brother Darius's new estate in Malvern.' The older man's expression brightened as he thankfully grasped this innocuous subject.

'I trust he is well, sir?' It had been far less than two years since Lucian had last seen his friend Darius—only seven months or so. But a lot had happened to the other man in that time…

The Duke's face took on a suitable look of melancholy. 'Bearing up, don't you know.' A glint of rueful humour entered his eyes. 'Some would say perhaps too well!'

There was an answering glint in Lucian's gaze as it knowingly met the older man's.

Lord Darius Wynter, Lucian knew, had taken himself a wife seven months ago. A Miss Sophie Belling, from the north of England. Her father owned several mills in the area, and so had been easily able to provide a more than generous dowry for his only child. It had not been a love-match, on either side: Miss Belling had wanted a husband with a title, and Darius had required a wife with a fortune. Conveniently—for Darius, that was— Lady Sophie had been killed in a hunting accident only a month after the wedding, leaving Darius in possession of the fortune but not the wife.

Darius had always been a rogue and a gambler. His profligate lifestyle meant that he had quickly gone through the fortune left to him by his father when he reached his majority, thus necessitating a need in Darius to marry for money. He had even, Lucian recalled with some amusement, offered for Lucian's young sister Arabella at the end of last Season. An offer Hawk, their haughty older brother and the the Duke of Stourbridge, had felt absolutely no hesitation in refusing!

'A brief diversion, for we're on our way to London,' the Duke of Carlyne continued lightly. 'For the Season. Or at least we were.' He frowned. 'Damned coach has developed a rickety wheel. But I mustn't keep you standing about here when you are obviously wet and un-comfortable.' He frowned as Lucian's greatcoat chose that moment to drip water on to the wooden floor. 'You surely aren't travelling on horseback, St Claire?'

Lucian grimaced. 'It was very fine when I set out from London two days ago.' After days, often weeks, spent in the saddle during his years in the war against Napoleon, the rain of an English spring did not seem like such a hardship to Lucian.

'That's the English weather for you, hmm?' The older man smiled ruefully. 'On your way to visit your brother and the family in Gloucestershire, are you?'

'I am, sir.' Lucian gave an inclination of his dark head.

'Inferior inn, I'm afraid, St Claire,' the Duke confided dismissively. 'But 'm reliably informed that the food makes up for the lack of other comforts. Join us for dinner once you have procured a room and changed out of those wet clothes.'

'I do not have the necessary clothes with me for dining in company—'

'Nonsense,' the Duke dismissed warmly. 'Do say you will join us, St Claire. I have no doubt the ladies will be relieved to have more diverting company than a crusty old man and his boorish brother.'

Ladies? Plural? Which obviously meant there would be another lady other than the Duchess present. And the Duke's 'boorish brother' had to be Lord Francis Wynter, the youngest of the three Wynter brothers—a young man Lucian had known for many years, and found pompous and opinionated in the extreme.

But good manners dictated that Lucian could not continue to refuse the Duke of Carlyne's gracious invitation. 'In that case I would be honoured, Your Grace,' he accepted stiffly. 'If you will allow me but half an hour in which to make good my appearance…?'

'Certainly, m'boy.' The Duke now looked pleased by this turn of events. 'I am sure m'wife will want to hear all about your brother and his pretty new Duchess.'

Lucian was equally sure, as he strolled upstairs to his

bedchamber several minutes later, having procured a room and demanded hot water for a bath, that his brother Hawk would not appreciate having his beloved Jane discussed in a public coaching inn or anywhere else!

'I am sure you will find St Claire extremely divert-ing, m'dear,' Grace's uncle, the Duke of Carlyne, con-tinued to assure her with a merry twinkle in his eye. 'Most of the single ladies of the ton seem to find his broodingly dark good-looks extremely appealing. Several of the married ones, too—eh, m'dear?' He gave his Duchess a knowing smile.

'I am sure I do not know what you mean, Carlyne.' Grace's aunt, a plump matronly woman still deeply in love with her equally smitten husband, dismissed him frowningly. 'Neither is it a fitting subject on which to converse in front of a young lady of Grace's sensibili-ties.'

'Certainly not,' Lord Francis Wynter agreed haugh-tily. 'In fact, George, I am not sure that it was a wise decision on your part to invite St Claire to join us for dinner at all, with two ladies present.'

'Don't be such a pompous ass, Francis. Oh! I am sorry, m'dears.' The Duke at once apologised to his wife and Grace for his outspokenness. 'But St Claire's entitled to sow a few wild oats,' he added defensively. 'What you should remember, Francis, is that Major Lord Lucian St Claire is a hero of the Peninsula War—and most especially that last bloody battle at Waterloo.'

Grace saw the flush of resentment on Francis's cheeks at this reminder that, despite being a youngest son, he had chosen not to enter into that particular war. A war, moreover, in which his only nephew, Grace's cousin, had lost his young life.

Grace was not sure either, after her aunt's whispered comments about Lord Lucian St Claire, and her uncle's more risqué ones, that the man was a fitting dinner companion. But she would not for the world have said so. She was deeply resentful of the almost proprietorial air that Francis Wynter had lately started to adopt towards her and her welfare. Especially as she had given him no encouragement, by word or deed, to behave in such a familiar manner.

Besides, Lucian St Claire sounded exciting, at least, and after weeks of Francis's tedious attentions Grace welcomed even the thought of that diversion.

'He sounds very—interesting, Uncle George,' she assured him softly.

'The man may well be a war hero.' Francis persisted. 'But rumour has it that since his return to Society he has become something of a rake and a—'

'That is enough, Francis,' his brother cut in warningly. 'I will not have any of our heroic soldiers denigrated in this way.'

Grace watched as another tide of resentment flashed across Francis Wynter's youthfully handsome features.

There was no doubting he *was* very handsome—his hair a rich burnished gold, his eyes a pale blue, his shoulders wide, waist tapered, legs muscled, in black evening clothes and snowy white linen. If only his nature were as pleasant as those looks. But his lengthy visit to his brother and sister-in-law's estate in Worcestershire, following on from a much shorter one to his brother Darius's new home at Malvern—the two younger brothers did not get on—had allowed Grace to learn that, besides being extremely opinionated, Francis was also completely lacking in a sense of humour.

He was not her Uncle George's full brother, of course, which could explain at least some of the reasons Francis was so different from his good-humoured eldest brother. George Wynter, aged eight and fifty, had been born to the first wife of the previous Duke of Carlyne; Darius Wynter, aged one and thirty, had been born to the second wife, and Francis Wynter, aged five and twenty, to the third and final one.

Grace could only assume, having now met and become better acquainted with all three brothers, that they must all favour their individual mothers—because they certainly bore little resemblance to each other. George was the warm, amiable-natured one, Darius the consummate rake—and Francis, she was sorry to say, was a complete bore.

Although it was distinctly ungrateful of Grace to think so, when the Wynter family had all been so warm and welcoming to her. Having lived quietly in the country with her parents for the first nineteen years of her life, Grace had suddenly found herself orphaned, her parents having both been killed in a boating accident a year ago. Her mother's sister and brother-in-law, the

Duke and Duchess of Carlyne, were now her guardians, the Duke also being trustee of her considerable estate and fortune until she married.

In fact, now that Grace's year of mourning was over, it had been her aunt's insistence that Grace really must have a Season that had necessitated them undertaking this uncomfortable journey to London in the first place—slightly earlier than was necessary, as her aunt intended to acquire a completely new wardrobe for Grace before any of the entertainments began. She had declared Grace's scant wardrobe of three day dresses and two evening gowns completely inadequate for a London Season, where she would be introduced to all the ton as the ward of the Duke and Duchess of Carlyne.

Grace was grateful for all the loving attention her aunt and uncle had bestowed upon her in the last year. She simply wished that Lord Francis Wynter were a little less proprietorial of her.

'Lucian was such a dear boy when he was younger,' her Aunt Margaret mused wistfully. 'Do you remember what great friends he and Simon always were, Carlyne? How the two of them were at Eton and then Cambridge together, before taking up a commission in the army on the same day?'

The Duke reached out and patted his wife's hand consolingly. 'There, there, m'dear. What cannot be changed must be endured.'

Grace's heart ached at how stoically her aunt and uncle bore the tragic blow of their only son's death. She had not known Cousin Simon very well, his being ten years her senior, but the little she did remember of him was as a man as good-natured and charmingly amiable as his father.

How strange, then, that he should be particular friends with a man her uncle described as possessing 'broodingly dark good-looks', and Francis claimed was 'a rake and a—' And a what? Grace wondered curiously. Whatever it was, as far as her uncle was concerned it was not a fit description for the ears of an innocent like herself.

Contrarily, Francis's disapproval of Lord Lucian St Claire only made him all the more appealing to Grace!

Lucian drew in a weary breath as he stood outside the parlour where the Wynter family were awaiting his appearance so that they might dine. The thirty minutes or so since Lucian had parted from the Duke had not improved his disposition. The accommodation at the inn had proved as inferior as Carlyne had claimed it to be, and the furnishings in Lucian's room were sparse, to say the least, with not even a lock on the door to keep his belongings safe while he was downstairs dining.

Which was perhaps the point…

Not that Lucian was carrying anything of particular value to a thief—chance or otherwise. Having arranged for his valet to depart for Mulberry Hall—the principal St Claire seat in Gloucestershire, and Lucian's home for the first eighteen years of his life—a day ahead of Lucian travelling on horseback, Lucian was carrying only the barest necessities with him. As he had already explained to the Duke, he did not even have with him appropriate evening clothes for dining in female company.

Stop delaying the inevitable, Lucian, he instructed himself severely. There was no getting out of dining with the Carlynes, so he might just as well get this initial meeting with the rest of the family out of the way as quickly as possible. After all, Margaret Wynter was pleasant enough, and if Francis Wynter was not to be tolerated he could at least be ignored. As could whichever elderly twittering female the Duchess had brought with her as companion for this visit to London.

He could hear the murmur of voices in the private parlour as he reached out and turned the door handle. One of those voices was raised much louder than the others, and the words reached Lucian as plainly as if he were already in the room.

'Say what you like about the man's war record, George, but I remember him as being wild and undisciplined in our youth. Neither do his years in the army alter the fact that St Claire has become nothing more than a rake since his return to polite society, and as such rendering him unfit company for the likes of Grace—' Francis Wynter abruptly broke off his tirade as Lucian stepped nonchalantly into the room.

Grace, along with everyone else present, turned her attention sharply towards the door as it was softly pushed open and an unknown gentleman stepped lightly into the room.

And what a gentleman!

Grace had never seen a man so tall, so fashionably

attired—in a superbly tailored jacket, waistcoat and cream breeches with highly polished Hessians, his linen snowy white, with delicate lace at the cuffs and throat—and so aristocratically and darkly handsome as Lord Lucian St Claire.

For surely this could be none other than the man Francis had just called a rake?

Grace's breath caught in her throat as she raised her gaze to Lord Lucian St Claire's face. His jaw was square and chiselled beneath cynically sculptured lips, and a straight nose was set below the darkest, blackest, most piercingly intense eyes Grace had ever beheld.

Eyes that coolly met her surprised gaze before he raised one dark brow with arrogant deliberation.

Grace quickly averted her gaze from that mockingly sardonic one—but not before she had noted that his overlong, slightly curling hair was almost as dark as those intense black eyes that seconds ago had looked at her so tauntingly.

'I seem to have interrupted your conversation, Wynter,' he drawled softly, challengingly. 'You were saying…?'

Grace felt a quiver of trepidation down the length of her spine at the warning she sensed behind the mildness of that tone, and knew by the way Francis's cheeks coloured that he was also aware of the air of danger that surrounded the slightly older man. Lord Lucian St Claire must have appeared a formidable officer to his men during his years in the army.

Francis's smile was forced. 'Nothing of any consequence, St Claire,' he dismissed determinedly. 'You know my sister-in-law, the Duchess of Carlyne, of course?' he added courteously.

'Your Grace.' Lucian St Claire stepped forward to take the Duchess's hand in his own before raising it to his lips.

'And this is Carlyne's ward, Miss Grace Hetherington,' Francis added, even as he took a proprietorial step that moved him pointedly to Grace's side, his hand lightly beneath her elbow in a gesture of possession.

It was a gesture that Grace, as she rose to bobble a curtsey to Lord Lucian, definitely took exception to, and she took a step away from that show of possession.

In fact, Grace acknowledged frowningly, Francis's manner was too pompously elevated altogether, when it should have been the Duke, as the host for the evening, who made the introductions.

'Miss Hetherington.' Lucian gave an inclination of his head, his dark eyes mocking as he gazed his fill on the youthfully beautiful Grace Hetherington.

It would have been impossible for Lucian not to be aware of Francis Wynter's unsubtle and protective move to Grace Hetherington's side—almost as if he suspected that Lucian might try to seduce her here and now, under the Duke and Duchess of Carlyne's watchful gaze, with his rakish ways!

He had also noted Grace Hetherington's instant removal of herself from Wynter's protection...

Francis's earlier claim that Lucian had been 'wild and undisciplined' in his youth had rankled more than Lucian cared to admit—especially as his own memories of visits to his friend Simon's home during school holidays were of Francis, the Duke's young brother and ward, constantly telling tales on the two older boys, petulant and whiny if he was excluded from their more mature pursuits.

But a single glance at Grace Hetherington had shown Lucian that he would be foolish to give in to the temptation he felt to use her in order to retaliate to Francis's barbs. There was no doubting that she was ethereally lovely, with her ebony hair curling enticingly about the pale delicacy of her face—a face dominated by unfathomable grey eyes surrounded by thick dark lashes, and a full pouting mouth that almost cried out to be kissed. She was also, Lucian noted dismissively, barely older than Lucian's nineteen-year-old sister Arabella.

Whilst Lucian might deserve the rakish reputation he had earned in the last two years, he had lately become tired of that life. Aware of his responsibilities, he had even come to the conclusion in the last few months that it was time he took a wife, to become mistress of his estate in Hampshire and provide the necessary heirs. An older woman, familiar enough with the ways of the ton to accept the little time and emotion Lucian felt able to give her…

'My Lord,' Grace Hetherington returned politely, her voice soft and husky.

A voice, Lucian recognised with frowning surprise, capable of raising a man's desire without any other effort being made on her part.

He gave Grace Hetherington a second, more searching glance from beneath hooded lids. Her hair was indeed lovely—black and silky, those curls enticingly impish—but the expression in her grey eyes was hidden by demurely lowered lashes that lay dark and thick against her creamy cheeks. Her nose was small and slightly uptilted, her lips full and lush in her heart-shaped face, her neck long and slender, her breasts surprisingly full and creamy above the low neckline of her cream silk and lace evening gown. The rest of her slender figure was indiscernible beneath the high-waisted gown.

Lucian's gaze returned to the delicate beauty of her face, still frowning as he tried to reconcile the come-to-bed huskiness of her voice with her otherwise youthfully innocent appearance. Was she aware of the effect her voice alone had upon a man? Those demurely lowered lashes seemed to say no, and yet—

Damn it, Grace Hetherington was his young sister's contemporary, Lucian reminded himself with impatient self-disgust. And as such she was completely untouchable for a man of his experience. Completely!

'I believe I have kept you all from your meal quite long enough,' he drawled in languid apology. 'Please allow me to escort you in to dinner, Your Grace.' He held out his arm politely to the Duchess of Carlyne.

Grace hadn't even been aware that she had ceased to breathe under the intensity of Lord Lucian St Claire's dark, unreadable gaze, until he broke that gaze as he turned away from her, in order to accompany her aunt through to the private dining room that had been set aside for their use this evening. Nor that her cheeks were hot and flushed. That her hands were shaking. Her legs feeling less than steady.

Lord Lucian St Claire, Grace had absolutely no doubt, even on such short acquaintance, was exactly the type of man—*exactly* the type of man!—that her mother had warned her to beware of if she were ever to find herself in tonnish society.

Exactly the sort of man it would be very dangerous—and heartbreaking—for any woman to ever fall in love with.

Not that Grace had any intention of falling in love with him. She definitely aspired a little higher than the tedious Francis Wynter as her lifetime companion, but at the same time she was not naïve enough to consider that a man as arrogantly handsome as Lucian St Claire had proved to be would ever fall in love with and marry someone like her. After the example of her parents' marriage, as well as her aunt and uncle's, Grace had already decided she would settle for nothing less than a love-match, either.

'Grace…?' Francis Wynter prompted impatiently as he stood beside her waiting to escort her into dinner.

Looking at him from beneath lowered lashes, Grace could not help but once again compare his petulantly blond good-looks to the saturnine handsomeness of Lucian St Claire. Day and Night. Good and devilish. Boring and dangerous…!

But with the mesmerising Lord St Claire now escorting her aunt into the adjoining room, Grace was able to take exception to Francis Wynter's proprietorial attitude, and she shot him a look of glittering reproof before turning to instead slip her hand into the crook of her uncle's arm.

'Shall we go through, Uncle George…?' She smiled up at him affectionately, all the time aware of the glowering dissatisfied gaze directed at the slenderness of her back as Francis Wynter followed closely behind them.

Chapter Two

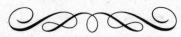

As expected, Lucian found himself seated between the Duchess of Carlyne on one side and Grace Hetherington on the other, with the Duke seated beside her and an obviously disgruntled Francis Wynter placed between his brother and sister-in-law. No doubt before Lucian's arrival the other man had expected to be seated beside the lovely Grace Hetherington, and so able to monopolise her attention.

A devilish impulse prompted Lucian to add to the other man's discomfort by focusing his own attention on the other man's more than obvious romantic interest. 'You are on your way to London for the Season, I believe, Miss Hetherington?' he prompted politely, turning towards her.

She paused in eating her soup. 'I am, My Lord.'

'Your first?'

'Yes, My Lord.'

'And have you ever been to London before, Miss Hetherington?'

Those long dark lashes were once more lowered over those smoky grey eyes. 'No, My Lord.'

She really did have the most sensuously arousing voice he had ever heard, Lucian acknowledged, and he found himself continuing to ask her questions just so that he could listen to that husky tone. It was a voice that possessed the potency of a caress against naked flesh. *His* naked flesh.

'And are you looking forward to all the excitement of your first Season? Perhaps hoping that the romantic prince of your dreams will appear and sweep you off your feet?'

Grace was frowning as she looked up at Lucian St Claire, having easily heard and taken exception to the light mockery underlining that drawling voice. She could now see the cynical curl to his lips, and the arrogant contempt in his expression towards the absurdity of the Season, and its accompanying plethora of marriage-minded mamas seeking a suitable husband for their daughters.

No doubt he felt all of those things towards Grace as she ventured into Society. As it happened, it was an unwilling venture on her part. She had agreed to this Season only after her Uncle George had explained to her that it would be a diversion for her aunt, who still suffered deep melancholy over the death of her only son.

'I do not believe in romantic princes, My Lord,' she assured him softly.

Those dark brows rose over eyes that seemed to laugh at her. 'You do not?'

'Not at all, My Lord,' Grace confirmed lightly. 'Divest even a prince of his title, and what do you see?'

Lucian St Claire's eyes were openly amused. 'Perhaps you would care to enlighten me, Miss Hetherington?'

She shrugged dismissively. 'That he is a man—like any other.'

Those sculptured lips curved appreciatively. 'You sound—contemptuous, Miss Hetherington?'

'Should I not? Perhaps I am wrong, My Lord, but it is my understanding that the rich and titled gentlemen of the ton are looking only for beauty in their future wives, for a woman of suitable lineage to produce their future heirs.'

'Really, my dear Grace!' her aunt interrupted sharply. 'I am sure that Lord St Claire does not wish to hear the—the perhaps less than genteel—' She broke off as Lord Lucian raised a placating hand.

'On the contrary, Your Grace, I find myself very interested in Miss Hetherington's conversation,' Lucian drawled assuringly, and once again found himself being surprised by Grace Hetherington. Especially as she had just described the sort of arrangement he had decided would most suit himself!

It was rare indeed to hear a young woman express herself so frankly when in public. Well, apart from his sister Arabella, of course. But, having grown up with three older brothers, Bella tended to be slightly different from the usual.

He gave Grace Hetherington a considering look from beneath hooded lids. 'You do not hold with the opinion that a titled gentleman is duty-bound to take himself a wife?'

'A wife he does not love nor perhaps even like?' Grey eyes frowned across at him. 'No, My Lord, I do not hold with that opinion.'

'This really is not suitable dinner conversation, my dear,' the Duchess of Carlyne reproved her again, lightly. 'You must excuse my niece, Lord St Claire; she has lived all her life in the country with her parents— my dear deceased sister and her husband. She does not yet know how to go on in Society.'

'On the contrary, I find Miss Hetherington's conversation very—refreshing,' Lucian assured her, his gaze fixed intently on the now slightly flushed face of Grace Hetherington. 'Tell me, Miss Hetherington, what is your opinion of the less financially fortunate gentlemen of the ton?' he prompted softly.

Grace was well aware that Lord Lucian was playing with her, deliberately provoking her into voicing her less than enamoured opinion of the Society in which he lived. And played. Even on such brief acquaintance Grace knew that this man played with words when no other diversion presented itself.

It was an arena in which her liberal-minded father and mother had encouraged Grace to hold her own. 'Those gentlemen are, of course, not so concerned with the way a woman looks, or indeed her lineage, so long as she has the fortune necessary for them to live the life-style they consider theirs by right.'

Lucian St Claire gave up all pretence of eating and

pushed his soup bowl away from him to focus all his attention on Grace. 'And which of those categories do you suppose I fit into, Miss Hetherington?' His voice was soft—dangerously so.

Grace pretended to give the question due consideration.

Pretended because, after Francis's description of the other man, she believed she already knew what type of man Lucian St Claire was.

Grace pushed her own soup bowl away from her before turning to meet that mocking dark gaze. 'It is my belief that there is a third category of man amongst the ton.'

'Which is?' The amusement was less in evidence now, and the darkness of Lucian St Claire's eyes had taken on a cold glitter.

Grace shrugged unconcernedly. 'It is, I believe, those gentlemen who have both money and a title but no use for a wife of any kind. They see women—married or otherwise—merely as playthings.'

'And you believe I am one of that category?' There was a definite edge to Lucian St Claire's voice now, a challenge in those sculptured lips as they thinned above the squareness of his arrogantly angled jaw.

'That really is not for me to say, My Lord,' Grace told him softly. Having glanced at Francis Wynter, she easily recognised the expression of malicious glee on his face as he listened avidly to the exchange. And another glance at her aunt's disapproving face told Grace that she should not pursue this conversation any further. That she had already pursued it too far.

That she had been goaded into doing so by Lucian St Claire was in no doubt, but nevertheless Grace accepted that she had been less than prudent in her opinions.

She lowered her lashes demurely, to hide the flash of temper she knew would be visible in her eyes. 'My aunt is correct, sir, when she claims I am not yet used to the subtle nuances of the ton. I apologise if you have found my comments in the least insulting. I have perhaps been too—candid in my views.' She looked up, her temper once again under control, her eyes calmly serene. 'It is also very wrong of me to have monopolised your attention in this way, when I am sure that my uncle is simply longing to tell you of the prime horseflesh he has recently acquired.' She gave her uncle an affectionate smile.

Surprisingly, Lucian was disappointed at this abrupt ending of his conversation with Grace Hetherington. For once in his life he had believed himself to be having an honest exchange with a woman—his sister Arabella once again excepted; Arabella was even more outspoken in her opinions than Grace Hetherington had been. Heaven help the male members of the ton if Grace Hetherington and Arabella should meet up in London during the coming Season and form a friendship!

But Grace Hetherington's introduction of the subject of the Duke's stables made the conversation less exclusive, and the three gentlemen began to discuss horseflesh, at the same time allowing the Duchess to once again gently reprimand her niece for her lack of discretion. Lucian noted this regretfully, as Grace Hetherington fell silent during the rest of the surprisingly excellent meal. Perhaps, as the Duke had claimed, the food *did* make up for the inn's lack of other amenities after all.

The good food and wine certainly helped to ease the earlier discord in their gathering. Even Lucian's mood had lightened somewhat by the time the ladies had drunk their tea and the Duchess had risen to suggest that the two of them would now retire for the evening, so leaving the gentlemen alone to enjoy their brandy and cigars.

'I believe I might retire too, m'dear.' The Duke rose more slowly to his feet than the two younger gentlemen. 'Forgive me, St Claire, but I'm feeling slightly fatigued. Too much good food and wine, I expect,' he added in rueful apology. 'There is no joy in getting older, I'm afraid!'

Lucian gave the older man a searching glance, noting as he did so the fine sheen of moisture on the other man's forehead, the slight pallor to his clammy skin, and the blue eyes dulled with pain. Obviously the Duke was suffering some discomfort after eating, but Lucian very much doubted that at the age of eight and fifty the reason for such discomfort could be attributed to age.

'Is it your heart again, George?' Francis Wynter looked up frowningly at his older brother.

The Duke's face became flushed with temper. 'No, dammit, it is *not* m'heart—'

'Calm yourself, Carlyne,' the Duchess soothed placatingly. 'I am sure that Francis was only expressing his concern.'

'It is a concern I can well do without.' Her husband scowled his displeasure.

'Remember what the physician you consulted in Worcester said about your heart and becoming too excited, Carlyne—'

'Damned quack,' the Duke dismissed disgustedly. 'Excuse the family exchange, if you will, St Claire.' He smiled across at Lucian ruefully. 'A touch of indigestion and everyone assumes 'm on m'deathbed.'

'I am sure that the Duchess and Francis meant well,' Lucian placated. 'Would you like me to accompany you up the stairs?' He frowned as he noted the way the Duke swayed slightly as he turned to walk to the door.

'Not necessary, m'dear fellow, when I have my dear Margaret and Grace beside me.' George Wynter smiled reassuringly at his wife as she took his arm concernedly, Grace at his other side. 'You two young bucks stay and enjoy your brandy and some congenial conversation.'

Lucian thought he would rather once again take up his commission and endure cold months in the saddle than spend any time alone with the pompous bore Francis Wynter had undoubtedly become! But as the Duke and Duchess of Carlyne left the room, accompanied by their solicitous niece, Lucian accepted that he had little choice than to partake of at least one glass of the brandy the young maid poured for them before she also left the room. After that he would acquire a decanter of his own to take up to his bedchamber, so that he might drink himself into oblivion.

Francis Wynter took advantage of the departure of

his brother and the two ladies to move into Grace Hetherington's seat, and the two men were sitting side by side as he leant confidingly towards Lucian. 'I beg that you will not think too badly of Miss Hetherington for her less than discreet conversation earlier.'

Lucian looked at the other man coldly, surprised at the younger man's chosen topic of conversation when his brother had just left the room in an obviously less than well state. 'I assure you I do not think badly of Miss Hetherington.'

Francis Wynter's eyes narrowed. 'But I am sure you will agree that she is yet slightly gauche when in polite society.'

Lucian had no idea where this conversation was going, but he certainly did not appreciate the younger man discussing Miss Hetherington in this familiar manner with someone who was, after all, a complete stranger to her. 'On the contrary,' he drawled slowly. 'It is my belief that Miss Hetherington's nature is such that over the next few months she will come to be considered an Original by the ton.'

'As to that, St Claire—' the younger man gave a supercilious smile '—I am sure it cannot have escaped your notice that Miss Hetherington and I...' He paused delicately. 'Well, there is an understanding between the two of us. Of course there has been nothing official announced as yet.' He grimaced. 'But I believe I can safely say that an engagement will shortly be announced.'

Lucian didn't react to the other man's self-satisfied announcement by so much as a flicker of an eyelid—

but inwardly… Inwardly! Was this young puppy actually warning him off pursuing any interest he might be nurturing in Grace Hetherington's direction? Did this man actually dare to presume—?

'Grace must be allowed to have her Season, of course,' Francis Wynter continued airily. 'But it is only to introduce her to Society. I have every confidence that George will consider no offer but my own.'

Damn it, he *did* dare to presume!

Lucian couldn't remember feeling this angry for a very long time. Certainly he had never been roused to such emotion before where a woman was concerned. 'Surely it is Miss Hetherington who will need to consider your offer?' he said. And from the little Lucian had observed this evening in Grace Hetherington's manner towards Francis Wynter, he had no doubt she would be in total disagreement with such an offer.

There was no doubting that such a match would be considered a very good one for a country miss such as Grace Hetherington. Lucian had guessed from the Duchess's earlier comments about her sister and her husband that Grace's parents had been simple country gentry. But, easily recalling that spark of rebellion he had seen in Grace Hetherington's eyes on more than one occasion this evening, and her earlier conversation concerning marriage, Lucian very much doubted that Francis Wynter was going to find it quite so easy to persuade Miss Grace Hetherington as to the suitability of his offer.

Not that it was any of Lucian's business *who* Grace

Hetherington chose to marry. Except that it would be a pity to see all of that originality subjugated by Francis Wynter's pomposity. Or her beauty given to him alone, Lucian allowed grudgingly, recalling those misty grey eyes and the fullness of Grace Hetherington's mouth, the creamy softness of her skin and the silky darkness of hair that, once unconfined, would no doubt fall in curling disarray to the slenderness of her waist.

Francis raised his brows. 'Grace will, of course, be guided by my brother and his wife when it comes to the acceptance of a marriage proposal. And a match between the two of us is more than suitable,' he claimed with certainty.

It might be suitable as far as Francis Wynter was concerned, Lucian acknowledged as he repressed a smile, but Grace Hetherington was another matter entirely. 'I wish you every luck in your endeavour, then, Wynter,' he drawled uninterestedly. 'Pass the brandy, would you?' he added briskly; if he had to endure this man's company then he might as well drink his fill of brandy now, and so be too drunk to take offence at anything the other man might say!

'You do not think that we should perhaps call a doctor, Aunt?'

Grace frowned her concern as she looked across the room at her Uncle George, where he lay back on the bed, his eyes closed, even paler now than he had been downstairs.

'Carlyne will not hear of it—claims it is only a touch

of indigestion.' Her aunt looked no less worried as she glanced across at her husband. Not surprisingly, when there had been several bouts of such indigestion in recent months.

'The opinion of another physician would perhaps be advisable, do you not think?' Grace ventured to suggest, knowing that her uncle had absolutely no time for the diagnosis of the local doctor who had been summoned to Winton Hall after his last bout.

Grace had become very fond of her aunt and uncle during the year she had spent under their guardianship, and could not bear to now see her uncle in such discomfort, or her aunt so obviously worried.

'I dare not go against Carlyne's wishes.' Her aunt gave a strained smile. 'I believe it best if we wait a while and see if this passes, as it has before. You are only next door, Grace. Be assured I will call upon you if I have need of you,' she added reassuringly as she saw Grace remained unconvinced.

Grace accepted the dismissal for what it was. 'Please do not hesitate if you are in the least concerned. After all, there is Lord Wynter and—and Lord St Claire to call upon if needs be.'

She felt a slight warmth enter her cheeks just at recalling her verbal exchange with Lucian St Claire at dinner. He had not been at all what she'd expected after Francis's description of him as a rake. He was very handsome, of course, as well as arrogant and mocking in his conversation, but there had been none of the overt familiarity that Grace had been expecting, nor the flirtation, nor indeed the faintest trace of a debauchee either in those arrogantly handsome features or the hard strength of his lithely muscled body. In fact, if anything, Grace had found him cold and emotionally removed.

She'd had the chance to observe him often from beneath lowered lashes during the course of the meal, and had come to realise that there was much more to Lord Lucian St Claire than the rake Francis had described him as being.

She had no doubt whatsoever that his affection for her aunt and uncle was completely genuine. And she had known that his contempt of Francis was equally sincere. But as Grace wholeheartedly shared that last view she could see no fault in him for that either!

In fact, as Mary, her maid, helped Grace to prepare for bed, before retiring to the room she was to share with the Duchess's maid, Grace found her thoughts lingering musingly on Lord Lucian St Claire.

She could find no faults in him whatsoever—apart from perhaps an excess of arrogance—and had even, to her shame, enjoyed that lively verbal exchange with him.

Could it be that she was ever so slightly infatuated with him? Grace wondered frowningly, as she sat in her nightgown on the seat before the window. She lifted the catch and allowed the brisk spring air to enter the stuffiness of the small bedchamber. Perhaps, she conceded self-derisively.

The gentlemen she would meet during her Season would certainly pale into insignificance beside his nonchalant elegance and arrogant handsomeness. If Francis

Wynter allowed any of those gentlemen close enough for her to be able to compare, Grace acknowledged with a tightening of her mouth as she crossed the room to climb into bed, before blowing out the candle and settling down sleepy-eyed amongst the pillows.

She had found Francis's proprietorial manner towards her this evening even more annoying than usual, his hopes of a match where she was concerned being more than obvious.

Surely her aunt and uncle would not seriously contemplate such a match for her? It would be the first note of discord in their relationship if that were to be the case. Because Grace had no intention, now or in the future, of accepting *any* offer of marriage that Francis Wynter might make her. She would not even consider such an offer.

She would think of the more fascinating Lord Lucian St Claire instead, Grace decided, and she hugged a pillow to her, her thoughts drifting off as she fantasised about herself held unwilling captive by a faceless spurned lover, and Lucian St Claire riding to her rescue before carrying her off to his deserted castle. Quite what she wanted to happen once they reached that deserted castle Grace wasn't sure, but no doubt it would include the placing of those finely chiselled lips upon her own, and the caress of his long, elegant hands upon her body.

A body that now warmed at the thought of such caresses. Her breasts were feeling strangely full, and there was an unaccustomed ache between her thighs as her thoughts wandered to considering what Lucian St Claire would look like without the benefit of the tailored perfection of his clothing. His shoulders would be wide and muscled, his skin soft and yet unyielding to the touch, his chest also, his stomach flat, his thighs—

Grace's thoughts came to an abrupt halt as she acknowledged that, as she had no real experience of the nakedness of a man's body below the waist, her imagination could take her no further.

But the little she had imagined had only increased the heat of her own body. The tips of her breasts were now tingling achingly, and there was a throbbing moistness between her thighs, a quiver of pleasure trembling through her body when she pressed her legs together, unlike anything she had ever felt before.

She touched herself wonderingly, feeling how slick and wet she was, how sensitive. Even the lightest touch of her fingers against that swollen flesh was sending tremors of feeling through her body.

How much more arousing would it be to have Lucian St Claire touch her in this way—to lie back and wantonly open herself to him as he…

Grace gave an aching groan as she turned onto her side and curled into a ball beneath the bedclothes, her face heated with embarrassment at her own unruly thoughts, and her eyes tightly closed against further imaginings as she willed herself to fall asleep.

He had drunk more brandy than usual during that enforced hour in Francis Wynter's company, Lucian acknowledged disgustedly, staggering slightly as he made his way slowly up the narrow stairs of the inn by the light of the candle he carried.

The younger man had to be the most crashing bore Lucian had ever had the misfortune to meet—more so even than Lucian had imagined. He certainly did not envy Miss Grace Hetherington if he had been mistaken earlier concerning her feelings and she *were* to accept the other man's offer of marriage; Wynter would probably be just as boring in the bedroom as he was in every other way!

Not his concern, Lucian told himself derisively as he concentrated on taking the measure of the stairs. Neither Wynter's tedium in the bedroom, nor the imagining of Grace Hetherington's slender loveliness going to such waste. No doubt if such a marriage should occur the two would deal very well together. Lucian certainly did not intend giving that lovely young lady or her future, with or without Wynter as her husband, another thought. All he required at this moment was his bed, and eight hours or so of complete oblivion, his sleep hopefully not visited by any of the nightmares that had so often beset him following that last horrendous battle at Waterloo.

Grace awoke with a start, having no idea why she had woken or indeed where she was for some seconds. Until she remembered the coach journey from Lord Darius Wynter's home at Malvern Hall with her aunt and uncle, and Francis riding his black hunter in front of the coach, so not noticing the faulty wheel that had necessitated an unexpected halt in their journey. A halt that had brought them to this less than comfortable coaching inn.

And so to her meeting with Lord Lucian St Claire.

Grace shied away from thinking of him again after the embarrassing thoughts she'd had of him before falling asleep, instead turning her attention to trying to discover why it was she had woken so suddenly.

There was someone in her bedchamber!

The realisation that she was not alone, that someone else was moving stealthily about the room, muttering softly under their breath as they stumbled into unseen obstacles in the darkness, held Grace frozen beneath the bedclothes.

Who could it be?

Her aunt, perhaps? To tell her that Uncle George's condition had worsened and they needed to send for the physician after all? But, no. Her aunt would have knocked on the door of the bedchamber before entering, and she would also have carried a candle to light her way, not be stumbling around in the darkness.

So the intruder was probably unknown to Grace.

A robber, perhaps?

But surely of all the guests staying at the inn— amongst them a duke, a duchess and two lords—the innocuous Miss Grace Hetherington was the least likely to have anything of value in her room?

Except herself, of course…

Grace's eyes widened in alarm as she acknowledged that it was perhaps her virtue that the intruder was intent on stealing.

Not without a fight on her part, Grace resolved determinedly, her mind racing as she considered how best to deal with the situation. She could just scream, of course—a move sure to bring at least four people running: her aunt and uncle, Lord Francis Wynter, and Lord Lucian St Claire. But that same scream would also alert the intruder to her wakefulness, allowing him the time to make good his escape and so be free to repeat the crime at some later date on a female perhaps less resilient than Grace. No, she would not scream. Instead she would deal with the intruder herself, before alerting her aunt and uncle.

Grace's movements were slow and quiet as she managed to slip from beneath the covers to crouch on the side of the bed furthest from the intruder, her intention being to grasp the empty water jug on the table before hitting him over the head with it.

Grace executed her move with surprising success, catching the intruder completely unawares as she literally smashed the jug over his head, so that he fell to the floor and ceased all movement.

Grace's hands were shaking very badly as she attempted to relight her candle, the flint refusing to spark until she had made several attempts, but the wick at last flickering into flame. She picked up the candle and turned to face her assailant.

Grace gasped her complete disbelief as she saw it was Lord Lucian St Claire who lay unconscious—and very naked!—on the floor of her bedchamber!

Chapter Three

Lucian's first thought upon awakening was that he appeared to be suffering from the worst hangover of his life. Which was strange considering that, despite the brandy he consumed on a nightly basis, he rarely, if ever, suffered the effects of it the following morning.

But the throbbing in his head, like a dozen or more tiny men wielding hammers, was definitely worse than anything he had ever experienced before or wanted to experience again, he acknowledged with a pained groan, as he attempted to move his head from the pillow. Those hammers began to pound even more violently.

'You're awake!'

Lucian became very still as he fell back on the pillow. He was sure that he recognised that huskily seductive voice from the previous evening, but just as sure that Miss Grace Hetherington should not—absolutely should *not!*—be in his bedchamber with him.

He kept his eyes firmly closed. 'Please tell me that this is just a manifestation of my imagination!'

'No, My Lord, I am afraid this is very real,' the voice that definitely sounded like Miss Grace Hetherington's confirmed wryly.

Lucian's lids rose abruptly even as he turned his head sharply in the direction of that voice, determinedly ignoring the painful hammering inside his head. His eyes widened accusingly as his gaze alighted on Grace Hetherington, where she sat on a chair beside his bed, apparently wearing only a silk robe over her nightgown, her black hair falling in enticing curls to her waist now that it was unconfined, just as Lucian had imagined it would.

'What the devil are you doing in my bedchamber?' Lucian demanded furiously.

More to the point, had he suffered any nightmares in her presence? Those dark, relentless dreams during which he cursed as he stabbed again and again with his sword at the French soldier who had just cut down Simon Wynter, in a bloodlust that left him shaken and numbed by his own savagery…

The fact that Grace had not run screaming from the bedchamber, nor now stared at him in horror, seemed to indicate that he had not.

Dark brows arched over clear grey eyes. 'I think, My Lord, that you will find that it is for *me* to ask what *you* are doing in *my* bedchamber.'

Lucian frowned darkly before shifting his gaze about the room. What he saw was a bedchamber very similar to his own. And yet strangely not his own…

None of his travelling clothes were draped over the chair, as he had left them the evening before, and his shaving things were not on the dressing table either. In their stead was a cream satin and lace gown—the one worn by Miss Grace Hetherington the evening before— and on the dressing table a silver brush set, obviously feminine, and the pearl earbobs this young lady had also worn the previous evening.

His gaze returned sharply to Grace Hetherington's face. 'What *am* I doing in your bedchamber?'

Those full and tempting lips twisted into a rueful grimace. 'I was hoping you might be able to tell me that.'

Lucian's frown deepened. He remembered stumbling up the stairs, and his infinite relief at escaping Francis Wynter's oppressive company at last. Then his wish for a peaceful night's sleep, and the opening of the door to his bedchamber—

The candle had blown out as he entered the room— Grace Hetherington's bedchamber rather than his own, apparently. Lucian remembered that now. He had been thrown into complete darkness, his irritation with Francis Wynter still such that he hadn't even bothered to grope around and relight the candle, but had instead undressed in the darkness—

He had undressed in the darkness!

Grace watched calmly as Lucian St Claire's hand shifted. He sharply lifted the bedclothes to look down upon his own nakedness. The same nakedness that had taken Grace completely by surprise when she had first

lit the candle and seen him lying unconscious at her feet.
The same nakedness that had initially shocked her into
being unable to do anything more than simply stand and
stare at so much male nudity.

As she had imagined, his shoulders were indeed
wide and muscled, his stomach equally taut. And Grace
now had her answer as to exactly what this man looked
like beneath those cream breeches…!

Beautiful. With a hard, masculine beauty that she
could never, ever have imagined. His legs were long and
muscled—possibly from the years he had spent in the
saddle whilst in the army—and a dark thatch of silky
hair surrounded his manhood.

Extremely—manfully—beautiful. There was no
other way in which Grace could possibly have described
the hard nakedness of Lucian St Claire's body.

Lucian let the bedclothes drop back over his nudity,
his mouth a thin, disapproving line, a nerve pulsing in
his jaw as he glared up at Grace Hetherington. 'Did I
touch you?'

'Touch me…?' she repeated softly.

Lucian closed his eyes only briefly before grating.
'Yes—touch you! Did I—before the brandy I had
consumed so obviously sent me into oblivion—did I
happen to take your innocence?'

Her eyes widened. 'You do not remember what
happened after you entered my bedchamber?'

'No, I—' Lucian broke off impatiently as he
frowned at her. 'I remember my candle blowing out as
I entered the room—'

She nodded. 'I had opened the window for some air.'

Lucian scowled at the admission—as if she were not perfectly at liberty to open her own bedroom window if she so chose. 'Miss Hetherington, did I or did I not make love to you last night?'

Grace stood up to move slightly away from the bed, sure that Lord St Claire would not follow her now that he was aware of his nakedness beneath the bedclothes.

He did not remember coming to her room. Did not remember undressing. Did not remember that, once Grace had helped him into the bed, he had been consumed by the most horrendous nightmares, during which he'd sworn and railed like a man possessed as he battled against a 'French bastard'…

Nor did he seem to remember that prior to that he had been hit over the head with a water jug…!

Grace chewed on her lower lip, unsure of what to do or say next.

It was obvious from Lucian St Claire's initial comment that he had believed himself to be in the privacy of his own bedchamber earlier, when he had moved so stealthily about the room, discarding his clothes before dropping them uncaringly on the floor.

She'd had time to ponder, as she sat helplessly in the chair beside the bed as witness to his nightmares, whether or not Lucian St Claire had *meant* to come to her bedchamber, and if so for what purpose. Although the fact that he was naked seemed all too readily to indicate that purpose!

But his surprise on awakening, at finding himself in her bedchamber rather than his own, and his anger and impatience with that fact, made a complete nonsense of her initial conclusion.

Disappointingly so? Perhaps, Grace allowed self-derisively. Even if she would have rebuffed his advances, it would still have been exciting—flattering, even—to be the object of the intimate interest of a man as arrogantly handsome as Lord Lucian St Claire.

But his mistaking her bedchamber for his own had obviously been genuine. A mistake—if they were not to be the centre of a complete scandal—that would have to be rectified as quickly and quietly as possible: namely by Lord St Claire's removal from her bedchamber!

'How long have I been here?'

Grace turned back to him. 'Only an hour or so.' She was reluctant to let him know that she had seen his disturbed dreams, already knowing him to be a man who would see such dreams as a weakness. A weakness he would hate anyone else to witness.

'An hour—' Lucian made the mistake of attempting to sit up. A mistake immediately brought home to him as the agonising pain that ensued caused him to place his hands on either side of his head in the hope of holding it in place should it attempt to topple from his neck!

Hell and damnation—what had been in the brandy this evening?

Ah—he had found the cause of the pain, his fingers having encountered a large bump on the left side of his head, just behind his ear. A lump that was tender and sore to the touch, as if—

He looked across at Grace Hetherington accusingly.

She swallowed, her throat moving convulsively, her eyes suddenly enormous grey pools of contrition in the pallor of her face. 'I—er—I struck you over the head with the water jug,' she admitted, with a self-conscious grimace.

Lucian winced. 'If, as you claim, I made no attempt on your innocence, might I enquire as to *why* you felt the wielding of the water jug necessary…?'

Her small pink tongue moved nervously across the fullness of her lips, moistening them. Enticingly so. 'I believed you to be an intruder, you see.'

Yes, Lucian did see—and heaven help any man or woman who ever tried to enter this young woman's bedchamber uninvited! It was certainly a pity he had been the recipient of her wrath this evening, but it was also reassuring to know that she was capable of defending herself if the occasion warranted it.

'What if your intruder had been Francis Wynter?' he drawled mockingly.

Angry colour darkened her cheeks. 'Then I would have used much more force than I actually did!'

'Really?' Lucian gave another wince as his fingers gently probed the tenderness of his scalp. 'I do believe that a heavier blow might have resulted in your killing him.'

'If Francis Wynter ever enters my bedchamber uninvited then it is a fate he will deserve!' Her expression was fierce.

Lucian's lips thinned as he repressed a smile. 'Perhaps it was as well that I conveniently fell upon the bed?'

She gave another grimace. 'You did not.'

He frowned. 'How the deuce did you get me from the floor to the bed…?'

He had noticed earlier this evening that Grace Hetherington only reached up to his shoulder in her slippered feet, and the fragility of her appearance certainly didn't indicate the strength of an amazon beneath her silk robe.

Colour brightened her cheeks. 'You were conscious enough to help a little, and I—I really could not leave you lying on the cold floor once I'd realised your identity!'

Lucian couldn't help but admire this young woman's fortitude.

He couldn't think of too many women—of any age—who would have the courage to knock an intruder unconscious with a water jug, let alone manage to drag him onto her bed. Before calmly entering into conversation with him once he regained his senses!

And Lucian *had* now recovered his senses.

All of them…!

Alone with her in her bedchamber, he found Grace Hetherington's beauty overpowering: her brow was like alabaster, her grey eyes mistily enigmatic, her lips full and poutingly tempting. The silk of her nightgown and robe flowed revealingly over pert breasts and curvaceous hips, and her feet peeped out daintily beneath its hem.

Desire stirred inappropriately in recognition of all those

womanly charms, and Lucian's breath arrested in his throat as his thighs hardened even more inappropriately.

Grace tensed warily as she sensed the sudden change in the quality of the silence that had fallen between them. There was almost an air of expectation—of awareness, Lucian St Claire's eyes having darkened to black as he looked at her through narrowed lids.

She straightened. 'I believe it is past time you returned to your own bedchamber, My Lord.'

'Really?' He turned on his side to lean his elbow against the pillows, raising himself to look at her. 'But I find your bedchamber so much more comfortable than my own, Grace.' His voice was low, huskily seductive.

Grace's eyes widened at the sense of intimacy his familiarity engendered. 'In what way, My Lord?'

'Why, because you are here, my dear Grace.' He grinned, instantly dispelling the impression of arrogant cynicism she had sensed as being such a part of him when they were first introduced. In fact he looked almost boyishly appealing now—especially so after the nightmares she had witnessed—and the dark hair that fell softly over his brow added to that illusion.

But it *was* an illusion. Lucian St Claire was far from being a boy. Not only was he a hardened soldier, but since resigning his commission he had also become known as something of a rake. A man hell-bent on the pursuit of pleasure. Pleasure that did not engage his emotions.

The warm intimacy of that dark gaze as it swept over her so slowly, from her head to her feet, gave the impression that she had now become the focus of that pleasure!

The warmth in Grace's cheeks spread to the rest of her traitorous body. Traitorous because Lucian St Claire's continued presence in her bedchamber in the early hours of the morning—or at any other time!—really was completely unacceptable. And dangerous. To her and to every rule dictated by the society they lived in.

Except he did look so dark and rakishly handsome, lying there in her bed, the sheet having fallen down as he turned to face her to reveal a muscled chest covered in hair as dark as that upon his head, and the flatness of his stomach, the hard curve of his hips, with the dark hair continuing in a deep vee towards thighs that were hard and—

Grace's stricken gaze returned to his face, the colour deepening in her cheeks as he raised mocking brows above eyes that openly laughed at her display of startled modesty. Her mouth tightened. 'If you are attempting to alarm me, My Lord, then you are not succeeding.'

'Am I not?' He sat up in the bed to place his feet upon the wooden floor, the sheet draped decorously across his hips, but doing little to hide the response of his body that had so flustered Grace seconds ago. 'Then you have me at a disadvantage, Grace—because being here alone with you like this is alarming the hell out of *me!*' he acknowledged self-derisively.

Her eyes flashed warningly. 'Do not attempt to trifle with me, My Lord—'

'Trifle, Grace?' His smile was wolfish. 'You describe the desire you have so obviously aroused in me as a mere *trifle?*'

In truth, it was some time since Lucian's interest in a woman had been strong enough to evoke any sort of reaction in him other than boredom. The married ladies of the ton, those beautiful and bored matrons looking for a brief and meaningless affair, that was all they required as a diversion from the tedium of their marriage, were proving far too easy a conquest of late.

Not that he had any intention of becoming genuinely involved with Miss Grace Hetherington, the marriageable ward of the Duke and Duchess of Carlyne, but Lucian couldn't deny that she was proving to be an interesting diversion to his otherwise jaded palate. Most young women in her situation would have run screaming from the room by now. So perhaps he could allow himself—and her—a few harmless kisses? After all, it would be a pity not to live up to Francis Wynter's lurid description of him earlier this evening!

'Come here to me, Grace.' He held out his hand to her invitingly. A gesture she recoiled from as if his hand had all the appeal of a snake about to strike. 'Or perhaps you would prefer it if I were to come to you?' His challenge—and his nudity!—were obvious.

Grace Hetherington predictably looked no more happy about that suggestion, and she scowled at him. 'I refuse to play this ridiculous game, My Lord—'

'Surely, my dear Grace, as I am at this moment in your bedchamber, actually seated upon your bed, it would be more appropriate if you were to call me Lucian?' he drawled comfortably, his relaxed and lazy posture totally deceptive.

'It would be totally *in*appropriate—as is your being in my bedchamber at all!' She glared across the room at him. 'If anyone were to find you here it would cause the most hideous scandal.'

Lucian couldn't deny the truth of that. Even Hawk, his older brother whose rigid code of conduct had become much softer and accommodating since his marriage to Jane the previous year, would baulk at Lucian debauching an innocent miss such as Grace Hetherington. Or giving the appearance of having done so!

He regarded Grace mockingly. 'Then the sooner you do as I ask the better for all concerned—do you not think?'

Grace regarded Lucian frustratedly, aware that he was once again playing with her, but not knowing, in this hitherto unknown situation, how to respond. It was unthinkable that she should actually take up the invitation of his extended hand. And yet not to do so, she was sure, would result in an even more unacceptable occurrence— that of Lucian walking naked across the room to her!

'No, I most certainly do not think!' she snapped, even as she crossed the room in three impatient strides. She'd ignored that outstretched hand even as she glared at him, her shortness in stature meaning that their faces were now on a level. 'There—I have done as you asked. Now will you please leave?'

Easier said than done, Lucian acknowledged self-mockingly as his arousal hardened to an almost painful degree; if he were to stand up now, erection magnificently on display, this innocent young miss would probably have a fit of the vapours. Or perhaps not...? She had, after all, already dealt quite capably with someone she had considered an intruder to her bedchamber.

'I think perhaps I would like you to kiss me better first.' He tilted his head invitingly.

Temper darkened her cheeks; those grey eyes were stormy. 'You are a man of almost thirty years, not three!'

Lucian gave an acknowledging inclination of his head. 'My years do not make the pain of my injury any less.'

'You are impossible, My Lord—'

'Lucian.'

'The familiarity of your name does not make your behaviour any less outrageous!'

He bared his teeth in a grin. 'A kiss, Grace. A single kiss. And then I promise that I will leave your bedchamber immediately.'

Grace's pulse was already racing at his proximity, and her heart was beating frantically in her chest just at the thought of placing her lips anywhere upon this man—even on the dark silkiness of his hair, where she had struck him with the water jug. To touch him in any way, while alone with him in the privacy of her bedchamber, would be highly improper—and yet if it meant that he would then vacate her bedchamber…

'One kiss?' She gave him a severe look.

His grin became boyish once again. 'One kiss, Grace.'

Her pulse began to race faster as he easily held her gaze. She leant towards him, her heart beating even more erratically as she breathed in the male scent of him, her legs shaking so much that Grace was no longer sure they would support her.

And then they didn't need to as, instead of remaining seated, Lucian St Claire surged powerfully to his feet, barely giving Grace time to register his nakedness before his arms moved about her like bands of steel. He pulled her body close against the heat of his and his head lowered towards hers.

Grace began to struggle against the strength of those arms. 'You said you wanted me to kiss you better—'

'Ah, but I did not say where, Grace,' he murmured huskily, before his lips claimed hers.

Grace became suddenly still in his arms, forgetting to breathe altogether as those lips moved purposefully, seductively, against hers. His tongue teased her own lips apart, deepening the kiss to intimacy as it continued on its marauding path, tasting her, claiming her, seeking out every soft and delicate contour of her mouth, his tongue running erotically along the edge of her teeth even as his arms tightened about her and he curved her body more intimately against his own.

Grace had been encouraged by her parents to have friends of both sexes during her adolescent years, and several of those friendships had developed into slight crushes as they'd matured. One of the boys had even dared to kiss her chastely on the lips on one memorable occasion.

But Lucian St Claire was no boy. And there was nothing chaste about this kiss. The imprint of his body seemed to sear into hers, even as he encouraged her to return the intimate caress, his tongue sweeping lightly across her sensitised lips an enticement in itself.

Grace felt as if she were on fire. Aflame. Pleasure rippled across and through her body as her fingers tightened on the bareness of his shoulders. His kiss was wondrous. Ecstasy. Beyond anything Grace had ever thought or imagined in her innocent musings of being kissed by a man.

'Please…!' she groaned achingly as his lips left hers to trail a path of arousal down the column of her throat.

The sound of Grace's voice—that softly husky voice that moved across Lucian's flesh like a caress—brought him back to the reality of exactly what he was doing. And with whom.

He raised his head abruptly, deeply shocked at the realisation of how aroused he had been by Grace Hetherington—Miss Grace Hetherington, the young, unmarried ward of the Duke and Duchess of Carlyne!

The shock Lucian could see upon her own face told him that Grace was just as stunned by her own response.

How could Lucian have forgotten, however briefly, that Grace was but twenty years of age? That she was an innocent about to enjoy her first Season?

What sort of man was he to use her in this familiar fashion? Lucian wondered with a self-disgusted groan. What sort of man had he become?

Was he now so armoured against the emotions of others, so centred on self, that he would have allowed himself to take this young woman's innocence without a qualm? Without a care for the consequences of such an action? Without a thought being given as to what that taking would have done to her? Made of her?

His hands tightened painfully on her waist and he scowled down at her darkly. 'Grace—'

'Grace, dear, I saw your candle was alight and—'

Margaret, Duchess of Carlyne, entered the bedchamber after the briefest of knocks—only to come to an abrupt, shocked halt in the doorway, her eyes wide and her cheeks paling as she took in the intimacy of the scene in front of her.

'Oh, my…!' she breathed faintly, even as she raised a stricken hand to her throat. 'Oh, my goodness…!' she groaned weakly. 'I—' She gave a dazed shake of her head. ' I—if you will excuse me…!' She turned and fled.

Chapter Four

Grace stared after her aunt in shocked dismay, even as she stumbled back to drop down weakly upon the window-seat, taking care, even in that numbing shock, that she didn't sit on the clothes of Lucian St Claire's, which she had so neatly folded and placed there earlier.

Not only had she forgotten every shred of caution the moment Lucian St Claire had taken her into his arms, but her Aunt Margaret—her Aunt Margaret—had been a witness to that wantonness! What must her aunt be thinking? What must she now think of Grace?

Grace closed her eyes as the hot tears rushed forward, aware of Lucian St Claire standing briefly beside her before he moved away again, the only sound in the room now her own heated sobs of mortification as she buried her face in her hands.

She had behaved the wanton in Lucian St Claire's arms. Had encouraged him. Had returned his kisses.

Had relished the feel of his lips and tongue against hers. With absolutely no thought of denial.

She—

'You will remain here, Grace,' Lucian St Claire rasped into the silence.

'Where are you going?' Grace lowered her hands, her head snapping up, and she saw that he was dressed now—in shirt and breeches and black Hessians, at least.

What manner of man was he that he could even think of leaving her to face this alone? She could not believe he was such a coward as to—

'To talk to your guardians, of course.' Lucian's expression was grim as he pulled on his tailored waistcoat and jacket. He might as well be dressed for the part, at least.

'My—?' Her face was stricken. 'What are you going to say to them? How can you possibly explain— excuse—? What are they going to think of me?' She gave a woeful shake of her head, her hair falling forward about her face like a black silky curtain.

Lucian eyed her coldly. 'No doubt they are going to congratulate you on succeeding in enticing the brother of the Duke of Stourbridge into a betrothal!'

Lucian could not believe he had been so stupid. So absolutely, bloody stupid! What game had he thought he was playing with this young woman? 'One kiss' be damned! He should have made his escape from her bedchamber whilst he still had the chance!

Instead, this surely had to take the place of honour as the most wanton piece of self-destruction he had ever allowed himself to fall into! A betrothal, followed by a marriage, to exactly the sort of young, inexperienced woman he had always been at such pains to avoid!

But there was no other way out of this situation that Lucian could see. Absolutely none. For either of them.

His mouth curled disdainfully. 'Do try to look a little happier, Grace, when I am about to ask your guardians for your hand in marriage.'

Grace stared at him dazedly, sure that she could not have heard him correctly. He could not seriously think—Could not imagine—'But I have no wish to marry you!'

'Wish?' He arched scathing brows. 'Wishes, Grace—either yours or my own—do not enter into the situation we now find ourselves in,' he assured her scornfully. 'We have broken the unwritten law of Society—'

'But we have done nothing that could result in—Well, in—' Grace was not so naïve that she did not know how babies were made. She was well aware that she should not have allowed this man the liberty of kissing her—had no idea how she was going to face her aunt again!—but surely that did not mean they had to actually marry each other?

Lucian St Claire gave her a pitying look down the long, arrogant length of his nose. 'The unwritten law, Grace—"thou shalt not get caught"! Society may behave exactly as it pleases behind closed doors—and very often does!—but in no way is it permissible to allow that behaviour to become public knowledge.'

'But only my aunt is aware—'

'Your aunt is no doubt relating this incident to her husband, the Duke of Carlyne, at this very moment,' he dismissed coldly. 'I have known them most of my life, Grace. Their son, your cousin, was my dearest friend. I am afraid that nothing less than marriage between us will satisfy that friendship.'

'No!' Grace protested as she rose sharply to her feet. This was wrong. All wrong.

She had behaved badly just now, yes. She had behaved stupidly, certainly. Recklessly, even. But surely that did not mean that she had to be tied for the rest of her life to a man who obviously loved her no more than she loved him?

Did it…?

'You have something else you wish to say to me before I talk to your uncle?' He was every inch Lord Lucian St Claire, brother of the haughty Duke of Stourbridge, as he paused in the doorway.

Frighteningly so. Grace found herself facing a complete stranger. The teasing lover of earlier was nowhere to be seen in this coldly arrogant nobleman.

Because he no more wished to be married to her than Grace wished to be married to him. Only Society, it seemed, and his friendship and regard for her aunt and uncle dictated that it must be so…

Well, if that were the case then Grace wanted no part of that Society. Nor would she remain with her aunt and uncle to bring shame upon them by her behaviour. If needs be she would return to the countryside from whence she had come.

Her chin rose determinedly. 'I will refuse any offer of marriage you might make, My Lord.'

His mouth twisted into a humourless smile, those black eyes cold and merciless. 'You will be given little choice in the matter, Grace.'

She gasped. 'But of course I will be consulted—'

'No, Grace, you will not,' Lucian assured her flatly, almost pitying her in that moment. Almost.

He was too angry, both with himself and with her, to feel genuine pity. Grace Hetherington was everything Lucian had already decided he did not desire in a wife. She was too young. She was too idealistic in her expectations. Expectations Lucian already knew, in the resolute way he felt he had to hold himself aloof from emotional entanglement, he would never be able to measure up to.

Her response just now to his kisses seemed to indicate they would both enjoy the bedding part of their marriage, but Lucian did not hold out hopes for the success of any other part of the alliance. Certainly he had no desire to see himself happily ensconced with Grace in the way that Hawk and Jane now were at Mulberry Hall. In fact, as Lucian had originally intended with any woman he took to wife, he would spend as little time with her as possible once they were married.

Grace had been brought up in the country. Once she was his wife it was to his own country estate in Hampshire that she would go, and there she would stay.

His mouth thinned with displeasure as he saw how

pale her face had become at his assertion. 'You have been caught in a compromising position, Grace, and the price of that compromise, for both of us, is marriage.'

And, oh, how he hated the very idea of it. Grace knew that without a shadow of a doubt. As did she. It would be horrible, unimaginable, to find herself married to a man who no longer seemed even to like her, let alone wanted to spend the rest of his life tied to her in marriage.

She straightened as she raised her chin challengingly. 'I will refuse to marry you, Lord St Claire.'

Those black eyes narrowed ominously. 'You will not, Grace.'

Grace stood her ground as she gave a determined shake of her head. 'You will not dictate to me, sir.'

A nerve pulsed in his tightly clenched jaw. 'My friendship with your aunt and uncle dictates it, not I!'

'Your friendship with my aunt and uncle…?' Her eyes widened with indignation. 'What of *my* feelings in this matter?'

His top lip curled with displeasure. 'They became unimportant, as did my own, the moment your aunt walked into this bedchamber and found the two of us together. It would seem I am to pay the price for the deed without even having enjoyed it to the full,' he added mockingly.

Grace breathed hard in her agitation. 'And neither *will* you!' she assured him forcefully. 'Not now. Or ever!'

Those black eyes narrowed dangerously. 'You are denying me our marital bed before we are even wed?'

'I am telling you that there will be no marital bed! I am refusing to marry you under any circumstances! For any reason!' Her hands were clenched tightly into fists at her sides.

She really was magnificently beautiful when she was angry, Lucian appreciated dispassionately. 'I really cannot agree to that, Grace—'

'I do not need your agreement, My Lord—'

'You would rather cause more distress to your aunt?' His eyes were narrowed coldly.

She flushed. 'No, of course not.'

'And your uncle?' Lucian continued remorselessly. 'Unless I am mistaken, the Duke is unwell…'

She swallowed hard. 'He has a—a condition of the heart. Although he refuses to believe it.'

Lucian gave an abrupt inclination of his head. 'Then do you not think a scandal involving his niece is the last thing that he needs?'

'You are being unfair, My Lord—'

'I am being practical, Grace,' Lucian rasped. 'Now, I advise that you tidy yourself in my absence. That you dress more appropriately for receiving the congratulations of your guardians on the good fortune of your future marriage.'

She gave a stubborn shake of her head. 'I do not believe my aunt and uncle would ever force a betrothal upon me brought about in such regrettable circumstances.'

Lucian gave her a pitying look. Grace really was very young if she honestly believed that would be the case. He already knew that the Duke and Duchess of Carlyne would grasp him eagerly to their bosoms and call him nephew as quickly as they would forget the circumstances of their betrothal, before congratulating themselves on the advantageous match they had secured for their young niece. Cynically, Lucian could not help wondering how long it would be before Grace saw that advantage for herself…

She would become wife to the war hero Major Lord Lucian St Claire, and sister-in-law to the powerful Duke of Stourbridge and his lovely wife Jane, also to the eligible Lord Sebastian St Claire, and to the beautiful Lady Arabella St Claire. And the prestige and wealth of those individual St Claires was such that in Society they were held to be a law unto themselves.

Except, Lucian knew, when it came to the question of besmirching the reputation of an innocent young lady such as Miss Grace Hetherington, ward of the Duke and Duchess of Carlyne, in a public inn…

Lucian gave a mocking shake of his head. 'Future events will prove you quite wrong, my dear Grace.'

'I am not your *dear* anything!'

Not yet, perhaps. But she would be. And if nothing else, once Grace was his wife, Lucian intended slaking at his leisure the thirst her body created in his. With any luck he could still continue with his earlier businesslike plans for his marriage. He would get Grace with child within months, and then he would deposit her at his estate in Hampshire—far away from London and the life he intended to carry on living there whilst his wife and child rusticated in the country.

Not for him the slavish devotion Lucian now saw in his brother Hawk. No, that was being unfair. Hawk worshipped the ground his beloved Jane walked upon, yes, but it was a love that was more than reciprocated as the two of them happily resided together at Mulberry Hall, awaiting the birth of their first child.

Completely unlike the businesslike arrangement that Lucian intended for his own marriage. Indeed, once Grace had produced the necessary heir they would not even have to see each other above once a year, and then only for appearances' sake.

'Indeed you are not,' he conceded hardly. 'But I advise you, for your own sake, that the sooner you learn to obey me the better we shall deal with each other.'

'*Obey* you…?' Grace stared at him incredulously, two bright spots of angry colour in her cheeks. 'The year is 1817, My Lord, not 1217, and the times of the feudal overlord are long gone!'

'Not on my estate,' he assured her coldly.

'But we are not on your estate,' she pointed out with insincere sweetness.

'Yet.'

'Ever!'

His dark gaze swept over her with chilling intensity. 'Your stubbornness in this matter is starting to annoy me, Grace.' His tone was softly warning—dangerously so.

Grace had never felt so consumed with frustrated

anger. No matter how many times she told this man she would not even consider the idea of marrying him, he still persisted in talking as if it were a foregone conclusion—as if Grace were already tied to him, answerable to him. Which she most certainly was not. And she never would be.

'Very well.' She finally nodded abruptly, her mouth set stubbornly. 'If your friendship for my aunt and uncle "dictates" it, then you may ask them for their permission to pay your addresses to me. It will be an offer I shall promptly refuse. And there the matter will be at an end.' She sat down in the window seat to arrange her nightgown as modestly about her as the circumstances allowed. It was a little difficult to look disdainfully elegant whilst wearing only her night attire!

Lord Lucian gave her another of those pitying smiles. 'Our betrothal will be announced before the week is out,' he predicted mockingly.

Her eyes sparkled rebelliously. 'I would rather agree to marry Francis Wynter than consent to enter into a betrothal with you!'

Lucian shrugged with complete indifference, knowing that this particular threat was an idle one. He was sure from watching the two of them together the previous evening that Grace would prefer even the prospect of marriage to *him* over a lifetime as Francis Wynter's wife.

'I am sure your guardians would even agree to that in order to avoid the scandal that would result if the events of tonight were to become public knowledge.'

'I have already assured you that my aunt will say nothing—'

'Your aunt, I am afraid, is probably already living in fear of the manifestation of the physical evidence of tonight's events.'

'Physical evidence…?' Grace looked startled.

'You really *cannot* be that naïve, Grace.' Lucian eyed her pityingly.

Her cheeks flamed anew as his meaning became clear. 'But we did not—' She gave a fierce shake of her head. 'Nothing happened tonight of which either of us needs be ashamed.'

'Shame…' Lucian repeated the word thoughtfully. 'Such a small word for the ruination of your life, is it not?'

'My life will not be ruined over one silly mistake—'

'Will it not, Grace?' he mused. 'I believe you will find you are mistaken about that. You see, Grace, a man is allowed his affairs—his mistresses, even—but a woman's reputation is a tenuous thing. As light and delicate as gossamer—and as easily destroyed,' he concluded hardly. 'I do assure you, Grace, physical evidence or not, if there is even the hint of gossip that you have been found by your guardians in your bedchamber with a naked man you are not even betrothed to, then your reputation will be ruined for ever, and any future marriage prospects completely destroyed.'

'Then I will retire to the country and remain an old maid—'

'I would not advise it for one with such a passionate nature as your own, Grace,' he drawled mockingly, knowing by the way her face paled that he had succeeded in shaking her.

'You are despicable, sir!' She glared at him vehemently.

'Probably.' Lucian shrugged off the insult. 'But a life in the country as an old maid really would not suit you, Grace. One day you would be sure to give in to temptation—with a local farmer, perhaps, or possibly a married neighbour. With the possible result that an illegitimate child would then bear the stigma of your shame for the rest of its days. No, Grace, you would be far wiser to accept your fate and marry me.'

She hated this man, Grace decided numbly. Hated him with a passion. With as much passion, if not more, with which she had only minutes ago returned his kisses. Any softer feelings she might have had towards him following his nightmares had completely dissipated in the face of his intractability concerning a marriage between them.

'Never.' She roused herself with an effort, so emotionally tired that she just wanted to sleep—to close her eyes and find when she woke in the morning that this had all been just a dream. A horrible, horrible dream.

Lucian St Claire's mouth twisted humourlessly. 'You really are not looking at this situation positively at all, Grace,' he taunted. 'After all, you will be marrying the brother of a duke—'

'I am already the niece-by-marriage of a duke.'

'I am also the *son* of a duke, Grace. A second son, admittedly,' he acknowledged dryly, 'but luckily my father was a man of vision. A man who saw that having three sons might one day present a problem. It was a dilemma that he solved by making provision for all of his children. As a result we are all, my sister included, independently wealthy. My own wealth has been increased considerably over the years by wise investments. I am wealthy enough by far, I do assure you, Grace, for my wife to live the life of a duchess without the onerous duties that necessarily accompany that role.'

Grace stared at him unblinkingly. What did she care for his wealth? Did this man really believe that if she agreed to become his wife she would be happy in the knowledge that at least he had the wealth to ensure her life was a comfortable one!

Comfortable?

Grace could not see any future life for herself as the unwilling wife of Lord Lucian St Claire's as being a comfortable one!

She gave him a narrow-eyed glare. 'My own father was also a man of vision, My Lord,' she assured him coldly. 'In as much as he did not see any difference between a male or female heir. I am my parents' only child. As a consequence, all of my father's considerable personal wealth, as well as his estate in Cornwall, were left in trust to me on his death.'

Lucian St Claire gave an abrupt inclination of his head. 'Then it appears I am to marry a woman with a considerable dowry, does it not?'

Her chin rose challengingly. 'The provisions of my

father's will ensure that a portion of that wealth remains in my possession even after I am married, with the rest to be put in trust for my children.'

Her parents could not have foreseen their premature deaths, of course, but it had always been a worry of her mother's, as well as her father's, that Grace would one day be pursued on the marriage mart not for herself alone, but for her father's considerable wealth. The property laws ensured that a woman's wealth automatically became her husband's on her marriage. It had been a law that neither of her parents had agreed with, and provision had been made to circumvent that law as far as was possible.

Lucian St Claire gave a brief smile. 'In that case it seems I will be able to forgo the task of arranging an allowance for you after we are married,' came his parting shot, as the door of the bedchamber closed quietly—decisively—behind him.

Grace stared after him blankly. His persistence in pursuing that particular line—his absolute conviction that a marriage between them was the only possible outcome of tonight's events—shook Grace more than she cared to admit. More than she cared for Lucian St Claire to know.

Because she was not so sure in her own determination that it would not be so as she wished it to be. Her aunt and uncle, the Duke and Duchess of Carlyne, although having been warm and kind to her this last year, were not as visionary as her own parents had been. Her parents would never have seen Grace married to any man for reasons other than a deep love existing between them. The fact that her aunt and uncle had known Lord Lucian St Claire for years—that he was a family friend, had been the best friend of her cousin Simon—already indicated that they would approve of a match between him and Grace.

A match Grace could never willingly agree to.

Never, ever willingly.

As Lucian St Claire would quickly learn for himself if he proceeded with this absurdity.

Chapter Five

'I know this is all terribly exciting for you, Grace, but you really must try to eat something.' Her aunt beamed at her encouragingly across the breakfast table from Grace, as the two of them sat in the private parlour of the coaching inn. 'After all, you do not want Lord Lucian to see his betrothed looking pale and sickly when he joins us.'

Grace looked at her aunt numbly. The two of them were alone in the parlour. Her uncle, having recovered fully from his upset the evening before, and Lord Francis had set off early to check on the progress being made on the repair of the ducal coach—it being the Duke's intention, her aunt had informed her archly, to tell Francis of Grace's betrothal to Lord Lucian St Claire during their absence, in the hopes that he would have accepted this startling change in circumstances by the time he returned.

As if it were of any interest to Grace whether Francis

were informed or otherwise—or indeed what his response was to the news!

Only Grace's own emotions concerning the announcement of her betrothal to Lord Lucian St Claire, imparted to her by her uncle when he and her aunt had come to her bedchamber in the early hours of this morning, were of any significance. Those emotions had been disbelief and horror. But Grace's protests had gone unheard as her uncle had proceeded to tell her how fortunate she was in her betrothed. How charming and worldly Lord Lucian was. How prestigious his family. How all the doors of Society would now be opened to her.

The list of advantages of being the wife of Lord Lucian St Claire were endless, it seemed.

Grace's numbness, following her aunt and uncle's return to their own bedchamber, had been so absolute it had resulted in her sitting in the window seat all night, staring sightlessly out at the slowly awakening day. It had seemed to her at the time that it was unacceptable that day should follow night, as it usually did, when such a momentous—horrifying!—occurrence was taking place in her own life. To add insult to injury, the sun had come out—as if to shine in blessing upon the union.

Her union to Major Lord Lucian St Claire.

He had been absolutely correct in his surmise that her aunt and uncle would look favourably upon such a match. In fact her aunt had gone so far in dampening her memory of exactly *why* the betrothal was felt to be necessary that she now chose to think of it as a love-match.

The only blessing of the previous night had been that Lord Lucian had not returned to Grace's bedchamber himself after he had proved so correct in his assessment as to her guardians' acceptance of his offer. A gloating Lucian St Claire would simply have been too much to bear on top of the other indignities Grace had already suffered that night! She certainly had not forgotten the humiliation of his remark about 'one with such a passionate nature as your own, Grace'!

Perhaps because she was still shocked at her own response to him the night before…

Indeed, it was the thought of seeing him again, of recognising the mockery in his dark, condescending gaze, that made it impossible for Grace even to contemplate the idea of eating breakfast. The tea she had requested also remained untouched.

'I am sorry, Aunt, I did not hear what you were saying…' She gave a pained frown as she realised how inattentive she had been while her aunt continued to chatter on regardless. In her preoccupation she might have missed the purchase of her wedding gown or the date of the wedding—possibly even where she was to go on her honeymoon trip!

'Your aunt was explaining how unfortunate it is that I have to continue my journey to my brother's home in Gloucestershire before I am able to return to London to be at your side,' Lucian drawled with lazy mockery, as he entered the parlour where the two ladies sat together.

Grace Hetherington, he noted frowningly, had stiffened at the first sound of his voice. Not an auspicious beginning to their betrothal, to be sure. But, in the circumstances, perhaps an understandable one.

Lucian was not particularly happy himself this morning. The effects of the brandy—and the blow to his head!—had now manifested themselves, leaving him with much more than a nasty taste in his mouth.

Lucian knew he would receive little sympathy from his family, either, regarding his imminent fate. In fact Hawk, as the patriarch of the family, had been making mutterings for some time about his own and Sebastian's unmarried state—even going so far as to remind Sebastian of a rash promise he had made the previous year, concerning looking for a wife in earnest once Hawk himself was happily married. A reminder Sebastian had so far managed to avoid satisfying.

In fact, Lucian had offered to act as escort to his sister Arabella during this Season in an attempt to surreptitiously seek a wife of his own. The meek, obedient wife of his imaginings. A woman so unlike Grace Hetherington as to be laughable! But his fate had been sealed the moment he had stumbled into the wrong bedchamber the previous evening, neatly entrapping himself in a web of his own making.

That did not mean that he had to like it. Or Grace Hetherington. 'Our separation will be hard for you to endure, following so quickly on the announcement of our betrothal, I know.' He looked down at his Grace mockingly. 'But you will not suffer alone, I do assure you,' he added tauntingly, instantly having the pleasure of watching indignant colour enter her previously pale cheeks.

Her beauty was undeniable. Her desirability also. It was only the thought of having to marry her, when Lucian had not even had the pleasure of satisfying his undeniable physical response to that beauty and desirability, that he found so intolerable. The parson's mousetrap, indeed! Lucian had been well and truly ensnared in it.

'I do believe I will survive such a separation well enough.' Grace met Lucian St Claire's gaze challengingly.

Hateful man. Hateful, *hateful,* mockingly horrid man!

If Grace never set eyes on him again it would be too soon! Even looking as rakishly handsome as he did this morning in brown superfine, tan waistcoat and breeches, brown Hessians, his linen very white against his throat, his dark hair untidily fashionable upon his brow.

Her betrothed.

A man she did not know.

A man she did not *want* to know.

But a man whose lips had intimately explored hers the previous evening. A man whom she had kissed back just as intimately.

Her cheeks burned at the memory of those kisses. 'As, indeed, no doubt will you,' she added hardly.

'I will bear up tolerably well, I believe, Grace. But only tolerably.' He folded his elegant length into the chair beside her own, his movements languidly graceful. 'Perhaps you would care to begin practising your wifely duties by pouring me a cup of tea…? Milk, no sugar.'

Grace's mouth thinned rebelliously as she lifted the cooling teapot and milk, wishing that her aunt were not present so that she might pour the two over Lucian St Claire's head, as she so longed to do. But her aunt's presence necessitated that she maintain a veneer of politeness between herself and Lord St Claire at least—no matter what her real feelings might be.

Society was an ass, Grace had decided as she'd sat broodingly staring out of the window earlier that morning, if it dictated that two such mismatched people as herself and Lucian St Claire should be forced to marry each other because of one small—one *very* small—misdemeanour. Not even a true misdemeanour, really. Only a small hiccup in those rigid rules the ton set such standard by.

'Carlyne and I thought that next month might be an agreeable time for the wedding…?' her aunt suggested lightly.

Grace's hand shook so badly as she handed Lucian St Claire his tea that the cup actually rattled precariously in the saucer. Her cheeks burned as she saw the hard mockery in his gaze as it so easily met her shocked one. Grace swallowed hard. 'Next month, Aunt? But I have always envisaged that I would have a June wedding…'

'June?' Her aunt frowned her consternation.

The reason for which was perfectly obvious, considering that her aunt believed Grace and Lord Lucian to have made love together the previous evening. The same reason that Grace was just as determined to have the wedding planned for two months hence.

Surely once her aunt realised that there were to be no repercussions from the incident—which there could not be!—then she would allow Grace to make an end to the betrothal?

Whether her aunt allowed it or not, that was fully Grace's intention. She simply could not—would not—marry a man she did not love, who did not love her, for something she—they—had not even done.

'Yes. June,' Grace repeated firmly, this time avoiding the mockery she knew would still be in Lord Lucian's knowing gaze.

'The weather is sure to be more agreeable then—do you not think, Lord Lucian?'

Lucian looked at her from between narrowed lids, not fooled for a moment by the innocence of Grace's expression as she looked at him enquiringly. Miss Grace Hetherington, he felt sure, was hoping to end their betrothal as soon as it became apparent to her guardians that she was not with child. An occurrence they already both knew was not even a possibility.

But it really would not do. Child or no, as far as the Duke and Duchess of Carlyne were concerned Grace's reputation was well and truly ruined, and the fact that no child would appear eight or even seven months after a marriage between them could not change that fact. Grace simply refused to accept that they had decided their own fates by the mere fact they had been found together by her aunt in Grace's bedchamber in a state of undress.

He met her gaze unblinkingly. 'I see no reason to delay the wedding until June when we are both so set on it.'

Those grey eyes flashed warningly, although her tone was calmly sweet. 'I believe the delay would give us more time to become better acquainted, My Lord.'

Lucian bared his teeth in a humourless smile. 'I assure you, your aunt and uncle believe us to be already acquainted well enough!'

The Duchess gave a strangled gasp at his candour, her hand going nervously to her throat as she became completely flustered. 'A wedding next month really would be preferable, Grace—'

'I am set on June.'

Lucian studied the stubborn set of Grace's mouth for several long seconds. Her stubbornness was another indication that she was far from the compliant wife he had wished for.

For all that Grace had probably not slept well the night before, once her guardians had informed her of their betrothal, she looked quite astonishingly beautiful this morning. Her high-waisted gown was of a shade of grey that was almost silver, a perfect match in colour for her eyes, and its low neckline showed a tantalising amount of her creamy breasts. Her hair was a riot of dark curls, with several wispy tendrils falling temptingly about her throat and nape, and her lips dusky pink in the otherwise paleness of her face. If he was going to have a wilful wife forced upon him, at least Lucian could be thankful she was a beautiful and desirable one!

He gave an acknowledging inclination of his head. 'If that really is your wish, Grace…'

'What an agreeable and accommodating husband you

are to have, to be sure, Grace,' The Duchess told her approvingly, seeming completely impervious to the way her niece's gaze had narrowed so suspiciously on Lucian.

But Lucian was aware of it, and met that look with one of challenge as he allowed a mocking smile to curve his lips. 'How could I be any other with one as beautiful as Grace?'

Grace wished very much that the two of them were alone, so that she might tell this man exactly what she wished him to do with her—and that was to release her from this bogus betrothal! Something he obviously had no intention of doing.

But the delay of the wedding until June was exactly what Grace wished for. She might then have just reason—in her guardians' eyes, at least—for ending the betrothal. Although it might be a little difficult to achieve with any degree of ease if St Claire were to continue being so accommodating.

Grace deliberately kept her lashes lowered over rebellious eyes.

'You are very kind, My Lord.'

'Then you are the first to find me so, Grace,' Lord Lucian drawled tauntingly.

'Oh, I am sure that cannot be true, Lucian,' the Duchess reproved indulgently. 'I remember you as being a most agreeable young man.'

Grace could not imagine Lucian St Claire as a young man at all, let alone an agreeable one. 'Age has a way of rendering cynical even the sunniest of spirits, Aunt.' She smiled sweetly.

No, definitely not compliant, Lucian acknowledged with reluctant admiration. But then, he doubted his interest would have been in the least piqued if she had been. He simply had not envisaged *marrying* her at the time!

'Obviously you do not yet have that excuse, my dear,' he drawled mockingly.

'Oh, I am sure that Grace did not at all mean the remark in a derogatory way, Lord Lucian.' The Duchess rushed to defend her. 'Indeed, maturity in one's husband is much to be admired. Carlyne is ten years my senior, and we have always dealt very well together,' she added fondly.

Lucian was well aware of the fact that the Duke and Duchess's alliance had been a successful one. But then, it had been a lovematch. Unlike his own and Grace Hetherington's. Although theirs promised to be a fiery one!

'If you will excuse me, ladies…?' Lucian stood up in one fluid movement. 'I believe it is time that I made my departure. You will allow Grace to walk outside with me for a few moments, Your Grace?'

'Of course.' The Duchess smiled up at him graciously. 'I am sure that you will wish to say your farewells in private.'

Lucian felt sure, after a brief glance at Grace Hetherington's flushed face, that farewell was the least of the things she wanted to say to him in private!

He took the Duchess's proffered hand and raised it to his lips. 'May I call on you at Berkeley Square when I return to town in a week's time?'

'Of course.' The older woman laughed happily. 'I am sure that Grace will be eagerly awaiting your arrival.'

Lucian bit back a smile as, in complete contradiction of her aunt's claim, he saw the brief look of disdain that Grace shot in his direction.

'My dear…?' He held out his arm to her pointedly.

Grace looked at that arm for several seconds as she debated whether or not she had the courage to refuse to accompany him outside. A futile gesture when being alone with Lord Lucian St Claire was exactly what she desired at this moment.

'My Lord.' She rose gracefully to her feet to rest her fingers very lightly on the sleeve of his jacket. 'I will not be long, Aunt.'

'There is no rush, Grace.' The Duchess smiled encouragingly. 'After all, you are betrothed, and you will not see each other for a week or more.'

The existence of a betrothal between them seemed to allow all sorts of liberties that would not otherwise be contemplated, Grace acknowledged frowningly as she accompanied Lucian St Claire from the inn. Apart from the obvious one, of course. But then, her aunt and uncle already seemed to believe her guilty of that!

'I am sorry to say you do not look any happier this morning than you did last night, Grace.'

'Did you expect me to?' Grace removed her hand from Lucian St Claire's sleeve before stepping away from him and linking her hands together behind her back. The bright sunshine was still doing nothing to lighten her mood.

He raised mocking brows over darkly brooding eyes. 'It is customary to be so when you are newly betrothed, surely?'

'Not when the betrothal is against one's wishes!'

'Grace—'

'My Lord?'

Lucian gave a weary sigh. 'Did I not tell you last night how it would be?'

'You did.' Her mouth was tight. 'I bow to your superior knowledge.'

'Even while you deplore it?'

'Yes!'

Lord Lucian's mouth was tight. 'Being angry and resentful towards me will not change what is now fact.'

Her eyes glittered silver. 'And are *you* not angry and resentful also?'

He shrugged wide shoulders. 'I am—resigned.'

'How commendable!'

'You would make yourself less unhappy if you were to adopt the same stance.'

'Unhappy?' Grace moved away from him agitatedly. 'I am not unhappy, My Lord. Neither am I resigned. What I am is determined on finding some way of bringing to an end this—this sham of a betrothal.'

Lucian eyed her pityingly. 'In circumstances such as these that might not be as easy to do as you might think.'

'Once it becomes apparent that I am not with child—'

'There is still the matter of your lost innocence.'

'We both know it is not lost.'

'And would you be willing to undergo a medical examination in order to prove that?'

Lucian knew from the sudden paling of her face that

Grace Hetherington believed he was being deliberately cruel in his bluntness, but he could see no other
way of bringing her to an appreciation of how serious
this situation was.

'Unless, of course, a medical examination might
prove the opposite…?' he added shrewdly. After all,
Grace Hetherington had been *very* passionate in her
response last night. Too much so…?

'You—you are disgusting!' Her expression was indignantly outraged.

Lucian gave a mocking smile. 'Far better that we
have honesty between the two of us, at least.'

'Honesty? *Honesty!*' she repeated scathingly. 'This
coming from a man whose reputation is far from untar-
nished!'

Lucian's mouth firmed. 'I advise you to tread carefully with this conversation, my dear.'

Even if his words had not been a warning, Grace
would have been alerted to the danger Lord Lucian now
represented by his sudden dangerous stillness, and the
dark scowl upon his brow. 'You are saying that you
agree with this double standard that a man is allowed
his experience while a woman is not?'

'I am not saying it at all, Grace. Society says it.'

Grace shook her head. 'But I am sure that you must
agree, My Lord, that this inequality when it comes to the
conduct of men and women is completely unacceptable?'

Lucian could feel a nerve pulsing in his tightly
clenched jaw. 'Not when it comes to the taking of a
wife, no.' It was an acceptable double standard in a

mistress, certainly, but Lucian was surprised at just how much he did not like the possibility of Grace Hetherington, the woman who was to become his wife, having known other lovers before him.

She gave a disgusted snort. 'You want innocence in your wife?'

He shrugged. 'It has its advantage, in that an innocent can be…tutored in the ways of pleasing her husband.'

'In the ways of pleasing—!' She drew in an angry breath. 'You are arrogant, sir!'

'I am,' Lucian acknowledged unrepentantly.

Her pretty mouth firmed while her eyes glittered. 'Then it is as well I have no intention of becoming your wife, Lord St Claire.'

Lucian looked at her from between narrowed lids, not liking that spark of rebellion he could see in her eyes at all. 'I advise you not to do anything rash in the next week, Grace.'

Her expression was too innocent. 'Such as?'

'Such as deliberately giving me reason for ending the betrothal!'

This man knew too much, Grace decided frustratedly. Saw too much. Because encouraging the attentions of another man—any man—was exactly what she'd had in mind, if there were to be no other way to bring their betrothal to an end. Reasoning with this man certainly did not seem to be having any effect.

She drew in a controlling breath. 'I will do whatever I deem necessary to bring about my own happiness, My Lord.'

'No, Grace, you will not.'

He was suddenly standing very close. Too close. Close enough for Grace to be aware of everything about him—from the dark, tousled hair that fell so attractively across his brow, to the width of his shoulders, the elegance of his tapered waist and thighs, to the highly polished Hessians upon his feet.

'If I so much as suspect,' he continued softly, 'or even hear the whisper of a rumour to the effect that you are encouraging the attentions of another man, then you will leave me with no choice but to force that particular issue myself. Do I make myself clear, Grace?'

Grace stared up at him, mesmerised. By the soft threat of his voice. By those dark, compelling eyes. Eyes that, in the sunlight, seemed to reflect gold flecks in their depths.

She started visibly as he raised a hand and gently lifted a curl that the warm breeze had brushed over her brow. His fingers seemed to burn her flesh where they touched, and the quiver she felt down her spine was one of complete physical awareness, rather than the revulsion she wished to feel.

What was it about this man, this man in particular, that made her react so? What spell had Lucian St Claire cast upon her that made it impossible for Grace to step away from him? The same spell that made her want to move closer? To once again know the hardness of his lips pressed against her own?

He smiled slightly, his gaze slightly softened as he gazed down at her. 'I intend making this betrothal as pleasant for you as possible, Grace,' he told her huskily. 'For us both to enjoy becoming—better acquainted,' he echoed her own words of earlier. But coming from him they had a completely different meaning, with a sensual undertone that was unmistakable.

A sensual undertone that made Grace's insides feel as if they were melting under the heat. Her breathing became low and shallow, and she couldn't break her gaze away from the darkness of his, felt as if he were slowly, inexorably, drawing her towards him by the sheer force of his will.

They weren't even touching, and yet Grace was aware of the swelling surge of her breasts, that suddenly made the bodice of her gown feel too tight, of the unfurling hardening of their tips.

She moistened dry lips, shaking her head as she strove for some sense of reason. 'I do not believe that your—appeal will improve upon acquaintance, My Lord.'

'Probably not,' he acknowledged with a taunting smile. 'But I have no doubt that yours will,' he promised meaningfully.

Grace's cheeks coloured hotly. The meaning behind that promise was easy to comprehend after Lord Lucian's earlier comment concerning an innocent being tutored in the ways of pleasing her husband. 'You—'

'Grace! Tell me it isn't true! Tell me you are not really intending to marry Lord St Claire!'

Grace stepped abruptly away from Lord Lucian to turn and look frowningly at Francis Wynter as he hurried up the pathway from the village towards them.

His handsome face was flushed with anger as he turned his glaring gaze on the older man who stood so confidently at Grace's side.

Contrarily, Francis Wynter's proprietorial assertion that Grace could not possibly be contemplating marrying Lord Lucian St Claire had the opposite effect from the one Francis so obviously desired. It completely turned Grace's earlier resolve to end her betrothal into a desire to do exactly the opposite. She deliberately put her hand into the crook of Lucian St Claire's arm to look challengingly at the indignant Francis Wynter.

'Have a care, Wynter,' Lucian warned the younger man softly as he raised his hand to lightly cover Grace's. 'I am feeling particularly mellow this morning, following Grace's acceptance of my proposal of marriage, but that does not mean I am open to insult.'

'No insult was intended I am sure, Lucian.' The Duke had arrived slightly after his brother, his breathing heavy from the exertion of trying to keep up with the younger man. 'Francis is merely surprised by the suddenness of your feelings for each other, I am sure. Is that not so, Francis?' he prompted his brother hardly.

Lucian looked coldly at the younger man, knowing as Francis Wynter fought an inner battle with his emotions that surprise was the least of them. Lucian read anger there, and frustration.

'I had no idea that your taste ran to innocents, St Claire.' Francis Wynter looked at him challengingly.

Insult was most definitely intended this time, Lucian was sure. But he was just as sensitive of George

Wynter's feelings this morning as he had been the previous evening, when caught in such a compromising position with Grace. A challenge to Carlyne's youngest brother for his insulting behaviour towards both himself and Grace would be just as detrimental to the older man's health.

He gave an acknowledging inclination of his head. 'The St Claire wives have always been above reproach.'

'Really?' The younger man looked scornful. 'But surely your brother's wife—'

'That is enough, Francis!' the Duke of Carlyne thundered imperiously. 'You will go into the inn forthwith and try to compose yourself.'

Lucian was tempted, so *very* tempted, to force Francis Wynter to finish the insult he felt sure he had been about to level at Jane, Duchess of Stourbridge. Only his respect and genuine affection for George Wynter prevented him from demanding satisfaction from this insolent young puppy.

Grace watched curiously as Francis Wynter obviously fought an inner battle with what he wanted to do and say against what his older brother demanded he do. Wariness suddenly darkened his gaze as he met the cold glitter of Lucian St Claire's eyes. Knowing Francis was right to be wary, Grace felt the tension of Lord Lucian's arm beneath her hand, like that of a leashed predator about to spring upon his prey.

'I will join you in a moment, Uncle,' she said lightly, her own gaze deliberately pleasant. 'Once Lord Lucian and I have said our farewells.'

'You are leaving your betrothed so soon, St Claire?' Francis taunted.

Lucian gave a stiff acknowledgement of his head. 'A previous family engagement requires me to be elsewhere, I am afraid.'

'Rumour has it that you are estranged from your family nowadays.' The younger man eyed him scornfully.

'Rumour is an ass.'

Lucian added no further explanation as the two men continued to stare at each other for several long, tense seconds. Francis's gaze was the first to drop. Although that did not prevent Lucian from scowling his displeasure at learning he and his family had been under discussion by the ton. Or the reason for it.

It had been impossible for Lucian, after Waterloo, to return to the warmth of his family when he had felt so alienated from them by the bloodshed he had witnessed, the friends he had lost. And the situation was made worse by the damnable nightmares that persisted in haunting his nights. So instead he had emotionally distanced himself from his family. From everyone. Choosing to hide what was left of his emotions behind a façade of boredom and uninterest.

His betrothal to Grace Hetherington seemed to have put an end to that façade…

The challenge with which the two men still viewed each other was intolerable, Grace decided frustratedly. On the one hand there was Francis—a man who obviously had intentions towards her but in whom Grace had absolutely no interest. On the other was Lord Lucian St Claire, a man who did not wish to marry her but to whom she so unhappily found herself betrothed. Ludicrous probably more aptly described their present behaviour—like two dogs fighting over a particularly tasty bone!

Grace felt nothing but relief when her uncle, obviously losing all patience with his brother, took a firm hold of Francis's arm and marched him into the inn, to close the door firmly behind them; Grace was easily able to guess at the unpleasantness of the conversation now taking place between the two brothers.

'Well, that was enlightening, was it not?'

Grace removed her hand from Lord Lucian's rigidly tensed arm before turning to him frowningly. 'Indeed, My Lord?'

'Indeed.' He looked amused now, his dark eyes glittering with suppressed laughter, a cynical twist to those sculptured lips. 'It would seem that I have a rival for your affections, my dear.'

Grace gave an unladylike snort of impatience. 'Francis is nothing but a fool if he imagines for a moment that I would ever have returned his interest.'

'Perhaps.' Lucian nodded tersely. 'But even fools have emotions that can be bruised or trampled upon.'

Her eyes widened indignantly. 'Are you implying that I did something to encourage Lord Francis's attentions?'

'No, I am not implying that. I am merely stating that a scorned man can sometimes be as dangerous as a scorned woman.'

Lucian sensed in Francis Wynter an underlying

remnant of the vindictiveness that had made him so un-pleasant as a child. That same slyness of character Lucian had noted in him when he had stayed with Simon during the school holidays, and Francis's sneaki-ness had left them no choice but to exclude him from their boyish pursuits.

He stared after the younger man thoughtfully. 'I am warning you to have a care where Francis Wynter is con-cerned…'

'Might I remind you, Lord Lucian, that I am not as yet your wife?'

Lucian's expression softened appreciatively as he met the challenge in Grace's expression. What a spitfire she was! So tiny, so delicately lovely, and yet she had a will of iron. A will that was almost—but not quite—as strong as his own.

'My dear Grace, I am counting the days until you become so,' he murmured softly, receiving a wary glance for his trouble. He laughed huskily. 'For the moment I will content myself—and you, I hope—with a single kiss.'

'You most certainly—!' Grace's protest was cut short as Lord Lucian swept her up into his arms and claimed her mouth with his own.

Grace was sure that, even betrothed to her as he now was, Lord Lucian should not kiss her so—so passion-ately, so intimately. He curved the slenderness of her body against the hardness of his, while his mouth plun-dered and claimed every inch of hers, rendering Grace breathless and clinging to the broad width of his shoul-

ders as her body responded in a most alarming manner.
The buttons on Lord Lucian's jacket were sensually
abrasive against her already roused breasts, inciting a
warmth between Grace's thighs.

Her face was flushed, her eyes fever-bright when
Lucian at last lifted his head to look down at her, with
satisfaction in the depths of those dark, compelling
eyes.

'I will count the *hours* until my return.' His voice was
mockingly low. 'No, do not ruin the moment with
another of your cutting remarks, Grace,' he added with
amusement as he released her, to step back and tap her
playfully on the nose. 'It will be far more pleasing to
leave with a pleasant memory to see me on my way,
rather than one of your sharp set-downs.'

Grace wasn't sure that she was at all capable of
making one of those sharp set-downs at this precise
moment. In fact, she wasn't sure she was able to speak
at all. In truth, this man—his kisses—had the ability to
render her speechless!

At the same time, she did not want Lord Lucian to think
she was in the slightest degree more amenable to the idea
of a betrothal or marriage between the two of them.

'You would rather take an illusion with you than the
truth?' Her voice was snappily dismissive.

His mouth twisted humourlessly. 'Most of life, I
have found, is an illusion. So a little more will make no
difference.' He drew himself up to his full impressive
height. 'I think I shall leave you now, Grace, before we
have the opportunity to argue again. My dear.' He gave

a brief inclination of his head before turning on his heel and walking away.

Grace watched with troubled eyes as he strode to the back of the inn where the stables and his horse were being kept. Lord Lucian St Claire, she was learning, was a man of contradictions. A man who, by his offer for her, placed honour and friendship above his own happiness. Yet he was also a man, from his words just now, who was disillusioned with the world and the people who inhabited it, who wore a mask of civility and boredom to hide that disillusionment. The same mask that no doubt hid the horror of his years spent in the army, and which Grace was sure, after last night, manifested themselves in nightmares instead.

A man who distanced himself from his family so that they should never learn of those nightmares…?

Did that unexpected vulnerability in a man who gave every outward appearance of being coldly controlled, even without emotion, make Lucian a man it would be all too easy to fall in love with…?

God—Grace hoped not!

Chapter Six

Lucian sat with his chair facing the fireplace, elbows resting on the arms, his fingers steepled together as he stared unseeingly into the unlit hearth in the comfortable high-ceilinged room at his club. He was totally unaware of his surroundings, or the comings and goings of the other men who felt the need to take refuge, in the same way Lucian did, from the demands of their womenfolk hell-bent on enjoying the Season.

He had been back in town for two days now, having safely delivered his sister, Arabella, and their aunt, Lady Hammond, to St Claire house, before taking his leave and returning to his own residence in Mayfair.

He was only delaying the inevitable, of course; he knew he could not continue to avoid calling on the woman to whom he had been betrothed for the last nine days. That betrothal was now public knowledge—the announcement, as Lucian had predicted, having appeared in the newspapers a week ago.

No doubt the ton were simply dying to see Lord Lucian St Claire and his betrothed Grace Hetherington together. Which was one of the reasons Lucian had delayed, and delayed yet again, his inevitable first foray into Society since his return to town.

Only one of the reasons.

Miss Grace Hetherington herself being the main one.

For Lucian had found himself thinking of her far too much for comfort while with his family in Gloucestershire.

'And I tell you there's something odd about the whole business. St Claire is avoiding her like the plague.' A man, young from the sound of his voice, announced this with satisfaction as he noisily entered the room. 'The girl has been in town for over a week, and he has not so much as paid her a call yet.'

'The whole thing is a sorry affair to my mind,' his companion came back disgustedly. 'Whoever would have thought an out-and-outer like St Claire would succumb to the parson's mousetrap?'

'I'm telling you that he didn't,' the other man assured him impatiently. 'Rumour has it that her guardian, the Duke of Carlyne, insisted on the marriage after finding St Claire in bed with her.'

'He'll never marry her if that's the case. Take my word for it—St Claire will find a way out of this coil.'

'Can't be done, old boy. Chit has to break the betrothal herself. And what woman in her right mind would do that?'

The other man gave a snort. 'Bank on it. St Claire will find a way.'

'The woman's the ward of a duke.'

'A passably pretty one, too, according to the mater. She paid a courtesy call on the Duchess of Carlyne yesterday and was introduced to the ward while she was about it. But what else is she? A nobody. A Miss Glynis Heathton? Daughter of an artist, or some such? Not a chance that St Claire is going to marry someone like that!'

'A wager on it,' his friend challenged.

Lucian listened to the exchange with rapidly rising displeasure. Not because the two young bucks did not have their facts more or less correct, but because they did. Too much so, in Lucian's opinion. No doubt he need look no further than Francis Wynter to find the one guilty of spreading such tittle-tattle. Had he not warned Grace over a week ago that Francis, feeling himself scorned, might be a dangerous man to cross…?

But Lucian would deal with that—and exactly whose daughter Grace was—later. For now, he needed to teach these two young bucks a lesson in manners, if nothing else.

He rose silently to his feet before turning. 'Good afternoon, gentlemen.'

The two young men in question, one blond, one dark, froze like insects on a pin, a look of horrified fascination on both their faces as they realised that Lord Lucian St Claire must have overheard the whole of their conversation.

'I believe that you will find the name of the young lady under discussion is, in fact, Miss Grace Hetherington.' He spoke softly, unthreateningly, but the faces of both men paled considerably. 'It is my impression that one or indeed both of you were just now seriously in danger of insulting my betrothed…' His voice had all the silent force of the sword he had once wielded with such success—on one memorable occasion with mindless ferocity!—on the battlefield.

Lucian's reputation had preceded his return to England almost two years ago, resulting in several headstrong young gentlemen of the ton, who had not joined the army, challenging him to prove his skill. When they had failed to conquer him in that field they had moved on to his pugilistic capabilities, which were rumoured to be just as lethal and had indeed proved to be so. In fact Lucian had stood as witness at his brother Hawk's wedding to Jane the previous year with bruised knuckles, having engaged in one such encounter that very morning!

The sickly pallor on the faces of the two young men now facing him confirmed that they had heard not only the tales of Lucian's heroism on the battlefield but also tales of those other equally successful encounters with young members of the ton who had not even had the misfortune to insult his betrothed.

They were not much younger than himself, Lucian acknowledged heavily. In years, at least. In experience, both on and off the battlefield, it was another matter, of course.

'*Was* that the case, gentlemen?' Lucian continued in a softly pleasant tone that deceived no one. 'If I am mistaken please do enlighten me…?'

'Not—not at all the case, St Claire,' the blond one stuttered.

''Course not,' his friend blustered at the same time. 'Merely congratulating you on your good fortune. The mater says Miss Hetherington is a stunner.'

'Indeed?' Lucian arched one condescending brow.

'Well. No. Er…' The dark-haired young man swallowed hard as he realised he had made yet another mistake. 'Very gracious and beautiful is how my mother described her.'

'How kind.' The hard mask of Lucian's face didn't alter by so much as a softening of the lips. 'Perhaps I will have the pleasure of introducing you two gentlemen to Miss Hetherington this evening, when we attend Lady Humbers's ball in the company of her aunt, the Duchess of Carlyne?' he challenged, knowing that rakish young bucks such as these two usually avoided such gatherings in favour of less genteel entertainments.

'Oh—of course.' The blond one nodded.

'Look forward to it,' his dark-haired friend agreed enthusiastically.

'Then no doubt I will see you both later.' Lucian gave a terse nod. 'If you two young gentlemen will excuse me?' He crossed the room in long, forceful strides, no doubt leaving the two younger men to congratulate themselves on their lucky escape.

At the same time he accepted that he had now committed himself to attending Lady Humbers's ball this evening, and also to seeing Grace again…

* * *

'You did not tell me that your father was the renowned artist Peter Hetherington.'

Grace's gaze was cool as she glanced up at Lord Lucian St Claire as the two of them danced together in the crowded ballroom of Lady Humbers's townhouse.

Grace had been in London for nine days now, and most of that time had been spent at dressmakers, milliners and cobblers as her aunt saw to the acquisition of the new wardrobe she said Grace was so in need of. Indeed, it had proved to be the case. Grace's three day dresses and two gowns for the evening were in no way sufficient for the at-homes her aunt held three mornings a week, and the numerous afternoon teas they had to attend in response to those morning visitors. And now the evening entertainments had begun in earnest too.

Lady Humbers's house was positively heaving with people this evening—the ballroom itself full to capacity, it seemed. But the crush of people, the noise of conversation and laughter, were not the reason for Grace's coolness of manner. No, that was for another reason entirely.

Her aunt had insisted that they did not move far from home these last two days, in the vain hope that Grace's betrothed, Lord Lucian St Claire, would call upon them—as he had said that he would once he returned to town. This had apparently taken place two days ago, Grace had been informed by Lord Lucian's sister, Lady Arabella, when she had called on them yesterday morning, in order that she might introduce herself to her future sister-in-law. The fact that Grace had taken an instant liking to the forthright and beautiful Lady Arabella did not in any way alter the fact that Lord Lucian had obviously been avoiding going anywhere near the Duke of Carlyne's residence, and Grace herself, since his return.

Grace continued to look at him coolly. 'You did not ask, My Lord.'

Lucian frowned his irritation with her reply. Damn it, it had been left to those two insolent young puppies at his club earlier today to unwittingly inform him that Grace was the daughter of 'an artist or some such'. The claim had easily been verified once Lucian had made the connection of Grace's surname with that of Peter Hetherington, a man who had had several of his paintings displayed at the Royal Academy's exhibitions at Somerset House, as well as hung in the numerous homes of every member of the ton here this evening; Lucian had two of them himself in his own townhouse; beautiful seascapes that captured the wild beauty of the southern coast of England.

'Perhaps if, as you said you would, you had presented yourself to the Duchess and myself when you returned to town, then there might have been occasion for us to have had such a conversation,' Grace added, with a sweetness that was totally at odds with the angry sparkle in her eyes.

Ah. Lucian breathed out ruefully. Grace had been aware of his return to town two days ago, and did not appreciate his lapse in not calling upon her during that time.

Lucian had had cause to wonder at the delay himself

when he had entered Lady Humbers's home earlier and spotted Grace across the crowded ballroom. She'd stood so tiny but confident at her aunt's side, looking dazzlingly beautiful in a satin and lace gown of the palest lavender. The colour was a perfect foil for her ebony hair, and somehow gave her eyes that same misty hue. Her complexion was like magnolia, her lips an inviting rose.

A *very* inviting rose.

An invitation Lucian was experiencing more difficulty in resisting than was comfortable!

'Shall we venture outside for some air?' Lucian's suggestion was a formality only as he took a firm hold upon Grace's elbow and steered her unerringly towards one of the doors opening out onto the terrace and garden—the evening having turned rather warm after a typically foggy day.

Grace had no idea how she came to be outside on the terrace with Lord Lucian, when being alone with him again was the last thing she had intended this evening. Although she had to admit that it was far easier to breathe outside than it had been in the overcrowded ballroom, it was an admission she had no intention of sharing with Lord Lucian.

'Is your sister attending the ball this evening, Lord Lucian?' She gave a nonchalant flick of her fan as she looked out over the lamplit garden, pretending an interest in Lady Humbers's pretty herbaceous borders.

Pretending an interest because the truth of the matter was that Grace had been unable to see anything or anyone else but Lord Lucian since he had entered the ballroom half an hour since, his dark hair fashionably tousled, the black evening attire and snowy white linen doing very little to hide the powerful width of his shoulders, muscled chest, and tapered thighs and legs.

Which were *not* the thoughts of a refined and innocent young lady!

Not that Grace was the only woman to have noticed and enjoyed Lord Lucian's appearance here this evening, she recalled sourly; women of all ages, it seemed, had turned to look at him appreciatively as he crossed the ballroom with elegance and purpose till he reached Grace's side, as several of those ladies had continued to watch the two of them together even while they distractedly continued with their own conversations.

'Arabella?' Lord Lucian replied with some surprise. 'No, I believe that she is attending a musical soirée at the Countess of Morefield's.'

The surprise in his tone at the mention of his sister was enough to tell Grace that as yet he had no idea the two women had already met. 'Your sister and your aunt were gracious enough to call upon my aunt yesterday morning.'

'Ah.'

Grace gave him another of those over-sweet smiles. 'I thought her both charming and beautiful.'

'Yes, Arabella is both those things,' Lucian confirmed dryly, aware that his sister was also a lot of other things—including interfering.

His family, as Lucian had predicted, had been delighted by the news of his betrothal. The fact that none of them knew Grace as yet had not seemed in the least important so long as he was embarking on the road to matrimony with someone who was not totally unsuitable—which Grace, as the ward of a duke, was not. But Lucian should have guessed that Arabella, that meddlesome minx, would feel no hesitation in taking matters into her own hands with regard to meeting Lucian's betrothed once she was safely ensconced in town.

And Grace was as much of a minx.

'I believe we were talking about your father…?'

'Were we?' She flicked him another of those cool glances. 'I believed that conversation to be over and done with, My Lord.'

Lucian was well enough acquainted with women to know that Grace was still angry with him for his tardiness in not calling upon her and her aunt, and that her anger was hidden—barely—behind a veneer of social politeness. A veneer Lucian had no patience with. He much preferred the Grace of their last meeting, when he had found her bluntness refreshing after the jaded ladies of the ton.

He gave a frustrated sigh. 'If you have something you wish to say to me, Grace, then I wish you would say it!'

She arched one ebony brow. 'The weather has been unseasonably oppressive today, has it not? I own, despite the shade of my parasol, that I felt quite fatigued by the heat as my aunt and I walked in the park this afternoon.'

Lucian scowled darkly at her prattling, knowing from their last meeting that Grace was far above such nonsense. 'I have no more desire to discuss the weather than you do, Grace.'

'No?' She maintained that infuriating coolness. 'Then perhaps the health of your family?'

'No.'

'The health of *my* family?'

'For the moment—again no!'

She gave a rueful shake of her head. 'Perhaps it would be as well if *you* chose the subject of our conversation, My Lord?'

Lucian's teeth grated together as he clenched his jaw. In truth, he didn't want to converse at all. He had spent the last ten minutes looking at the grace and beauty of Grace's delicate profile as she kept her face averted from his: the swan-like arch of her creamy throat, the smooth line of her tiny pointed chin, and those rose-coloured inviting lips. Lips that Lucian felt a strong compulsion to claim with his own...

A kiss.

A single kiss—

No, damn it. It had been claiming a single kiss from this woman that had put them both in the untenable position of finding themselves betrothed to each other in the first place. Because he had not wanted to stop at kissing Grace that night. He had wanted to share so much more than kisses with her—to feel her skin as soft as velvet to the touch, her breasts full and responsive as he cupped them—

'Shall we stroll in the garden?' Lucian stood back abruptly even as he made the suggestion, to allow Grace to precede him down the stone steps.

Grace hesitated, eyeing Lord Lucian warily. Being alone with him like this was dangerous. More dangerous than she had imagined even during the times she allowed herself to dwell on the night they had met at the coaching inn. Then he had appeared rakishly handsome to her—if arrogantly so. But this evening, surrounded by the glittering and bejewelled members of the ton, Grace had been made even more aware of the differences between them.

There had been a lull in the conversation when Lord Lucian had appeared in the doorway of the ballroom, looking down his arrogant nose at the company gathered there. Men and women alike had stood aside for him to pass as he made his way determinedly to her side. And those same men and women had watched his every move—the men enviously, the women covetously— telling Grace that Lord Lucian St Claire was a much admired and yet at the same time feared member of this select and prestigious company.

Grace felt a quiver of apprehension down her spine as she recognised that same fear of him within herself— if for a totally different reason.

'Perhaps we have been absent from the ballroom long enough, My Lord…?'

His smile was hard. 'We are betrothed, Grace. I sincerely doubt that anyone would dare to accuse me of ravishing my betrothed in Lady Humbers's garden!'

Grace sincerely doubted that anyone—man or woman—would dare to accuse Lord Lucian St Claire of anything, without fearing the cold retribution that accusation would bring down upon their head.

Why had she not recognised the darkness within him the first time she had set eyes on him? Or, having recognised it in the nightmares she had witnessed, why had she not been sensible enough to avoid a situation that would put her so completely in his power?

Grace straightened her shoulders determinedly. 'It is my own wish to return to the ballroom, My Lord.'

Lord Lucian returned her gaze just as assuredly. 'And it is *my* wish, dear Grace, to go where I might discuss something of importance with you, to a place where our conversation will not be overheard.' He turned to scowl pointedly at another couple as they strolled out onto the terrace. The man appeared sensible to the darkness of that scowl, and he bent to whisper something into the ear of the lady at his side before the two of them turned and swiftly re-entered the ballroom.

Grace's gaze was derisive as she turned back from witnessing their behaviour. 'Did you rout Napoleon's army single-handed, My Lord?'

He bared his teeth in a humourless smile. 'Not quite.'

'That is what I thought.' Her smile was mocking. 'Very well, My Lord.' She gave a gracious inclination of her head. 'I will walk in the garden with you, so that you might tell me what is so important you have to discuss it with me where our conversation will not be overheard!'

This girl was barely out of the schoolroom, Lucian acknowledged ruefully as he accompanied her down the steps, in experience if not in years, and yet there was no doubting that Grace held his interest, that he did not find her company in the least boring or tedious. In fact, he found himself waiting in a state of anticipation for what she might say or do next!

It was perhaps unwise of Lucian to linger outside with her in this way. Perhaps? It *was* unwise! But for the moment, with Grace so elegant and beautiful as she walked beside him, Lucian chose to put aside his usual caution.

She barely reached to his shoulder as they strolled away from the house. Those dark curls appeared blue-black in the moonlight, her face an ethereal white, her eyes silver as they too reflected the moonlight, and the firm swell of her breasts was rapidly rising and falling—*too* rapidly rising and falling?

Could it be that Miss Grace Hetherington—that paragon of young maidenhood who had claimed their time together in her bedchamber had been an aberration of the moment—was as curious to repeat the experience as he was…?

Chapter Seven

Grace watched Lord Lucian from beneath lowered lashes as they stepped off the lamplit pathway in order to wander amongst the trees. The sound of the music playing in the ballroom was becoming softer, more distant, and the stillness that now surrounded them made it appear as if there were not at least two hundred people in the house such a short distance away, but as if they were completely alone amongst the moonlight-dappled bushes and trees. Completely alone…

Grace came to an abrupt halt. 'I believe we have gone far enough, Lord Lucian.'

He turned to face her, his face dark and almost satanic in the moonlight, his eyes appearing an unreadable black. 'Do you?' he murmured softly.

Grace swallowed hard, aware of the slight trembling of her body, of the erratic rise and fall of her breathing. 'Do not presume to flirt with me, sir,' she rebuked sharply, in an effort to hide how disturbed she was by the sheer force of his presence.

Had she really spent over an hour alone in her bed-chamber with this man just over a week ago? Gone willingly into his arms? Allowed him the liberty of kissing her intimately? The mere thought of the intimacy of those kisses made Grace tremble with longing.

His teeth gleamed very white in the moonlight as he gave a wolfish smile. 'You do not care for flirtation, Grace?'

Her eyes flashed silver as she raised her chin in challenge. 'I do not care to flirt with a man who, despite all claims to the contrary, does not honour his promises!'

'Ah.' Such a small sound, and so softly spoken, and yet it conveyed the fact that Lord Lucian was well aware of the promise Grace was referring to.

Grace glared up at him. 'I have been in town for over a week now, My Lord, and during that time I have, for my aunt and uncle's sake, behaved as if I am actually pleased, even honoured, to find myself betrothed to you. I have had to suffer the good wishes of numerous people on my good fortune in acquiring such a man as you as my betrothed, and yet you, who have been in town these past two days, have not even had the decency to call upon that so-called fortunate woman!'

Lucian had difficulty in holding back a smile as he looked down into Grace's furiously indignant face. She really was wonderfully beautiful when she allowed her anger full rein. Even her hair seemed to glow a deeper ebony. 'Would such a call have been welcome, Grace?' he prompted softly.

'Do not be ridiculous, Lord St Claire—'

'Lucian, Grace. I wish, when we are alone, for you to call me Lucian,' he explained huskily at her sharply questioning glance.

'Unfortunately, My Lord, your wishes are not, and never will be, of particular importance to me!' Her eyes flashed.

Yes, Grace was *very* angry at his tardiness. But how could Lucian explain to her, without revealing too much of his own unwelcome emotions, that his reluctance to see her again did not arise from a desire not to see her again, but the opposite?

Lucian had known many women in his life since his first initiation into the pleasures of the flesh at the age of seventeen, and his eligibility as the second son of a duke had made those conquests easy and numerous. His years in the army as a so-called hero had only increased the number of women who wished to share his bed and body. A fact that had, quite frankly, sickened him—to the point where Lucian had avoided anything more than brief physical relationships since he had resigned his commission.

But Grace, with her tiny delicacy and lush breasts, had re-ignited his interest, his desire. So much so that Lucian wanted nothing more than to take Grace in his arms right now and make love to her, not gently or courteously, as her innocence deserved, but with a mind-numbing fierceness that would probably frighten her half to death.

Lucian forced down those emotions as he raised a

hand and gently cupped the curve of her cheek. Her skin was as smooth and pale as alabaster, but with none of its coldness. 'Would a kiss suffice as apology for my tardiness?'

'Certainly not!' She moved her head back sharply from his touch, her gaze reflecting her alarm at his suggestion. 'I have not forgotten, My Lord, even if you appear to have done so, that it was a kiss that first placed us in this ridiculous position of being betrothed to each other!'

He gave a humourless smile. 'My behaviour these past two days may have been tardy, Grace, but I assure you my memory is not.'

'Then do not add insult to injury by so much as suggesting—'

'Insult to injury?' Lucian echoed softly. 'You believe our betrothal to be injurious to you? You consider my kisses an insult?'

Grace was fully aware of the underlying edge to the huskiness of his tone, and of the sudden tension in the broad width of his shoulders. Like a cat about to pounce. But in Lord Lucian's case not a cat of the domestic variety, that were so numerous on her father's estate in Cornwall, but something much more wild and untamed. And dangerous.

She breathed slowly, carefully, aware that the slightest wrong move could result in her becoming mauled—verbally if not physically. 'No, of course I do not, My Lord—'

'Lucian,' he grated hardly.

'Lucian,' Grace echoed obediently even as she continued to eye him warily. 'They are merely unnecessary in a betrothal which is nothing more than a sham—'

Her explanation was cut off abruptly as Lord Lucian gathered her up into his arms and fiercely claimed her lips with his own.

Grace fought his assault initially, but as his mouth continued to plunder hers she felt her anger and impatience completely evaporate, to be replaced by a strange, yearning ache that threatened to overwhelm her in its intensity.

Her lips parted beneath his to allow the captive surge of his tongue into the heat of her mouth, and that tongue duelled with hers as Grace's fingers clung to the broadness of Lucian's shoulders. His hands were sliding down her body now, to grasp her hips and pull her in tight against his body. A hard, throbbing body that clearly indicated the force of his desire.

Lucian's desire for her.

It was heady indeed to know of the effect she had on a man of Lucian St Claire's years and obvious experience, and it increased Grace's own arousal. Her gasp was only slight as one of his hands moved to cup her breast. That breast swelled against his palm, the nipple hot and throbbing, crying out for his touch.

Grace groaned in protest as Lucian wrenched his mouth from hers to look down at her searchingly. Whatever he read in her expression was enough for him to move back slightly and wrench off his jacket impatiently, to lay it down upon the grass at her feet.

'Lie with me, Grace,' he pressed urgently, the

darkness of his gaze alone holding her captive now, glittering with satisfaction as, after the slightest hesitation, Grace moved to his bidding.

The muscled hardness of his body was soon against the length of hers as he lay beside her to once again capture her mouth with his.

This was madness. Insanity of the worst kind. And yet Grace had no strength, no will to deny the clamouring needs that swelled so uncontrollably inside her as she heatedly returned the demand of Lucian's lips against hers, moaning low in her throat as his hand stroked and caressed the fiery tip of her breast.

Lucian could feel the response of that breast through the silk of Grace's gown and chemise, and revelled in its softness, its heat. But he knew that he wanted more—that he wanted to touch her bare flesh, to suckle and lave her with his tongue, to taste her.

Would Grace allow it? Could she—could either of them—do anything to stop this now that it had begun?

Lucian dealt deftly, swiftly, with the buttons at the back of Grace's gown, holding her gaze with his as he pulled the material over her shoulders and arms, before slipping down the thin straps of her chemise and freeing her breasts completely, only then lowering his gaze to drink his fill of her.

Grace was so tiny elsewhere—her waist slender, her hips narrow—but her breasts were full and firm, the nipples hard and thrusting, their very fullness crying out for his touch.

His hand looked very large, its skin dark against the

paleness of her more delicate flesh, and Grace cried out softly as Lucian ran the soft pad of his thumb across her nipple, her back arching in invitation, thrusting her breasts temptingly upwards. Lucian accepted that temptation, that invitation, placing his lips about her sensitised nipple as he slowly laved that heated tip with his tongue, gently suckling as he felt the trembling of her body beneath his touch, the razor-edge of her nails as she clung to his shoulders.

Lucian continued slowly, taking his time as he introduced Grace to all the heady pleasures that awaited her, not wanting to push her too quickly, allowing her time to adjust, to accept those pleasures. His own wants and desires came a poor second to pleasuring Grace.

Minutes, hours later, Lucian knew, as her hips moved restlessly against his, that Grace was ready for more—that her body now cried out for something else, something her body was sure *he* could give her.

For once in his life Lucian wasn't quite sure how to proceed. He had known from the first that he could not make love to Grace out here in Lady Humbers's garden, but his desire for her had been such that he had needed to kiss and touch her. But now he was aware that Grace was too aroused, too needy, for him to just leave her wanting in this way. She needed—craved—release.

Would she allow him that intimacy? Allow him to give her that release with his hands, lips and tongue? Or would he only succeed in shocking her?

It was a dilemma. On the one hand he knew that Grace, once alone, would feel resentful and frustrated if he left her as she was. But on the other she could quite possibly end up hating him if he were to give her the release her body clamoured for.

'Lucian…?'

It was her whispering of his name, the feverish glitter he could see quite clearly in her eyes, that finally decided Lucian. His lips were against her throat now, and her skin so soft and silky, the perfume of her innocence much headier than any of the spring blossoms that surrounded them.

Grace burned at the touch of Lucian's lips as he kissed slowly, leisurely, along the length of her throat and down to her breasts. The evening air had cooled her flesh so that his lips and tongue were like fire against her, igniting delicious tremors through her body, increasing the aching heat between her thighs—an ache that made her restless for—

For what?

Grace had no idea. But as Lucian shifted her gown slightly, lifting the hem so that one of his hands could move slowly along the bare length of her thigh, higher and then higher still, creating fire wherever it touched, Grace knew that she could safely leave everything to Lucian, that he knew exactly what he was doing—

'I assure you, Margaret, I have strolled about the garden and they are not here.' The sound of Francis Wynter's irritated voice was unmistakable. 'You must have missed seeing them when they returned to the ballroom.'

'I tell you I did not,' the Duchess of Carlyne came back impatiently. 'I noticed the moment they came outside together—as did everyone else!' She sounded distressed by the fact. 'And I assure *you* that I have not taken my eyes from the doors for a single moment since.'

Grace stared up wide-eyed at Lucian, knowing by his stillness that he too had recognised both voices in conversation—and heard that they were the subject of it! His expression was grim as he raised a silencing finger in front of her dazed face.

As if Grace needed any warning to remain silent!

The music was still faint and distant, but the voices of Francis Wynter and the Duchess of Carlyne were completely audible. Which meant that they must be standing very close to where Grace lay upon Lucian St Claire's coat, her own clothing in complete disarray, possibly on the other side of the bushes that surrounded them. If either Francis or her aunt should walk only a little further in this direction—

'Then they must have returned by another door,' Francis dismissed briskly. 'They are probably taking refreshment even as we speak. It is certainly uncomfortably hot enough in the house for that to be the case,' he added disapprovingly. 'Come along, Margaret—or no doubt the gossips will start to wonder what you and *I* are doing out here alone in the garden for so long!'

'It really is too bad of Grace to behave in this reckless manner…'

The Duchess's worried voice began to fade as the pair obviously moved back towards the house.

'I do not blame Grace at all.' Francis sounded as

pompously self-righteous as ever. 'St Claire has been, and continues to be, a very bad influence upon her! I did warn you and George that this was an unsuitable match, but…' His voice faded away completely as he and the Duchess obviously returned to the crowded ballroom.

Grace's gaze was stricken, completely mortified, as she looked up at Lucian—the man she had allowed to make love to her without a single protest. A man who was indeed a bad influence on her.

Somehow it was all made worse by the fact that either Francis Wynter or her aunt could have so easily walked a little further in this direction and discovered them together.

What had she been thinking? *Had* she been thinking? No, she had not, Grace accepted miserably even as she sat up to turn away and begin righting her clothes, arranging her camisole over her still sensitised breasts before pulling her gown back into place.

'Here—let me.' Lucian pushed her trembling fingers aside as Grace tried unsuccessfully to fasten the buttons at the back of her gown.

'Thank you.' Grace waited only long enough for him to deal deftly and quickly with those buttons before getting to her feet, still deeply shaken. Both by Lucian's lovemaking and their almost-discovery by Francis and the Duchess. 'We should return to the ballroom—'

'Grace—'

'We have no time to discuss this now, My Lord.' Her eyes flashed a warning in the moonlight as she turned sharply to face him. 'In fact, I do not believe I ever wish

to discuss it. I am mortally ashamed of my behaviour.'
She shook her head self-disgustedly.

Lucian's gaze frowningly held hers and he took his
time before answering, giving his jacket a brief shake
before shrugging back into it and straightening the lace
cuffs of his shirt. '"Mortally" ashamed, Grace?' he
finally repeated dryly. 'I assure you that you were still
some way from that "little death" when we were so
rudely interrupted.'

She looked puzzled. '"Little death"…?'

What an innocent she was, Lucian acknowledged
with grim self-reproach. Of course Grace did not know
that the physical release a man and woman could give
each other was called a little death. It was cruel of him
to tease her when she already looked so devastated by
their near discovery.

'It does not signify for now,' he dismissed impatiently, and took a light hold of her arm.

'But—'

'We *should* return to the ballroom, Grace. Before
your aunt becomes any more distressed by our absence.'

Her aunt *had* sounded distressed, Grace acknowledged frowningly. But surely the fact that Grace and
Lucian were betrothed allowed them a little more
freedom in each other's company than might otherwise
have been approved? Not to the point of almost making
love together in Lady Humbers's garden, certainly! But
surely enough that they might spend some time together
alone without it being cause for gossip?

Although not, Grace felt sure, if they returned into

company looking as if they had just been making love together!

Not that Lucian *did* look like that. His appearance, apart from a more pronounced tousling of his hair, was as impeccable as always. But Grace doubted her own appearance had suffered so little. She was sure that her hair was no longer neatly styled, and her lips were feeling fuller than usual, and her gown was slightly crushed in the front from being crumpled about her waist for so long. She supposed that she should be grateful to Lucian, because by lying upon his coat she had prevented grass stains upon the back of her gown, too!

Grace didn't feel grateful. She wasn't quite sure what she did feel. But it wasn't gratitude.

She would think about it later, once she was alone in her room. For now the two of them really *did* have to return to the ballroom, and the curious eyes of 'everyone else', whom her aunt claimed had noticed their departure together earlier.

'Let me,' Lucian said again gruffly, as he saw Grace's attempts to tidy her hair back into neat curls. His fingers were gentle in contrast to his grim expression as he coiled several of those curls back into place.

Not that the tidying of Grace's hair was going to stop most of Lady Humbers's guests—the males in particular—from knowing exactly what had taken place between Lucian and Grace during the last few minutes; her eyes were over-bright, her cheeks were flushed, and her lips had that slightly swollen appearance that came after a woman had been made love to.

Lucian frowned darkly. 'We still have not had an opportunity to talk.'

He had intended telling her of the conversation he had overheard at his club earlier today—of the rumour of their betrothal being a forced one which was obviously circulating around the ton. But after their behaviour this evening, perhaps there was no need for that conversation? Who could now doubt, after their prolonged absence in the garden together, that there was more to their betrothal than expediency?

'And whose fault is that?' Her tone was waspish as she bent down to retrieve her fan from where it lay abandoned on the grass.

Lucian's mouth twisted mockingly. 'Yours, I believe.'

'Mine?' Grace's eyes were wide with indignation.

He shrugged. 'You should not be so beautiful.'

Those grey eyes narrowed in warning of her rapidly evaporating patience. 'I told you not to flirt with me, Lucian.'

'So you did.' He reclaimed his hold upon her arm as they began to walk back towards the noise and clamour inside the house, noting with satisfaction that Grace did at least address him as Lucian now rather than 'My Lord'. 'But it cannot be called flirting when one is simply stating the truth.'

Grace eyed him suspiciously. She was young when compared to this man—and not only in years. Her inexperience with the Society he had lived amongst all of his life, her complete lack of artifice when compared to the other much more beautiful women present this evening, made her appear—and feel—gauche in comparison. Telling her that she could not possibly hope to claim, or retain, the interest of a man of such sophistication as Lucian St Claire.

'I do not think that I believe you…'

'You wound me if you believe I would make love to a woman who was not beautiful!'

Grace's mouth firmed. 'I believe it would take a lot more than my opinion to wound you, My Lord.'

'Do you, Grace?'

He was suddenly once again much too close, causing a strange fluttering sensation in Grace's chest. 'What was it you wished to talk to me about this evening, My Lord?'

Lucian eyed her impatiently. Although whether that impatience was directed at himself or at Grace he was not sure. If he was to be forced into marrying this chit, then it would be under his own terms, not hers. Certainly he did not intend to become a slave to the desire he knew that he felt for her.

His mouth firmed. 'Come for a ride in Hyde Park with me tomorrow morning, Grace. We will discuss it then.'

'A ride in the park?' Her eyes lit up excitedly. 'You could not have suggested anything I would enjoy more than the freedom of a brisk gallop upon one of my uncle's mounts—'

'I had meant for us to ride in my curricle, Grace,' Lucian put in dryly, aware that Grace could have no idea of the honour he was bestowing upon her by the suggestion. He did not—*ever!*—take ladies riding in the park in his curricle.

'Oh.' Her excitement faded as quickly as it had appeared. 'I should have realised.' She grimaced. 'Yes—if my aunt allows it, I will certainly join you in your curricle tomorrow morning.'

Lucian felt unpleasantly as if he had just taken something away from Grace, denying her a treat. He also found—irritatingly—that he did not like the feeling. 'I am willing to exchange the comfort of my curricle for a ride on horseback, if you would prefer that.'

'Oh, I would!' Her eyes glowed once again.

Lucian shrugged. 'However, I should warn you that galloping, briskly or otherwise, is really not the done thing.'

'Why ever not?' The frown was back upon her brow.

Lucian gave a mocking smile. 'Because, my dear Grace, the ladies and gentlemen of the ton who choose to ride in the park do it to see and to be seen—not to gallop!'

Grace grimaced. 'That sounds rather boring, if you do not mind my saying so.'

'I do not mind your saying so in the least, Grace.' His mouth twisted derisively. 'In fact, I agree with the sentiment.'

'I suppose I also have to sit decorously side-saddle, wearing one of those beautiful riding habits my aunt has felt it necessary for me to acquire this past week?'

Lucian eyed her frowningly. Grace's disgust with the idea seemed to imply that she did not usually ride side-saddle… What sort of life had Grace enjoyed on her father's estate in Cornwall? Of course her father had been an artist, and possibly a bohemian, but her mother had been Lady Amelia Hopgood before her marriage—sister to the Duchess of Carlyne. Surely she must have known how to go on in Society? If she had, then it appeared she had not passed that knowledge on to her daughter.

The image of Grace he instantly had in his mind, riding astride her mount, wearing figure-hugging breeches that clung to the length of her legs and rounded bottom, caused Lucian to shift uncomfortably as his body hardened in response.

Grace watched from beneath lowered lashes as a disapproving scowl appeared on Lucian's arrogantly handsome face. 'Anything else would cause a scandal, I suppose?'

'It most certainly would!' he assured her grimly.

'Perhaps you should not have told me that…' Her eyes glittered challengingly.

His mouth thinned with impatience. 'Grace—'

'Lucian!'

Grace turned towards the terrace to look at the outrageously good-looking young man who had just warmly greeted the man at her side. Teasing brown eyes gazed guilelessly back at her. Closer inspection showed Grace that he bore a startling resemblance to Lucian and Lady Arabella—except that his eyes had none of Lucian's coldness, nor Lady Arabella's brittle cynicism. This surely must be Lord Sebastian St Claire—the youngest of the St Claire brothers.

'And your betrothed, I gather?'

The man she believed to be Lord Sebastian St Claire smiled with pleasure as he moved down the terrace steps to join them in the garden.

'Introduce me, Lucian,' he invited mockingly.

'I am more interested to know what *you* are doing here,' his brother came back dryly. 'I did not believe such entertainments were to your liking.'

The younger man raised taunting brows. 'I was persuaded to come with two friends of mine. I believe you met them earlier today...?'

'So I did,' Lucian acknowledged hardly, eyes narrowing. 'Grace, may I present my brother, Lord Sebastian St Claire? Sebastian—Miss Grace Hetherington. As you have already guessed, my betrothed,' he added dryly.

'Miss Hetherington.' Lord Sebastian St Claire raised her hand to his lips, that teasing laughter still in his eyes as his gaze met hers, almost as if the two of them shared a joke of some kind. 'What a shame we did not meet first, Miss Hetherington. I assure you I am by far the easiest of the St Claire brothers to get along with!'

Grace liked him immediately, sensing none of Lucian's reserve in him, nor any of what she had heard to be the Duke of Stourbridge's haughtiness. 'I am pleased to meet you, My Lord,' she returned shyly.

'And I you.' He grinned back unabashed, still maintaining a hold upon her hand. 'I don't suppose Lucian has told you that you have the most—?'

'Sebastian!' Lucian cut in warningly, having seen the way his brother's gaze had darkened appreciatively at the sound of Grace's huskily sensual voice. 'You may safely leave any compliments for my betrothed to me!' He gently but firmly took Grace's hand from his brother's and placed it upon the sleeve of his own jacket.

He had predicted over a week ago that once in Society Grace would quickly become known as an Original—but he had not expected to have to protect Grace from the flirtation of his own brother!

Not that Grace looked as if she needed protecting, as she shot him a narrow-eyed glance before turning away to smile warmly at Sebastian. The sort of smile she had never bestowed upon *him,* Lucian acknowledged scowlingly.

'And does Lucian pay you *many* compliments, Miss Hetherington?' Sebastian encouraged lightly.

'Not that I have noticed, My Lord,' Grace answered softly.

He fell into step on her other side as they all walked towards the house. 'Then it falls to me to correct the omission. Your eyes are like—'

'Sebastian, you are becoming tiresome!' Lucian rasped harshly.

His brother still looked unabashed. 'He believes he is still in the army, you know, and that we are the troops under his command,' he confided to Grace in a deliberately over-loud whisper.

'I would not have tolerated such as *you* in my regiment,' Lucian assured him impatiently.

'You see.' Sebastian gave a dramatic sigh. 'Such is the fate of a younger brother.'

Grace was greatly enjoying this exchange between the two brothers, and already liked Lord Sebastian tremendously. It was impossible *not* to like his teasing good humour. Grace felt sure it had to be good for the more reserved and troubled man that she knew Lucian to be.

Did his family know of his inner turmoil? Of the disturbing memories that haunted his dreams? Did she sense a certain subtlety of purpose behind Sebastian St Claire's teasing? As if any response from his taciturn older brother was better than no response at all…? She turned to give the younger man a considering look, receiving a barely perceptible wink in return.

Lucian saw that exchange with a darkening of his brow. 'Sebastian, do you not have somewhere else you need to be?'

'Would you care to present us, St Claire?'

Lucian turned scowlingly to find the two young bucks from his club standing beside him. The blond, more outspoken one was acting as spokesman for the pair, and he looked at Lucian expectantly. The admiration in the eyes of the dark-haired one was obviously genuine as he goggled at Grace. A fact that did not please Lucian in the least. He had thought the evening bad enough with Sebastian's interruption, but it had just deteriorated to a greater degree!

But, having ensured that these two young sprigs would present themselves here tonight, Lucian really had left himself with no choice but to make the introductions. Which he did so—stiffly. 'Gentlemen—my betrothed, Miss Grace Hetherington.'

'Sir Rupert Enderby.' The blond-haired man bowed formally over her hand.

'Lord Gideon Grayson.' The dark-haired one also bowed. 'Might I request the honour of this next dance, Miss Hetherington?' he prompted politely, as a brief pause could be heard in the music before the next dance began.

So it was that seconds later Lucian found himself standing with Sebastian and Sir Rupert Enderby at the side of the ballroom, doing his best to conceal the grinding of his teeth as he watched Grace gliding elegantly around the room in the arms of the obviously enchanted Lord Gideon Grayson.

Chapter Eight

'You seem preoccupied this morning, My Lord?' Grace looked at him from beneath lowered lashes as they rode their horses side by side along the busy bridle-path in the park, with the young groom her aunt had sent along for propriety's sake riding some distance behind them. A dozen or so other riders were there with their mounts, despite the earliness of the hour, and all of them, it seemed, were acquainted with Lucian— although his replies to their greetings had so far been taciturn to say the least.

Her Aunt Margaret, having been assured the previous evening by Lord Sebastian St Claire—not quite truth-fully!—that Grace and Lucian had been taking refresh-ment and talking with him for the past half an hour, had readily agreed to Lucian's request that he take Grace out riding with him this morning, so long as a groom ac-companied them.

Grace was wearing one of her new riding habits, in

a deep grey velvet, and a matching bonnet over her wayward curls that, even if she did say so herself, looked very well with the sleek black mare her uncle's groom had provided for her to ride.

Lord Lucian looked very handsome, of course— Grace seriously doubted that he could ever look anything else! A fine black hat was upon his head, his tailored jacket was of severe black, his linen snowy white, and his cream riding breeches and highly polished Hessians emphasised the muscled hardness of his calves. As was to be expected from a man who had spent years as a commissioned officer, he rode very well, easily maintaining control of his frisky black stallion. In fact, the only thing that marred Lucian's appearance this morning was the equally black scowl upon his brow…

'I have received a note from Arabella this morning, requesting that I accompany her to your aunt's house for tea this afternoon.'

Grace's brows rose. 'No doubt in response to the fact that my aunt and I called upon her and Lady Hammond two days ago.'

Lucian's mouth thinned. 'No doubt in response to the fact that Sebastian has already informed her it is his intention to call, along with Viscount Rupert Enderby and Lord Gideon Grayson!'

'That will be pleasant.' Grace kept her voice deliberately neutral.

In truth she had very much enjoyed the company of the three other young men the previous evening, finding their light-hearted banter a distinct contrast to the ever-increasing darkness of Lucian's mood.

Lucian's mouth thinned as he nodded acknowledgement to yet another gentleman who only had eyes, it seemed, for the beautiful young woman riding at Lucian's side. It had been this way since the two of them had first appeared in the park together this morning. Unsurprisingly so, when Grace rode with an elegance and surety—even side-saddle—that was much to be admired.

Grace's appearance at Lady Humbers's ball the previous evening seemed to have garnered her many admirers. Amongst them his own brother Sebastian, as well as Sir Rupert Enderby and Lord Gideon Grayson. Those three young bucks had claimed their single dance with her, and then remained within Grace's circle of admirers for the remainder of the evening. Much to Lucian's annoyance.

Grace's smile was warmly mischievous as she glanced across at him. 'I am sure Sebastian has only decided to call in order to annoy you.'

Lucian was absolutely positive that Sebastian meant to annoy him; his younger brother had been doing just that for most of his life! No, it was the presence of Rupert Enderby and Gideon Grayson that had irked Lucian.

He could not in all honesty say that Grace's behaviour towards the two men, or the other half a dozen or so young gentlemen who had requested a dance with her during the remainder of the evening, had been in the least familiar. It was Lucian's own feelings of resentment towards those gentlemen, though completely unjustified, that mystified as well as irritated him.

He eased the tension from his shoulders with an effort. 'As it happens, it was Sebastian's friends Sir Rupert Enderby and Lord Gideon Grayson who were instrumental in bringing to my attention the subject I wished to discuss with you yesterday evening.'

Grace frowned her puzzlement. 'But I had not even been introduced to those two gentlemen at the time…'

'You misunderstand me,' Lucian rasped. 'It was a conversation I overheard between those two gentlemen that I wished to discuss with you.'

Grace's brows rose. 'You seem—angry, My Lord?'

'Not with you this time, Grace.' He sighed before proceeding to tell Grace the gist of the two young gentlemen's conversation the previous afternoon. 'Such speculation was only to be expected, I suppose, when our betrothal happened so suddenly. Although I intend to find out exactly who was responsible for instigating such a rumour,' he concluded grimly.

Grace looked troubled. 'Perhaps someone at the inn…?'

'I find that highly unlikely, when I paid the innkeeper a vast amount of money in exchange for his silence on the subject of our first meeting!'

Grace could not help agreeing with the unlikelihood of the innkeeper having broken his oath—not because of the money Lord Lucian had paid him, but because she seriously doubted that any man, innkeeper or duke, would deliberately choose to oppose a man who projected such an aura of danger as Lord Lucian!

She wrinkled her brow. 'Then perhaps my aunt's maid?' She trusted the silence of her own maid implicitly. 'Household servants very often do know much more than we give them credit for,' she added ruefully, remembering all the gossip she had heard on her frequent visits to the kitchen in the sprawling manor house she had called home for the first nineteen years of her life. And which she hoped to call home again some day...

Lucian shot her a hard glance. 'I had Francis Wynter more in mind. Especially as I was made privy to another piece of gossip yesterday evening that indicated you had rebuffed Francis's proposal in favour of the second son of the Duke of Stourbridge rather than a third son of another!'

Grace's initial denial froze on her lips as she realised that such an action sounded very like something Francis Wynter would do. But *why* would he do such a thing? For spite? Because Grace had rebuffed all of his own advances towards her, both before meeting Lord Lucian and since? It seemed a distinct possibility!

There had only been the five of them present at the inn if the servants were to be excluded. Grace and Lord Lucian were definitely not to blame for the gossip, and her aunt and uncle would certainly not have instigated such speculation concerning Grace's betrothal to Lord Lucian St Claire. Only Francis remained, it seemed...

Just thinking of the way she had made her appearance so innocently into Society the evening before, completely ignorant of the speculation about her betrothal to Lord Lucian St Claire, made Grace cringe with embarrassment.

'This is awful!' She gave a pained groan, her face very pale beneath her grey velvet bonnet. 'Absolutely awful.' Especially so as the announcement of her betrothal to Lord Lucian St Claire was supposed to have precluded such gossip.

'Intolerable.' Lucian nodded tersely. 'But I think you may safely leave me to ascertain the identity of the culprit and then deal with him appropriately.' His expression was coldly determined.

Grace's gaze avoided meeting his. 'I think—I think, if you do not mind, that I would prefer to return to my aunt's house now—'

'That will not do at all, Grace,' Lord Lucian bit out abruptly. 'Do you not see,' he explained at her questioning glance, 'that the best and quickest way to silence the gossips is for us to spend time together? For us to show them over the next few weeks that ours is a love-match after all.'

Her eyes widened. 'A—a love-match?'

Lucian gave a hard laugh at her startled expression. 'You could try looking a little less dismayed at the prospect of being thought my love, Grace!'

Grace swallowed hard, not knowing quite how to take this last remark. She was not his love. As he was not hers. How could they possibly pretend, even for Society's sake, that it was any different between them?

But hadn't they done just that the evening before, by

disappearing into the garden together for that almost indecent length of time…?

Grace gave an indignant gasp. '*That* was why you took me off into the garden last night! The reason you made love to me!' Her expression was accusing as she glared at him, her cheeks flushed and hot.

Lucian looked at her from beneath hooded lids. Did Grace really think that? Did she really believe that he'd had any control over what had occurred between them in the garden the previous evening? For his own sake Lucian would dearly have liked to claim that he had, but the truth of the matter was, if Francis Wynter and the Duchess of Carlyne had not interrupted them the way they had, then Grace would have so much more to accuse him of than duplicity!

He assumed a bored expression. 'You are becoming hysterical, my dear.'

'I am never hysterical!' Grace assured him cuttingly, even as she pulled on the reins and turned her mount back in the direction they had just come. 'Neither do I believe, despite your actions yesterday evening, that you have any desire to continue such a deception. Especially when you are aware that it is my own intention to end our betrothal at the earliest opportunity,' she snapped as Lucian pulled his own mount in beside her own.

Lucian drew in a sharp breath. This conversation had not gone as he had expected or hoped that it would. Mainly, he accepted, because of their closeness in Lady Humbers's garden the previous evening. But could Grace not see that now there really was no escape for her from a marriage to him? That Society would not allow her to end their engagement? Not with any semblance of her reputation remaining intact, at least.

He grimaced. 'As much as it pains me to do so, I really must disagree with you—'

'You surely are not claiming that you *do* wish to continue such a deception?' she scoffed, looking neither to left nor right as she urged her mount towards the gate.

'That was not the subject with which I wished to disagree,' Lucian drawled lazily, raising dark, mocking brows as Grace cast him a suspicious glance from beneath her bonnet. 'You are hysterical, Grace,' he assured her softly. 'Hysterical as well as headstrong.'

Grace reined her horse to a sudden halt in order to turn and glare at him from between narrowed lids. He looked so arrogant, so superior, as he sat astride the black stallion, so easily keeping its waywardness in check. If she were ever to become his wife, Lucian would no doubt attempt to keep what he obviously considered her own waywardness in check!

Never, Grace vowed determinedly. No man, husband or otherwise, would ever control her!

'Then it is as well that you discovered such character faults before we were wed, is it not?' she told him, with a sweetness that was not intended to be believed. 'I will tell my aunt and uncle on my return that you have changed your mind concerning our betrothal—'

'You will do no such thing!' Lucian had reached out with one gloved hand and grasped her reins to prevent her headlong flight, his jaw tight, his teeth clenched. 'You will obey me in this, Grace.'

'You will let go of my reins, My Lord!' Bright wings of angry colour stood out lividly on her cheeks.

He raised dark, arrogant brows. 'And if I do not?'

Her mouth tightened, a light of challenge in her eyes. 'Then you will leave me with no choice but to make you do so.'

Once again, while in Grace's undoubtedly enjoyable company, Lucian had trouble holding back a smile that he knew without a doubt would not be appreciated. She stood just over five feet tall in her slippered feet, weighed almost half as much as he, and yet she still thought to make him do something he was not prepared to do. He could not help but admire her total belief in her ability to best him.

'Grace—'

'You have had your chance, My Lord!' Grace, having seen the light of confident amusement in Lucian's patronising dark eyes, raised the loose end of her reins and slapped him sharply across one arrogantly carved cheek.

The action so took Lord Lucian by surprise that he flinched back in his saddle, causing the stallion to dance nervously and pulling Grace's reins from Lord Lucian's grasp. It took every bit of his considerable expertise to steady the animal.

Grace took one look at the red welts that had appeared on his arrogant cheek before digging the heels of her soft grey leather boots into the flanks of her own mount and taking off at a speed she hoped Lord Lucian, for the several minutes it would take to make good her escape, would be too preoccupied to match.

She gave an exhilarated grin as she saw the gaping surprise on the groom's face as she and the black mare rushed past him, not caring one way or the other whether he was able to follow her as she bent low over the mare's back and urged her on to even greater speed.

The sound of hooves thundering behind her filled Grace with even greater urgency. But she dared not take even the few seconds to glance back to see if her pursuer were the groom or Lord Lucian as she deftly negotiated her way between other riders hell-bent on getting out of her path.

She had almost—almost—reached the gate to the road that would take her back to the Duke's stables, when the black stallion, Lord Lucian astride it, drew level with her, and one glove-covered hand reached out to grasp the mare's reins, pulling her to a skidding halt that would surely have unhorsed Grace if she had not been such an adept horsewoman.

Her face was deeply flushed with anger as she turned. 'That was without doubt the most dangerous, stupid piece of horsemanship—'

'I warn you not to push me any further this morning, Grace!' he grated between gritted teeth, those dark eyes glittering furiously as he glowered down at her.

'*I* am not to push *you?*' Grace was completely at a loss for words.

Lucian gave a disgusted shake of his head. 'You are

without doubt the most wilfully reckless woman it has ever been my misfortune to meet!'

Grey eyes narrowed on him balefully. 'I will ask you one last time to release your hold upon my reins, Lord St Claire.' Her tone was frosty.

Lucian glared at her frustratedly. His cheek stung from the slash of her reins, and his heart was still palpitating from the shock of seeing Grace urge her mount hell-for-leather down the busy path. He had expected at any moment to see either Grace or some other innocent rider tumbling to the ground in a dangerous tangle of limbs, possibly beneath the lethal hooves of their mount.

In comparison, Grace sat there, so magnificently beautiful in her defiance of him, that it was all Lucian could do not to slide from the stallion's back before pulling her from her saddle and crushing her mouth beneath his, in an attempt to force her compliance that way. She was, Lucian acknowledged grimly, becoming more hazardous to his health than any of Napoleon's army had ever been!

He drew in a ragged breath. 'Very well, Grace.' He released her reins. 'Hopefully you will be of a more reasonable state of mind when I accompany Arabella to your aunt and uncle's house later this afternoon.'

Her eyes flashed warningly. 'That is something I would advise you not to put too much hope upon!'

Lucian's mouth set grimly. 'I trust you will not mind if I allow your groom to be the one to accompany you back to your aunt's house…?'

Grace glared. 'On the contrary. I would prefer it!' She left him with a terse nod of dismissal and signalled for her groom to follow her.

Lucian held the stallion reined in as he sat on the path and watched Grace ride away, her head held proudly high.

When Lucian had begun to consider the idea of taking a wife over these last few months, he had never—not even in his wildest musings—imagined her as being someone as impossibly headstrong and wilful as Miss Grace Hetherington was proving to be…

'Grace, may I say how beautiful you are looking this morning—'

'No, you may not!' Grace turned angrily on Francis Wynter as she encountered him in the hallway, after returning from her ride in the park with Lord Lucian. 'In fact, do not talk to me at all!' she added scathingly, her chin high. 'You are despicable, sir. Beneath contempt. A worm. Worse than a worm!'

Lord Francis looked startled by the vitriol of her attack. 'Really, Grace, I do not think such behaviour—'

'I do not recall giving you leave to address me so informally, My Lord.'

'But Grace—'

'I said do not speak to me!' Grace was shaking in her anger, still far from recovered after that verbal exchange with Lucian St Claire earlier. 'From all accounts you have spoken far too much already!' she added disgustedly.

Francis looked even more bewildered. 'I do not—I have no idea what—'

'Do not force me to name you a liar as well as a gossip, sir!' Her eyes glittered warningly.

He drew himself up stiffly. 'If you were a man I would call you out for such—'

'If *you* were a man I would accept!' Grace assured him forcefully. 'Deny it—if you can!—that you are responsible for spreading gossip about the—the suddenness of my betrothal to Lord St Claire!'

His look of bewilderment faded, to be replaced by his usual expression of pomposity. 'I thought only to give you a means of breaking the engagement—'

'By shaming me?' she gasped. 'By embarrassing me?'

'By publicly offering myself as an alternative to the embarrassing situation you found yourself in,' he corrected gently.

'The only embarrassment I have suffered has been at *your* hands, sir!' Her mouth twisted scathingly and she eyed him pityingly. 'But I have no doubt that I may leave any retribution to St Claire. He is not, I believe, a man it is wise of you to have made an enemy of.'

'You are over-emotional, Grace.' Francis was fast regaining his composure, his expression once again pompously condescending. 'Even hysterical—'

'I am furious, Francis,' Grace corrected icily, her cheeks bright with that emotion, as he made the mistake of extending to her the same accusation that Lord Lucian had earlier. 'In your own interest, I believe it would be better if you were to learn to perceive the difference between the two emotions. At least as far as I am concerned.'

He gave a disapproving shake of his head. 'You used never to behave or talk in this unbecoming fashion before you became acquainted with St Claire…'

'How can you be sure of that when you have never really known me—either before I became acquainted with Lucian or since?' Grace challenged.

'I believed that I did—'

'Then you were wrong, were you not?'

'So it would appear.' He gave a stiff inclination of his head. 'In the circumstances, I believe it is as well that I had not already made the mistake of offering for you myself.'

Grace eyed him coldly. 'The only pity in that is that I have been denied the pleasure of turning down such an offer!'

Francis eyed her with dislike. 'Then we are agreed we have both made a fortunate escape?'

'The only thing *I* am agreed on, sir, is that you are a despicable worm—'

'What on earth is all this commotion about?' A perplexed Duke of Carlyne appeared in the hallway. 'I could hear your raised voices behind the closed door of my study.' He looked at them both reprovingly.

Grace instantly felt uncomfortable at having caused such a scene here in the hallway, where not only her uncle had been disturbed by it but the servants might have overheard too.

But before Grace could make her apologies to her uncle, Francis Wynter spoke to him instead. 'Only one raised voice, I am afraid, George. I believe Grace—Miss Hetherington—to be…indisposed,' he said, after receiving a glaring look from Grace. 'No doubt a tiff of some kind with St Claire is to blame for her uncharacteristic shrewishness.'

Grace stared at him incredulously. This man—this excuse for a man—thought to turn the blame for this exchange on to *her?* Perhaps the inappropriateness of the place of their exchange was her fault, but its content most certainly was not.

'On the contrary, sir. I can assure you that, unlike some gentlemen of my acquaintance, Lord St Claire was everything that is amiable this morning,' Grace assured him with saccharine sweetness.

Francis Wynter's mouth tightened at the obvious implication of her cutting remark. 'Amiable is not a word I would ever associate with St Claire!'

'But then, you do not know Lucian as…as well as I do.' Grace eyed him challengingly, knowing by the tightening of his pompously pursed mouth that he would dearly have liked to add something equally cutting.

A glance at his listening older brother obviously deterred him from doing so. He bowed stiffly. 'Then I can only wish you joy of each other.'

Grace shot him another look of narrow-eyed dislike before turning to give her uncle a wan smile. 'I believe I have a headache, Uncle George. If you will both excuse me…'

'Of course, my dear. Of course.' The Duke looked relieved to have whatever unpleasantness had taken place between his brother and his ward over and done with.

Except that Grace doubted it *was* over and done with...

She had never met a man such as Francis Wynter before. Her father had been everything that is amiable— an easy-going man who had cherished both his wife and his daughter. The Duke of Carlyne was equally kind-hearted, and still deeply in love with her Aunt Margaret. Even Lucian St Claire—well, Grace had no doubt that Lucian had a fondness for his brothers and sister, at least, that was affectionate as well as forbearing.

Francis Wynter seemed to be a man who loved only himself and his own interests.

Such a man had deserved to feel the edge of her tongue, Grace decided stubbornly as she slowly made her way up the staircase...

Chapter Nine

'Your aunt was not sure you would be awake when she gave me permission to come up to see you…' Lady Arabella beamed her satisfaction as she stood in the doorway to Grace's bedchamber.

Grace reclined on a chaise in front of the window that looked down into the square, which allowed her, in between reading the novel she had quickly hidden in the folds of her robe when Arabella knocked on the door, to glance outside occasionally and see the arrival of her aunt's afternoon callers.

Lady Arabella looked cheerfully beautiful in a pretty gown of buttercup-yellow that suited her blonde colouring and cream complexion to perfection. 'I must say you do not look stricken down by a headache.' She eyed Grace's elegant appearance in the fitted cobalt-blue velvet robe Grace had donned this morning on reaching her bedchamber, in an effort to convince her aunt of her indisposition when the Duchess later came to visit her.

Guilty colour washed over Grace's cheeks at the truth behind Arabella's teasing remark. Grace was *not* stricken down by a headache, but had continued the ruse in an effort to avoid spending any more time today in the company of Arabella's brother! Not that Lucian St Claire and Lady Arabella had been the only visitors this afternoon; Grace had also seen several other young gentleman from yesterday evening come to call.

'My brother Sebastian, and Sir Rupert and Lord Gideon also, are most disappointed that you are indisposed,' Arabella remarked mischievously, as if she had read some of Grace's thoughts.

But only some of them, Grace hoped; it would be too awful if Arabella were aware of Grace's present aversion to being anywhere near Lucian—the brother she so obviously adored!

'Lucian is pacing the drawing room like a caged tiger in his agitation at your absence,' Arabella added speculatively.

Grace avoided that searching gaze. 'I am sure he is doing no such thing.'

Arabella gave a tinkling laugh. 'I assure you that he is.' She sat down on the end of the chaise, forcing Grace to sweep her robe aside, and at the same time dislodging the book Grace had so recently hidden there. 'Why, Grace!' Arabella bent down to retrieve the book. 'I do believe you were just avoiding your visitors, after all…'

'Not at all.' This young lady saw altogether too much for comfort, Grace decided frowningly as she took the book and impatiently disposed of it on the table beside her. 'It is only that it becomes a little tedious, just lying here with nothing to occupy me.'

Arabella's eyes glowed a teasing brown. 'But the alternative was equally unpalatable, I am sure!'

'I really have no idea what you mean, Lady Arabella—'

'Arabella. We are to be sisters, after all.' Arabella's glowing smile faded slightly. 'I believe I would be avoiding Lucian too, if I were the cause of his present scowling countenance.'

Ah, so Lucian was still scowling, was he? It was just as well, then, that Grace had decided to stay in her room for the rest of the day.

'Although,' Arabella added frowningly, 'I must say it is a relief to see him showing *any* emotion.'

Grace gave her a searching glance. 'What do you mean?' Lucian had shown Grace nothing *but* emotion since the two of them had met, his initial formal politeness in front of her guardians having given way to irritation, desire and anger—most of all anger! Although Arabella's comment *did* seem to confirm Grace's suspicions that Lucian's isolation from his family since he had left the army had been deliberate…

'I—Ah, another visitor!' Arabella announced excitedly, as a carriage could be heard drawing up outside the Carlynes' townhouse. 'You do not suppose that it is yet another one of your admirers, come to make my brother grind his teeth so jealously?' she prompted laughingly, and the two women stared unashamedly out of the window as they waited for the passenger to alight from the carriage.

Grace gave an exasperated shake of her head. 'I do not believe you understand my relationship with your brother at all. Our betrothal is—was brought about by events I really cannot discuss with you or anyone else—'

'You are referring to the gossip, are you not?' The laughter had faded from Arabella's countenance. 'I heard some murmurs of speculation yesterday evening at the Countess of Morefield's,' she explained sympathetically. 'But as I have been quick to point out, Lucian has shown these last two years that he does not give that—' she gave a snap of her fingers '—for the dictates of Society.'

'Not for his own sake, perhaps,' Grace acknowledged uncomfortably, her cheeks once again hot with embarrassment as she accepted that Lady Arabella had also heard the gossip about them. Who hadn't? 'But for the sake of his friendship with my aunt and uncle, and the damage that would be done to my own reputation if—well, if he did not make an offer for me.'

'Hah! Lucian would—Why, I do believe that is Lord Darius Wynter…' Arabella stared down into the street, where a gentleman had at last alighted from his carriage.

Grace also recognised Lord Darius, the middle Wynter brother, as he stepped down onto the pavement, the sunlight glinting on golden hair and his supercil- iously handsome face as he took his hat and cane from a waiting groom before glancing up at the house with eyes the same cobalt-blue as Grace's robe.

Arabella moved guiltily back from the window. 'I had not thought to see him in town this Season…'

Grace nodded. 'We stayed with him at his estate in Malvern before coming here, and I believe there was some talk then of his coming up to town for a few days. Something to do with his late wife's estate. You are aware that Lord Darius was married for a short time and recently widowed…?'

'Oh, yes, everyone is aware that Lord Darius married a woman of great fortune.' Arabella assured her ruefully. 'There has been much talk since that his wife's death was not an accident.'

'I did not know…' Grace was taken aback at the disclosure. Especially in light of the views she had expressed at the inn just over a week ago, when she had made her opinion more than plain concerning men who only married for fortune. She would not have voiced such an opinion—not even to annoy Lucian St Claire— if she had known that Darius Wynter was considered by the ton to be such a man… 'Still, he *is* very handsome,' she added ruefully.

'Very.' Arabella acknowledged abruptly as she stood up. 'Such beautiful golden hair, eyes of unfathomable blue, and with the face of an angel. Or a devil.' She gave a hard laugh. 'A very wealthy devil now, if gossip is to be believed.'

'But I thought you had just assured me that it is not…?' Grace teased.

'I do not believe that it is in Lucian's case,' his sister insisted firmly. 'However, Lord Darius is another matter entirely. He barely knew his heiress before their wedding—and then for her to die only a month later…!' Arabella shook her head. 'It was all very convenient. Not for her, of course.' She blushed uncomfortably.

'Arabella, you are about to be indiscreet!'

Grace had stiffened at the first sound of Lucian St Claire's voice, and her face was very pale as she slowly turned to see him standing in the doorway of her bedchamber. One look at his harshly disapproving face as he looked at his sister told Grace that he had overheard some of the conversation between the two women, at least. She could only hope that did not include any of the remarks made about him!

Although Grace could not help but recall that this was the second time Lucian had entered her bedchamber uninvited…

Lucian, having taken in the elegant beauty of Grace's appearance when he had first opened the door to her bedchamber—those ebony curls loose down the length of her spine, her waist and bosom clearly emphasised by the cut of her soft velvet robe—deliberately kept his steely gaze fixed firmly upon his sister. That did not mean he was not still completely aware of Grace's state of déshabillé, or the way her robe clung so revealingly to her tempting curves…

'I believe, Arabella, that you owe Grace an apology.' He spoke coldly to his sister. 'Lord Darius is her uncle-by-marriage, and you have just insulted him,' he pointed out.

Arabella's face stiffened in challenge. 'By telling the truth?' His sister met his gaze defiantly.

Lucian's mouth tightened. 'By repeating unfounded gossip.'

'I believe you are mistaken, Lucian.' Grace was the one to answer him softly, but equally challengingly.

Lucian looked at her with hard dark eyes. 'You believe Lord Darius to be guilty of the crime my sister accuses him of…?'

'No, of course I do not!' Her cheeks coloured in her impatience. 'I am referring to the fact that Lord Darius is only the brother of my uncle, and I do not believe Arabella was accusing Lord Darius of any misdeed, only relating to me what others think concerning his tragically brief marriage.'

Lucian gave an abrupt shake of his head. 'It is still unfounded gossip.'

'Oh, tosh!' Arabella snorted dismissively. 'Anyway, people who listen to other people's conversations have no right to complain as to the content of that conversation!'

'I believe it would be better if you were to return downstairs, Arabella.' His sister really had become an outspoken little madam, Lucian decided frowningly. It was time—past time—that Hawk did something to curb that recklessness. Preferably by marrying her to a man who would not tolerate Arabella's frequent acts of rebellion.

Her eyes opened wide at this suggested impropriety. 'Better for whom?'

'Yes, Lucian. Better for whom?' Grace looked at him incredulously; she would never be able to extricate herself from this betrothal if Lucian continued to compromise her in this manner. But perhaps that was his intention…? Although Grace couldn't understand why; after this morning he must be even more aware of how unsuitable a wife she would make him.

He turned icy black eyes on her, his handsome face cold and forbidding. 'For Arabella, of course. Unless you would prefer that my sister remains during yet another of our arguments…?'

So it was to be like that, was it? Grace acknowledged heavily, already more than a little impatient with Lucian's rebukes about her behaviour. Although he did perhaps have cause to complain after she had struck him with her reins this morning, Grace accepted guiltily as she noted that the mark from that blow was still slightly visible in a narrow red welt on his right cheek.

'Perhaps you *should* leave, Arabella, if your brother is going to deliver yet another one of his interminable lectures.' She gave the other woman an encouraging smile.

Arabella walked gracefully to the door, pausing beside her brother. 'The Duchess will not approve…'

A nerve pulsed in Lucian's tightly clenched jaw. '*I* approve.'

'Oh, well, then—I am sure that makes it acceptable!' Arabella laughed tauntingly. 'Although I believe I will ask to be shown out into the rose garden until you return downstairs, in order that the Duchess does not become too…concerned by your absence.'

Lucian's mouth thinned. 'That will not be necessary, Arabella. After all, Grace and I are betrothed.'

'Nevertheless, I believe I will take a stroll outside,' his sister insisted, before standing on tiptoe to give him an affectionate peck on the cheek, pausing only long enough to shoot Grace one last mischievous glance before leaving them alone together, and leaving an awkward silence in her wake.

Grace was very aware of how alone she now was with Lucian. And Lucian—well, Grace could only guess at his feelings on the matter. From the arrogantly disapproving look on his face as he stepped fully into the bedchamber, closing the door softly behind him, she could only assume that his being alone with her in her bedchamber when Grace was wearing only a thin velvet robe over her silk nightgown was not in the least disturbing to him!

Grace wished she could claim the same unconcern at being alone in her bedchamber with him. But Lucian looked too arrogantly handsome, in a superfine of royal blue over an embroidered silver waistcoat and white linen, breeches of soft grey, and black Hessians moulded to the muscled curve of his calves, for Grace to feel in the least comfortable in his presence.

Requesting that Arabella leave him alone in the bed-chamber with Grace had perhaps not been his most sensible move, Lucian acknowledged grimly as he realised how intimate their situation had now become. Grace was so alluringly beautiful, with that ebony hair cascading loosely down the slenderness of her back, and the low neckline of her robe allowing him a tempting glimpse of the creamy swell of her full, unconfined breasts. And the intimacy of the bed was so tantalisingly close...!

Lucian clasped his hands together behind his back as he began to pace the bedchamber impatiently, his gaze averted from the beautiful cameo Grace presented by the window. 'I believe I owe you an apology for my behaviour this morning.'

'An apology...?' Grace's eyes widened; this was the last thing she had been expecting from Lucian after he'd requested the two of them be left alone.

He nodded tersely. 'I have considered our disagreement and believe my manner may have been more dictatorial than one reasonably has a right to be with one's betrothed.'

'The dictatorship only begins *after* the wedding?' Grace made no attempt to keep the scorn from her voice.

'I also believe I am guilty of having made certain—remarks,' Lucian continued hardly, as if she had not interrupted, 'Personal remarks, concerning your character, that I should not have made, and which resulted in your behaving...rashly.'

As an apology it was rather poor, seeming to imply that it was Grace's own behaviour that had caused Lucian to behave in the way that he had. But it was an apology nonetheless...

'Apology accepted.' She nodded graciously.

Dark eyes narrowed on her suspiciously. 'That is very—generous of you...'

Grace gave a dismissive shrug. 'I am a very generous person.'

Lucian's lips twitched on the edge of a smile at her magnanimous attitude, some of the tension leaving his shoulders. But not all. He was still too aware of Grace's loveliness, her near-nakedness beneath her velvet robe, to be able to relax completely. 'The Duke tells me that there was some sort of upset between you and Francis when you returned from our ride this morning…?'

Grace's chin rose challengingly. 'He annoyed me.'

Lucian gave a tight smile. 'By breathing, perhaps…?'

She nodded abruptly. 'Perhaps.'

Lucian gave an understanding nod of his head. 'If, as we think, Francis is the one responsible for the rumours concerning our betrothal—'

'He *is!*'

'He has admitted as much?'

Her mouth tightened angrily. 'As good as, yes.'

'Then you have every right to be annoyed with him.'

Her eyes flashed. 'How kind of you to give me permission to be so, My Lord!'

Why, Lucian wondered irritably, did every conversation he had with Grace result in an argument of some kind? Even when he was attempting to be reasonable—*especially* when he was attempting to be reasonable!—Grace seemed to take offence over something he either said or did.

He sighed his impatience. 'I am merely suggesting that it might be better if you were to leave any reprimand to Francis Wynter to me. Better as regards your aunt and uncle, I mean,' he rasped at Grace's fierce glare. 'After all, he is the brother of your guardian, your uncle, and for the moment you are all residing under the same roof.'

Grace found she couldn't disagree with this argument. Although, contrarily, found she would have liked to do so. There was something so deliciously…exciting about inciting Lucian to anger. Especially when both his brother and sister seemed to imply that their brother was no longer capable of deep emotion…

For the last two years, anyway. It had been a bloody war against Napoleon, of course, and many of those who had fought in it had not returned. Perhaps—perhaps that was the very reason Lucian had those disturbing dreams? Because he was one of the ones who *had* returned?

If that were the reason then it was ridiculous of him to feel that way, of course, but in the short time that she had known him Grace had come to realise that Lucian *was* a man capable of very deep emotions. Anger and desire to name but two…

'Perhaps you are right.' Grace spoke quietly, her gaze slightly shy beneath the sweep of her lashes.

'Good God…!' Lucian looked astounded.

Grace gave him a startled glance. 'What is it?'

'I do believe, Grace—' he grinned widely '—that is the first time in our acquaintance that you have ever agreed with me without argument!'

'I am sure that cannot be right, Lucian.' She frowned. 'What about—? No. Well, there was the time—No.' She gave a heavy sigh. 'But surely I did agree—? No, I did not.' Grace grimaced as she realised that his claim was correct. 'Perhaps if you were not always so determined to be right—'

'No, Grace, I will not allow you to spoil this moment for me!' Lucian moved forward to place a triumphantly silencing finger against her mouth.

He was instantly aware of his mistake as he felt the softness of her lips beneath his fingertips, the warmth of her breath against his skin. The nearness of the soft rise and fall of her breasts…

Grace's startled gaze met his, their faces only inches apart, misty grey captured by dark, compelling black, her breath only the softest of whispers against his fingers. Lucian's own breathing had become somewhat erratic.

Time seemed to stand still as Lucian gazed deeply into Grace's eyes, watching as the pupils became enlarged, leaving only a rim of grey at their edges as she stared up at him in rising expectation, as if willing him to kiss her.

Lucian wanted to kiss her.

More than anything he had ever wanted, he *needed* to kiss her!

Lucian wanted to take Grace in his arms and crush her body against his, even as his lips claimed hers in a kiss that demanded what her eyes already promised she was prepared to give.

But Lucian knew that if he once started kissing Grace he would not want to stop. That he would not be able to stop. And, once again, they were not in a place where it was safe for him to give in to that impulse—let alone lose himself in all Grace's ripe loveliness.

She was not only a young woman of tender years, but also one of inexperience—certainly no match for the force of the passion that threatened to break loose from Lucian.

Damn it!

Lucian drew in a harsh breath and moved back abruptly, straightening as he once again clasped his hands together behind his back, so that he would not be tempted into touching Grace again. 'Your aunt explained your absence downstairs earlier was because of a headache. I trust you are recovered now?' His manner was stiff and unyielding.

Grace frowned, completely ruffled by what had just transpired between them. She was not mistaken, she was sure of it; Lucian had been on the point of kissing her. Yet now he was behaving almost like a polite stranger, his arrogant face remote, even the expression in his eyes hidden by hooded lids.

In contrast Grace was filled with a trembling awareness, her body heated, that familiar tingling in her breasts, the nipples hard and thrusting as she found her gaze drawn to those sculptured lips that had pleasured those aching tips so thoroughly yesterday evening. As she longed for them to pleasure her again...!

Her gaze dropped, her hands trembling slightly as she smoothed her gown over her thighs. She had never thought of herself as a woman who would enjoy a man's hands upon her body. No, not *any* man's hands—it was Lucian's touch alone that she craved, that she ached for. It was a craving she *would* not—could not!—see fulfilled.

She moistened lips that felt sensitive to the touch, her gaze no longer meeting his. 'Unfortunately not, My Lord.' Her voice sounded strained even to her own ears. 'To the point that I believe I will now have to lie down in my darkened bedchamber in order to find any relief from the pounding in my head.'

Lucian had been convinced earlier, when the Duchess had made her niece's excuses, that the headache was nothing but a ruse. But he could see now that Grace's face was very pale, her eyes having a slightly bruised look beneath them. 'I should not have intruded when you are unwell.' He frowned darkly. 'Please accept my apology—'

'Two apologies in one afternoon, My Lord?' Grace's smile was taunting. 'Such an occurrence will only bring about a further relapse, I am sure!'

Lucian gave a hard smile at her obvious derision. The previous moment of intimacy between them seemed as if it had never happened. Perhaps for Grace it had not…? 'I see we are back to our usual daggers drawn!'

Grace gave a dismissive shrug. 'I am not sure we were ever anything else…'

Lucian's smile became self-derisive now. 'Perhaps not.' He bowed stiffly. 'With your permission, I will call again tomorrow, when hopefully you will be feeling better.'

Her eyes widened. 'There is really no necessity for you to be quite so attentive, My Lord. I am sure that a verbal enquiry, carried by one of your servants, will be quite sufficient if you really feel that you must show an interest.'

He appeared very tall and forbidding as he turned in the open doorway. 'Your aunt and uncle will expect that interest to be of a more personal nature.'

Of course, Grace accepted heavily. Her aunt and uncle *would* expect it. Society dictated that he must be attentive to the woman he was betrothed to. How silly of her, how naïve of her, to have thought that Lucian might have actually *wanted* to call on her tomorrow in order that he might be with her again.

She gave a gracious inclination of her head. 'I am sure you must do whatever you deem to be correct, My Lord.'

His mouth was tight. 'Must I, Grace…?'

She blinked, sensing another meaning beneath that casual enquiry. A meaning she did not understand. 'My Lord?'

'Never mind, Grace.' He gave a shake of his head, his expression one of bored dismissal. 'I will leave you to your rest.' The door closed softly behind him.

Grace sat unmoving after Lucian had left, an uncomfortable fluttering sensation in her breast, her skin feeling hot and feverish. Her lips were trembling slightly, her eyes deeply troubled as she continued to stare at that closed door.

Could it be—? Was it possible—? Could she possibly have done what she had not wanted to do and actually fallen in love with Lord Lucian St Claire…?

Chapter Ten

'There is a Miss Hetherington to see you, My Lord.' Reeves, Lucian's elderly butler, stood stiffly just inside the library, where Lucian sat before the fireplace enjoying a glass of brandy before retiring to his bed. 'A Miss Grace Hetherington.'

Lucian didn't need the 'Grace' part added to that statement—he knew of only one Miss Hetherington!

A Miss Hetherington who should not—most definitely should not!—be calling on him at his home at almost eleven o'clock at night. As a single young lady, even one who was his betrothed, Grace should not be calling on Lucian at his home at *any* time!

'The devil—!' Lucian sat up abruptly in his winged armchair, scowling darkly. 'I trust she is not alone?'

'No, My Lord, there is a maid with her.' The rigidity of Reeves's back showed his disapproval of this strange turn of events.

Rightly so, Lucian accepted grimly. Since his move

to London ten years ago Lucian certainly hadn't lived the life of a monk, but he never, ever brought women into his home who were not related to him, and—maid or no maid—Grace had behaved completely inappropriately by visiting a single gentleman in this way. Which Lucian had every intention of telling her as he escorted her straight back to the Duke of Carlyne's residence—

'Miss Hetherington seems rather—emotional, My Lord,' Reeves added, with a slight softening of his stern demeanour.

Lucian frowned warily. 'In what way emotional, Reeves…?' If Grace had taken some new hare-brained notion into her head that had necessitated her coming here at this time of night just so that she could challenge him with it, then Lucian would personally put her over his knee and—

'Miss Hetherington appears…to have been weeping, My Lord.' Reeves informed him softly.

Weeping? Grace? The outspoken, refusing-to-be-cowed-in-any-situation Grace, appeared to have been weeping? What or who had dared to distress her to the point that she had been reduced to shedding tears?

Lucian frowned darkly as he stood up. 'Lucian!' A distraught-looking Grace—having obviously tired of waiting—appeared in the doorway behind Reeves, her hair in disarray, the evidence of those tears upon her pale cheeks. 'Oh, Lucian!' Reeves just managed to step to one side as Grace rushed into the room to launch herself into Lucian's arms. 'It's just too awful, Lucian!'

she sobbed as she clung to him. 'And I am to blame! *I* am to blame!'

An angry or defiant Grace was easily understood, if not dealt with. A distressed and weeping one was completely beyond Lucian's comprehension. He shot Reeves a frowning plea for assistance even as his arms moved to cradle Grace against him, her face buried against his chest as she continued to cry.

The butler looked no less at a loss. 'I will take Miss Hetherington's maid to the servants' quarters, My Lord, and leave you to talk with Miss Hetherington...privately.' Reeves beat a hasty retreat, closing the door softly behind him as he did so.

Deserter! Lucian accused him frustratedly as he looked down helplessly at Grace. She felt so tiny in his arms, so delicate, and her helpless sobbing was bringing out every protective instinct he possessed.

Several minutes later, having moved to sit in the armchair with Grace seated upon his knee, with her tears showing no sign of abating, Lucian knew he had to do or say something to stop them. 'Grace, I really doubt, considering the damp state of my shirt, that there can be any more tears inside you left to weep!'

Grace slowly came to an awareness of exactly where she was and what she was doing, sitting up dazedly to stare down at Lucian's white shirt. Damp hardly described its condition. The fine linen material was completely transparent as it clung to him, clearly revealing the dark hair Grace already knew grew upon his chest.

Lucian had discarded his jacket, waistcoat and

cravat, and was now wearing only tailored cream breeches and the damp white shirt—that shirt unbuttoned to reveal the strong column of his throat. He obviously had not been expecting visitors this evening—let alone one who wept all over him!

Grace attempted to stand up as she realised she was unashamedly perched upon his knee as he sat in the winged armchair, her expression one of guilty embarrassment as she modestly lowered silky dark lashes.

'No, do not move,' Lucian rasped as his arms tightened about her. 'Now that you are calmer I wish you to remain exactly where you are and tell me what has so distressed you.'

The tears instantly returned to her eyes as Grace recalled exactly what had brought her here. To Lucian. To the man she might constantly spar with verbally but whose strength she did not doubt for a moment. To the man she might, in fact, love…

She swallowed hard. 'My uncle—the Duke—has had a—a seizure of some kind. The physician—the physician is not sure that he will recover!' The tears once again fell hotly down her cheeks. 'And it is all *my* fault, Lucian!' She fell to weeping once again.

'Grace, I really must insist that you calm yourself.' Lucian's voice was deliberately stern. Enough to stem her flow of tears, he hoped. 'There is nothing I can do to assuage your fears whilst you continue to caterwaul in this unbecoming fashion,' he added brusquely, when his sternness had no visible effect upon her tears.

That last remark certainly did. Grace's expression

was one of indignation as she glared at him. 'Caterwaul, sir? Ladies do not caterwaul!'

'Usually not, no,' Lucian drawled.

Her cheeks became flushed. 'I insist I was not caterwauling!'

Lucian gave an unrepentant grin. 'Whether you were or were not, my remark had the desired effect, did it not? Your tears have now ceased, and along with them my own discomfort.' He gave a pointed look at his wet and clinging shirt.

Grace gave him a reproving look as she moved out of his arms and rose to her feet. 'It is unkind of you to tease me when you can see how upset I am.'

Lucian studied her. She really did not look anything like the elegantly fashionable Grace Hetherington she had become these last ten days. Her hair was secured precariously in a riot of curls, her face was blotchy and her eyes red from the tears she had cried, and her pale blue high-waisted gown was crumpled and creased from the time she had spent in his arms. But Lucian knew by the sparkle that had returned to her eyes and the high colour in her cheeks that his remark had had the desired effect. That, although obviously dishevelled, Grace was rapidly returning to her determinedly outspoken self.

'It was unkind.' Lucian gave an acknowledging inclination of his head. 'Even if true, it was unkind.'

Her mouth firmed. 'My Lord—'

'We are not going to argue again this evening, Grace,' he reproved with a dark frown. 'The Duke of Carlyne is ill, you say?'

Grace instantly forgot her annoyance with Lucian as she recalled the terrible scene that had transpired at Carlyne House earlier that evening. Her uncle had staggered from the direction of his library to where Grace and her aunt sat in the family salon, his face bright red as he clutched his chest, appearing to be struggling for breath. Grace and her aunt barely had time to rise from their chairs before the Duke had collapsed onto the carpet at their feet.

Aunt Margaret had instantly begun to scream hysterically, bringing both Francis and Darius running to the salon. Francis had seemed at a loss as he just stood and stared at his older brother; Darius was the one who had remained completely calm as he sent one of the servants for the physician, before he and his younger brother carried the Duke, still unconscious, up to his bedchamber.

Grace had tried her best to calm her aunt as they'd followed the men up the wide staircase—to little effect. Her aunt had been almost on the point of collapse herself by the time the physician had arrived, some time later, and sent them all out of the room so that he might examine his patient in peace, as well as privacy.

All the time Grace had soothed and offered words of comfort to her aunt she had been guiltily aware of the altercation that had occurred between Francis and herself that morning—an event that had so disturbed the Duke…

'I am to blame,' she said again softly.

Lucian stood up impatiently. 'You have already said that, Grace. Several times. I have no idea why you should think it so—'

'Can you not see?' She glared her irritation at him. 'If I had not argued with Francis this morning—If our raised voices had not disturbed my uncle—'

'Let me see if I understand you correctly, Grace.' Lucian eyed her impatiently. 'You believe that it was your argument with Francis that took place—what? Twelve or fourteen hours ago?—which caused the Duke to collapse this evening?'

She shot him a reproving frown. 'Of course that is what I mean.'

'I admire your arrogance in thinking it might be so, Grace, but—'

'It is not arrogance!' She glared. 'What other reason could there possibly be for my uncle to collapse so suddenly?' Grace began to pace the room restlessly.

Lucian could think of several reasons off the top of his head. The London Season could be extremely tiresome as well as tiring for a man who lived his life mainly in the country—although Lucian decided against mentioning that to Grace, knowing it would only bring on another bout of guilt when *she* was the reason the Carlynes had come to London for the Season! The Duke might possibly have financial worries that none of them knew of. Francis Wynter had to be the most trying of lingering house-guests. Darius had arrived earlier today too, and although he was by far easier to get along with, the Duke's two younger brothers had little time for each other. Having the two of them staying together at Carlyne House would no doubt be cause for tension.

Grace's little spat with Francis earlier this morning was unimportant by comparison with any of those things!

Lucian shook his head. 'Your aunt and uncle may have had a marital disagreement—'

'Ridiculous!' Grace snapped her impatience with such a suggestion. 'Aunt Margaret and Uncle George have the most harmonious of marriages!'

So did Lucian's brother Hawk and his Duchess, but even *they* had been known to have their disagreements on occasion! 'Some unpleasantness between Darius and Francis, then,' he dismissed. 'There are any number of things that could have caused the Duke's collapse, other than your own disagreement with Francis this morning. Or none of them,' Lucian added gently. 'Perhaps it is just that the Duke's physician in Worcestershire was right all along, and he does have something wrong with his heart…?'

Grace looked a little less certain in her conviction that she was to blame for her uncle's collapse. 'The physician this evening did say, after examining my uncle, that he believed it had been a seizure of the heart.'

'There you are, then.' Lucian shrugged.

'But even if that is true, surely there must have been a reason for his collapse?'

'Grace, I really think you are taking far too much upon yourself by imagining that anything you or Francis did or said could have resulted in such a collapse.' Lucian was fast losing patience with her stubborn belief that she was to blame for what had happened.

She looked less certain. 'You do…?'

'I do.'

Now that Grace had calmed down somewhat she was fast coming to a realisation of just how impetuously she had behaved in coming to Lucian's home this evening. Not only was it completely improper of her to have done so, but—as she once again took in Lucian's state of undress—she could not help but realise how rakishly handsome he looked in the billowy white shirt and thigh-hugging breeches.

How much she loved him…

Grace was left in no doubt that Lucian was also aware of the intimacy of their situation, and their gazes met, the very air between them seeming to still.

Her breasts quickly rose and fell. She found it impossible to look away from the intensity of Lucian's dark gaze, her own eyes widening in alarm as he took a step towards her.

Lucian stood only inches away from her now, very tall and handsome, so close that Grace could feel the heat emanating from his body, and admire the way his damp shirt clung to the muscled width of his powerful chest.

'I should take you home.' His voice was huskily soft.

'Yes…'

'Now.'

'Yes.'

'Right now.'

'Yes.'

But neither of them moved. Grace couldn't move. Didn't want to move. Unless it was into Lucian's arms!

Lucian was the one to take the single step that brought Grace into his arms, before his head lowered and his lips captured hers. Not gently, but forcefully. Not asking, but demanding. A demand Grace met as her lips parted beneath the onslaught of his, her pulse racing as Lucian's tongue gently probed the moist heat of her mouth.

She felt warm and softly yielding as he moulded her body against the length of his, his arousal pressing against her softness.

Lucian continued to plunder the moist cavern of her mouth for long delicious minutes, his arousal leaping in response as her tongue moved shyly to duel with his and her hands moved between them, so that she might fully unbutton his shirt to touch his heated flesh. But even that wasn't enough, it seemed; Grace pushed the shirt from his shoulders and down his arms, to leave the whole of his torso bared to her touch.

Her fingers were initially like butterfly wings against his flesh, and then her caresses grew bolder, kneading him, nails scraping erotically against his nipples, creating a pleasure Lucian had never known before. His neck arched as she broke their kiss to trail a path of fire down his throat. Tasting him. Biting him. Her tongue flicking at his nipples in the same way his had once sucked hers.

Dear God…!

Lucian wanted to touch and taste her in the same way. *Needed* to touch and taste her in the same way! All of her!

He moved a hand beneath her chin so that he might look into her face, his gaze searching, asking the question and seeing the answer in eyes that were dark, with only a rim of silver. Her cheeks were flushed, her lips full and swollen from the demand of his kisses and her own arousal.

Grace found the tense silence between them unbearable. Unacceptable.

'Do not stop, Lucian…!' She moved close enough to rub herself sensually against the hardness of his arousal. 'Show me what to do next,' she encouraged throatily. 'I know there is more. There *has* to be more! Show me how to please you…'

Lucian gave a choked groan. 'Grace, I am not sure I will be able to maintain control if you please me any more than you have already done!'

'Perhaps I do not want you to maintain control?' Her gaze continued to hold his even as her hands moved caressingly across his shoulders and down the hard length of his chest, those hands appearing pale and delicate against his much darker skin.

He drew in a ragged breath. 'Grace—'

'Please, Lucian!' She moistened swollen lips. 'I want—I ache…!' Grace could not bear even the thought of a repeat of the dissatisfied ache Lucian had left her with yesterday evening. An ache she had no experience, no idea, how to assuage.

Continuing to hold Lucian's dark gaze with hers, Grace slowly unfastened the buttons at the front of her gown, before slipping it from her shoulders and letting it fall to her slippered feet. That dark gaze slowly shifted down to her breasts, now concealed only by a cream silk camisole that reached to mid-thigh, the thin material a sensuous caress across her roused and thrusting nipples, the dark triangle of hair at the apex of her thighs was also tantalisingly visible…

'Grace—' Lucian's groan of protest was strangled in his throat as Grace lifted delicate white arms and removed the pins from her hair, to allow it to fall free and curling down the slenderness of her back, her breasts rising temptingly with the movement.

Lucian found it impossible to resist that temptation and his hands lifted to cup beneath those delicious orbs, before his head lowered and his lips claimed one turgid nipple through the delicate material of her camisole, drawing it fully into the heat of his mouth. Any idea of gentleness evaporated as Grace arched into him, and he felt her fingers become entangled in his hair as she held him to her.

Lucian suckled greedily, laving the roused nipple with the rough rasp of his tongue while his hand kneaded and caressed its twin, hard beneath the soft pad of his thumb. Grace mewled softly in her throat at this dual assault upon her senses.

He continued to suckle her as his hand shifted, moving down over the slenderness of her waist to seek the heat between her thighs. He felt the silkiness of her ebony hair, her slick wetness against his fingers, before he sought and found the hardened nub that nestled there, his fingers sure as he began a rhythmic caress that matched the suckling of her breast with his lips and tongue.

Grace felt her knees buckle slightly as Lucian caressed her, her fingers tightening in his hair even as she felt the pressure of some new pleasure building between her thighs. She pressed against him, feeling the pleasure grow stronger, parting her legs instinctively as Lucian's hand shifted slightly and she felt the long length of a finger entering her welcoming wetness slowly, inch by pleasurable inch, and then stilling to allow her time to adjust to the invasion before he entered her fully.

Grace groaned as the pad of his thumb continued its rhythmic caress, clinging to his shoulders as that invading finger was joined by another. Her nails dug into Lucian's flesh as he slowly began to thrust inside her, and she felt herself expand and become wetter still, so hot and wide that she easily accommodated those caressing thrusts. Her eyes closed as once again she acted on instinct and began to move against those invading fingers, riding them as the pleasure grew to almost unbearable heights.

Lucian was aware of the tightening, the arching of Grace's body as her climax began to grip her—felt it as she began to convulse inside, her breath coming in shallow gasps as the pleasure rippled through her, becoming stronger, more intense.

He raised his head to look at her as she trembled and shook on the edge of release, deliberately holding her at the pinnacle of that pleasure, feeling himself filled with a fierce satisfaction as she whimpered and cried for that release, only relenting in his control as she moved pleadingly against him, when a slight pressure of his thumb against her hardened nub sent her spiralling out of control.

She looked beautiful as she rode that release, her face flushed, her eyes tightly closed, her mouth full and moist, her breasts thrusting forward. Those dusky-rose nipples were tight and hard, and her long dark hair curled enticingly over her shoulders, down the length of her spine.

For long, timeless minutes she continued to convulse and gasp as her climax took her through that journey of pleasure. Her forehead was damp against the bareness of Lucian's chest as he drove her relentlessly on, knowing pleasure himself in his ability to drive Grace so completely and wildly out of control.

Grace felt as if she were on fire, every particle of her aflame with excitement, as spasm after spasm of aching release possessed and held her. As *Lucian* possessed and held her, still caressing, still thrusting, Grace's eyes opened wide as she felt a second wave of intensity building deep inside her.

'Yes!' Lucian encouraged her fiercely, before his mouth once more claimed hers, his tongue thrusting inside the heat of her mouth in the same rhythm as his fingers, that dual assault on her senses sending Grace spiralling into a second climax. This time the pleasure was almost pain as it reduced her to bodyracking sobs.

Lucian's arms were like steel bands about her waist as Grace finally collapsed against him, her legs no longer able to support her as her body quivered and quaked in the aftershocks of release.

She should feel mortified at her complete abandon. Grace knew that she should.

Except she didn't.

Not only was she in love with Lucian, but what they had just shared made her feel exultant—this secret knowledge of sexual release made her feel more truly feminine, more womanly than she had ever felt before.

Grace had no idea how long she lay in the strength of Lucian's arms, her body sluggishly replete, her senses filled with a satiated euphoria. But slowly she came back to awareness, to a remembrance of Lucian's arousal—to the knowledge that she had been selfish in her pleasure, and that Lucian had not come anywhere near finding the release that he must surely crave as desperately as she had.

She moistened lips swollen and sensitised from his kisses. 'Lucian—'

'I sincerely hope that you are not going to come out with any words of regret for what just happened...' His voice was harsh in its rebuke.

Regret? How could Grace possibly regret anything so wonderful? So liberating?

She swallowed. 'No.'

'No?' He raised dark brows.

Grace shook her head, her smile slightly self-derisive. 'I could never regret something so—so beautiful.'

Lucian knew that most women in Grace's position

would certainly have done so—that women of the ton did not give themselves so generously as she just had. Or if they did they did not admit to the emotion so freely.

But, as Lucian already knew, Grace was not 'most women'. She was different from any woman Lucian had ever met—of the ton or otherwise.

He looked down at her searchingly, noting her almost shyness as she avoided meeting his gaze. 'But something is troubling you…?'

Her throat moved convulsively before she spoke huskily. 'You did not—' She looked up at him searchingly. 'Is it that you do not want me…?'

Lucian gave a disbelieving grimace. 'How can you possibly think that when we have just made love together?'

A delicate blush coloured her cheeks. 'Because although I lack…experience in such matters, I know enough to realise that you have not—you did not find the same release…'

'Feel how much I want you, Grace.' Lucian took one of her hands and guided it down to where his arousal was still rigidly hard beneath his breeches, groaning low in his throat as he felt the tentative caress of her fingers against him. 'I want you, Grace,' he assured her gruffly. 'I very much want you. In fact, I would enjoy nothing more at this moment than to sit naked in that chair over there—' he looked ruefully across at the winged armchair beside the fire '—and watch as you remove the last of your clothes before you come to me, placing your legs either side of mine, and lower yourself upon me, taking all of me inside you. Do you remember telling me that you like to ride astride…?'

Lucian recalled their conversation on that subject very clearly. Just as he remembered the eroticism of his own fantasies following that claim.

'I remember.' Her cheeks were flushed, her eyes bright.

Lucian nodded. 'I would like you to ride astride *me,* Grace. Slowly. And then with increasing speed.' His jaw clenched just at the thought of it. 'I would like you to ride me in that way until I reached the same release as you have just experienced.' He gave a shake of his head. 'I fantasise about your doing all that with and to me, Grace. I just have no intention of it becoming a reality.' His voice hardened over the last.

She tilted her head quizzically to one side. 'Why not?'

Lucian gave a rueful smile. 'You are a virgin, Grace—do not deny it when I have felt the barrier of your innocence for myself,' he added with gentle rebuke as she would have spoken. 'What we just did—what you experienced just now—did not take away that innocence. It is an innocence I wish you to keep until you marry, Grace.'

Grace had felt the leap of his hardness against her caressing fingers as Lucian talked of her nakedness, of her taking him inside her as she mounted him. 'If you are so determined on that—'

'I am.' His tone brooked absolutely no argument on the subject.

Grace nodded. 'Then is there no way that I could—? That you could—? Is there no way that I can give you the same pleasure, the same release you have just given me, without the taking of my innocence…?'

His jaw clenched. 'There is a way, yes…'

'Then I would like you to show it to me.'

Lucian groaned low in his throat as Grace looked up at him so trustingly. How could he refuse her? How could any man refuse her when he wanted her so desperately and she so innocently offered him paradise?

Nevertheless, Lucian knew that was exactly what he had to do. 'You are an innocent in the ways of men, Grace. It would be wrong of me to—to take away any more of that innocence than I already have.'

She shook her head. 'I do not feel as if you have taken anything from me, Lucian. On the contrary, I feel liberated! Is that how men feel too after—after—?'

'It is called a climax, Grace.'

'It is that "little death" you once talked of, is it not?' she realised astutely. 'And it *is* a little like dying. As if you have glimpsed a brief piece of heaven.'

This woman would be the death of him, Lucian acknowledged achingly. She was so trusting, so open and honest about the things she had felt, that it almost brought him to his knees. That gentle caress of her fingers against his pulsing arousal *was* almost bringing him to his knees!

He gave a rueful shake of his head. 'It is exactly the same for a man as for a woman, Grace. But the moment has passed. *My* moment has passed.' He gently but

firmly removed her hand from his arousal and lifted it
to his lips, to run them caressingly over her delicate
fingers. 'It is time I returned you to your aunt and
uncle's house,' he added, as she looked confused and
hurt by what she obviously saw as his rejection. 'Do you
not see that if anyone has discovered your absence from
the house you will only be adding to their worry?'
Lucian felt he had no choice now but to be cruel to be
kind.

He could not—would not—make love with Grace as
the hardness of his arousal demanded he should. Their
lovemaking so far tonight had only opened her eyes to
the joy to be found in physical intimacy. To introduce
her to any more would be unforgivable on his part.
Besides, Lucian had every intention of making this
woman his wife. After tonight's events, sooner rather
than later!

Grace was shocked. Stunned. For during those last
minutes in Lucian's arms she had totally forgotten her
reason for coming here. Had forgotten her uncle's
collapse earlier tonight, followed by her aunt's distress.
How could she have done such a thing?

What spell had her love for Lucian cast upon her
that she had so forgotten the loyalty and love she owed
to the couple who had taken her into their own home
when her parents died? Her aunt and uncle had treated
her this last year as if she were a beloved daughter
rather than just a niece. They were only in London at
all at this time because her aunt had insisted that Grace
must have a Season!

She turned away, stricken, feeling ill as she grabbed up her gown from the carpeted floor and quickly pulled it on over her near nudity, her fingers shaking as she refastened the buttons.

'Grace…?'

'Do not say anything!' She turned fiercely on Lucian, the colour high in her cheeks.

'Grace, what has happened here between us this evening is a—a normal reaction—to illness, to the realisation of our own mortality,' Lucian told her gently. 'I have seen it time and time again following battle. The need to—'

'We will never speak of this again.' Grace was shaking with the intensity of her emotions. 'I should never have come here, let alone—let alone… We will *never* speak of this again!' she repeated vehemently.

Lucian frowned grimly, knowing by Grace's very fierceness that he had not handled the situation correctly.

He had not intended to hurt Grace by reminding her of her aunt and uncle, only to put an end to his own torment, to the urge he had to lay Grace down upon the carpeted floor before experiencing the joy of thrusting inside her and giving them both another brief glimpse of heaven! But he knew it was too late for him to retract now.

Grace agitatedly stabbed the pins back into her hair, once again securing it in loose curls upon her head, seemingly uncaring of the pain she was inflicting upon her own scalp.

He drew in a harsh breath. 'I will arrange for my

carriage to be brought round immediately.' He strode forcefully towards the door.

'Lucian!'

He turned frowningly at Grace's admonishing cry. 'Yes…?'

Grace swallowed hard, her cheeks very pale. 'Should you not—not dress yourself before appearing in front of your servants?' The sight of Lucian's bare chest, the rippling muscles of his back, reminded Grace all too forcefully of how she had almost ripped his shirt from him minutes ago, in her need to touch his bare flesh.

Lucian's movements were impatient as he pulled the shirt back into place before refastening it. 'Are your sensibilities satisfied now, Grace?' His gaze was darkly challenging.

Her sensibilities were shattered, if not utterly destroyed by the wantonness of her recent behaviour! So much so that Grace was not sure she would ever regain them…

She gave a haughty inclination of her head. 'Thank you.'

Lucian's mouth twisted mockingly. 'What a little prude you are, after all!' He gave her one last arrogantly sweeping glance before leaving the room.

A prude? Lucian could still call her a prude after—after—? Grace couldn't even bear to think of the intimacies she had allowed—encouraged!—between the two of them only minutes ago. Of the way she had pleaded with Lucian to show her more. Of the way she had asked him to show her how to give *him* the same pleasure!

A request he had refused…

What must he think of her?

A young lady of breeding and refinement simply did not behave in that way.

Grace's self-recriminations at her wantonness were immense. But how much more shocked and disgusted by her behaviour must Lucian be…!

Chapter Eleven

'I believe it would be for the best, once we reach your uncle's home, if I were to talk to Darius alone,' Lucian told Grace firmly as she sat across his carriage from him, her maid beside her.

'Very well.' Grace nodded after the briefest of pauses. 'But I wish to speak with you again before you leave.'

Lucian could easily guess the subject of *that* conversation!

Despite what Grace had said to the contrary, Lucian had no doubt she deeply regretted their earlier intimacy. How could he doubt it when she had so studiously avoided any physical contact with him since that time, even to shunning any assistance from him in ascending into his carriage a short time ago?

But with Grace's maid present Lucian knew it was impossible for them to discuss the subject further now. Although he feared they would not be able to discuss it later either, with her uncle's household in such emotional turmoil.

'Very well.' He nodded distantly. 'It would perhaps be advisable if you were to be in your bedchamber when Darius sends for you.' He shot the young maid an impatient glance, well aware that although she was not a part of this conversation she could nevertheless hear it. 'I do not believe it will serve any purpose for your relatives to know that you came to my home this evening. I would suggest that we allow them to believe your maid came in your stead, to inform me of your uncle's collapse and that you felt a need for me to be at your side during this time of distress.'

Grace appreciated exactly what Lucian was trying to do. It *had* been extremely improper of her to have gone to his home this evening. In light of what had transpired between them it had been much worse than improper!

'I am sure you are right,' she acknowledged distantly. 'If asked, I am sure that Mary will agree.' Mary had been Grace's maid since childhood, accompanying Grace from Cornwall when she had gone to live with her aunt and uncle in Worcestershire.

Grace lapsed back into silence, her thoughts far from pleasant as they persisted in dwelling on her behaviour this evening. The ache of her breasts and thighs refused to let her think of anything else!

Lucian had touched her breasts. Kissed her there. Taken her nipples into his mouth to suckle and caress them. As for the way he had touched her between her legs… Just thinking of those caresses, the hard thrusts of his fingers inside her, the unimagined pleasure she had known from those caresses, was enough to re-ignite that aching heat and bring a flush to her cheeks. Her breathing became low and shallow, her breasts pressing tautly against the bodice of her gown.

It didn't help Grace's discomfort that she was so aware of Lucian as he sat opposite her, looking so cool and distant, so much his arrogantly confident self, in the cream breeches and with a topcoat over his dark blue jacket, his necktie tied meticulously at the throat of the clean—and dry!—white shirt he had changed into before rejoining her in his study. Looking every inch as if their earlier intimacy had never occurred…

Grace dearly wished that it had not.

She had even more reason to wish that were the case when Lucian joined her in the drawing room, following his conversation with Lord Darius!

'The prognosis is not good, Grace.' Lucian did not see the point in prevarication concerning the Duke of Carlyne's state of health; Grace would need to know the truth of the situation if she were to be of benefit to her aunt during the coming days and weeks. Besides, as he knew only too well, Grace was not the sort of woman who appreciated being protected from the truth. 'The physician is to remain at your uncle's bedside tonight. It is his belief that a second, more serious seizure may occur during the next twenty-four hours.' His expression was grim.

The only colour in Grace's face was the dark, smoky grey of her eyes. 'And if that were to happen…?'

Lucian grimaced. 'He doubts that your uncle would survive a second seizure.'

Grace turned away to blink back her tears, her hands tightly linked together as she faced the prospect of another death in her family. But her own feelings were instantly set to one side as she thought of her aunt's pain and distress if that were to happen. Her aunt and uncle were so devoted to each other, and had already suffered the loss of their only son. It was unimaginable that her aunt should lose her beloved husband too.

'I have, of course, offered any assistance I can give during this time.' Lucian continued talking as he allowed Grace to assimilate the information he had given her. He was already acquainted with her well enough—after tonight, some would say too well—to know that she had the fortitude of character to see her through the strain of the days ahead.

Even if the Duke did survive, the Duchess would need a stalwart companion. Not Darius or Francis, but a female companion whom she might lean upon, depend upon, to give her the strength she would need. Lucian had no doubt that Grace was in possession of that strength.

Despite the pallor of her face, Grace's chin was bravely high when she turned back to him. 'Thank you,' she accepted gravely. 'I am sure that my aunt, Lord Darius and Lord Francis will be most appreciative of your generosity.'

The Duchess and Darius, perhaps, but Lucian seriously doubted that Francis Wynter would see Lucian's presence as anything more than interference in what he considered a private family matter. Fortunately Lucian had absolutely no interest in Francis Wynter's feelings on any subject!

'Fond as I am of George, Margaret and Darius, my offer was made for your benefit, Grace. Not theirs,' Lucian said quietly.

Grace's brow puckered into a frown. 'I am upset, naturally, but that does not mean that I expect you to inconvenience yourself on my behalf.'

'We are betrothed, Grace.' Lucian's mouth thinned as he saw the way her mouth tightened at his reminder of their betrothal. 'Do you not see that in these circumstances it is even more essential that you do not proceed with your plans to end our betrothal?' His impatience with her stubbornness made his tone curt.

Unfortunately Grace *did* see. Just as she accepted, on brief reflection, that it was not the time to add to her aunt's worry and distress. But that did not mean Grace was at all comfortable with continuing this forced betrothal.

'Besides,' Lucian continued with mocking gentleness, 'did our earlier intimacy not prove to you that marriage to me would not be such an unpleasant prospect after all…?'

Grace felt the colour blaze in her cheeks even as she glared at him. 'I believe I said that I do not wish to discuss that particular subject!'

He shrugged those broad shoulders. 'Fortunately for us Darius was too distracted just now to notice that you had arrived in the carriage with me, let alone to question too deeply how I come to be here at all at this time of night. Let us hope that on that subject, at least, he remains distracted.' His mouth twisted ruefully. 'Otherwise, my dear, whether you like it or not, we could find ourselves standing before a preacher much sooner than anticipated!'

Grace gave him a chilling glance. 'Lord Darius is not my guardian.'

'He nevertheless takes on that role until the Duke recovers,' Lucian drawled.

Her cheeks felt very warm. 'Lord Darius's own life has been far from blameless!'

Lucian gave a mocking smile. 'Have you not heard that reformed rakes make the strictest guardians?'

Grace's eyes glittered angrily. 'You speak from experience, of course?'

'As it happens, I do,' Lucian acknowledged tauntingly. 'My brother Hawk—a reformed rake if ever there was one—was very briefly guardian to the young lady who is now his Duchess.' He met Grace's gaze challengingly, knowing that had not been her implication at all.

Was *he* a reformed rake?

There had been no women of any consequence in Lucian's life since his return from the Peninsula, admittedly, but that had been for quite another reason than any transformation on his part. The same reason he now had to drink himself into a stupor most evenings in order to find any respite.

The same reason that marrying Grace, or indeed any woman, being with her night and day, and consequently she being with him, was not something Lucian welcomed. How can he possibly relish *any* woman seeing him after the visitation of one of the nightmares that had haunted his nights these last two years, resulting in exhaustion and self-disgust?

Lucian's only hope was that the maintaining of completely separate bedchambers once they were married would take care of that. As long as he did not actually fall asleep in Grace's arms once they had made love, he could see no reason why she need ever know of the horrors that possessed his nights.

His mouth tightened grimly. 'I do not intend to discuss this with you any further tonight, Grace.' His tone brooked no further argument. 'It is time for me to leave, and for you to retire to your bedchamber. I will return in the morning, when we can discuss this further if that is your wish.'

Grace's wish was that she had not acted so impetuously earlier this evening by going to Lucian's home in such a brazen way. More than that she wished that brazenness had not become wantonness once she had been left alone with him in his study!

It was a wantonness that Grace knew neither she nor Lucian would ever forget...

'Our aunt is still abed.' Arabella answered Lucian's unspoken question when he was shown into the breakfast room at St Claire House the following morning. 'Is this not a shockingly early hour for you to be abroad, Lucian?' she added mischievously. 'It was my belief that male members of the ton stayed abed until noon!'

Lucian dismissed the footman once he had poured him a cup of tea. 'The Duke of Carlyne suffered a heart seizure yesterday evening.'

Much as he loved his sister, Lucian was not in the mood for Arabella's teasing this morning.

'Oh, how awful!' His sister was instantly concerned at his news, her creamy brow creasing into a frown. 'How is the Duchess? And Grace? Dear Grace,' she added worriedly.

'Grace is the reason that I am here at such a shockingly early hour.' His mouth thinned, his expression grim. 'Grace had a note delivered to me a short time ago, informing me that her uncle died at four o'clock this morning without regaining consciousness.'

Arabella gasped her dismay, her face paling. 'That is—I cannot believe—' She gave a dazed shake of her head. 'How truly awful!' Her gaze sharpened. 'But should you not go to Grace, Lucian?' She frowned. 'She must be terribly upset.'

Lucian could hear the rebuke in Arabella's tone. A rebuke Lucian knew he richly deserved. As her betrothed, Lucian knew he should be at Grace's side this morning—that Grace's letter, although it did not state it, tacitly requested it. Lucian had every intention of complying with that request, but he would prefer it if Arabella accompanied him to Carlyne House.

For his dreams last night had not consisted of those vivid nightmares that had haunted him for so long.

Instead he had dreamt of Grace. Of her lusciously responsive curves. Of the pleasure he had given her. Of the satisfaction her pleasure had given him.

As usual Lucian had awoken pale and exhausted, but fully aware that this time his physical dilemma had been caused by his own aching need to possess Grace's body rather than those nightmares that took him back to the blood and gore of battle.

He thought he almost preferred the bloody nightmares…

Lucian nodded tersely. 'I am sure she is. Which is why I think it would be beneficial if you were to accompany me to Carlyne House. You find the suggestion not to your liking?' His frowning gaze followed Arabella's abrupt movement as she stood up to cross the room and stand in front of the window that looked out into the garden.

'The Duke is dead, long live the Duke…' she murmured softly.

Lucian frowned darkly. 'I beg your pardon?'

Arabella's smile was scornful as she turned. 'I was thinking how strange it is that Lord Darius, a man who was considered to be an unmitigated rake just one short year ago, now finds his fortune completely turned around!'

Lucian gave a reproving shake of his head. 'I fail to see…'

The sunlight shining in through the window behind her turned Arabella's blonde curls to gold. 'A year ago Lord Darius was on the verge of bankruptcy, was not? And yet within the last seven months he has married an heiress, who conveniently died and left him in sole possession of her fortune, and now his brother has also died, leaving him in possession of a dukedom.' Arabella gave a scathing shake of her head. 'A change of fortunes, indeed!'

Lucian scowled. 'I trust you are not implying anything untoward, Arabella?'

'I am not implying anything, Lucian,' she assured him brittly. 'I am merely commenting that Lord Darius has been blessed by this sudden change of circumstance.'

Lucian's brows rose. 'I do not believe he would consider himself blessed in having just lost his older brother.'

'You would not feel that way if it were Hawk, I am sure, but…'

'I had no idea you disliked Darius so much.' In the circumstances it was perhaps as well that Arabella did not know of Darius's offer for her the previous year!

Arabella shook her head. 'I do not know him well enough to dislike him.'

Lucian frowned. 'Perhaps it would be better if you did not accompany me this morning, after all.'

'Oh, I am most definitely coming with you, Lucian,' his sister informed him determinedly. 'I assure you I will not allow my prejudice towards Lord Darius to prevent me from being of some comfort to Grace.' She moved to the door. 'I will go upstairs now and inform our aunt of our visit, before collecting my bonnet and cloak.'

Lucian's expression was thoughtful as he continued to sit at the breakfast table, mulling over Arabella's comments concerning Darius Wynter's sudden change of circumstances.

Darius's nephew Simon, Marquess of Richfield, had died two years ago, during the horrific battle of Waterloo.

Darius's wife of only one month had died in a hunting accident six months ago, leaving him in possession of her considerable fortune.

His brother George had now collapsed and died—the fact that he had not regained consciousness meant they would never know now what had caused that collapse—making Darius the new Duke of Carlyne.

Coincidence, Lucian dismissed as he rose briskly to his feet, to move into the hallway and collect his hat and cane in readiness for departing to Carlyne House. He had known Darius since childhood, and whilst the older man might have been a womaniser and a gambler before his marriage, seven months ago, Darius had by all accounts settled down to country life on his estate in Malvern.

No, Lucian was convinced this was just a course of unfortunate events. Although George Wynter's death *did* now make Darius Grace's guardian…

'My aunt, with the help of the draught the physician left for her, has finally fallen into an exhausted sleep,' Grace informed Darius and Francis Wynter wearily as she joined them in the library, wearing the only gown she had with her that was in the least suitable for mourning: a deep grey, high-waisted silk gown that exactly matched the colour of her eyes.

Darius gave a grave shake of his head as he stood in front of the window. 'I still cannot believe it. It is as well that I happened to be here and not in Malvern.'

'It is, is it not?' Francis didn't even attempt to hide his resentment as he sat in one of the high-backed chairs before the unlit fireplace. 'I, of course, would never have been able to manage without you!'

Grace gave a gasp at this unwarranted attack by Francis upon his elder brother. As far as she could tell there had never been any love lost between them—they were far too different in character to have anything in common—but surely they could ignore those differences now, in deference to their older brother's recent death?

Darius, despite his grief and lack of sleep, this morning looked every inch that handsome angel/devil that Arabella had described him as yesterday.

'I will excuse your rudeness, Francis,' he rasped harshly, those cobalt-blue eyes narrowed warningly. 'You are obviously overset by George's death.'

'Of course I am.' Francis drew in a shaky breath, his face very pale. 'Are you not equally upset, Darius?'

'Damn it, of course I am upset. Yes, Reynolds?' Darius turned scowlingly to the butler as he quietly entered the room.

'Lord Lucian St Claire and Lady Arabella St Claire have called to see Miss Hetherington, Your Grace.'

Grace could not help but recoil at the butler's use of Darius's new title. It *was* his title now, of course, but it

seemed somehow irreverent when Grace's Uncle
George had only been dead a matter of hours.

'Curiosity seekers!' Francis muttered disgustedly.

Grace looked at him coldly. 'They are here because
I sent Lord Lucian a note earlier this morning, informing him of my uncle's death.'

Francis gave a humourless smile. 'Of course you did.'

Grace bit back her sharp retort, turning to the butler
instead. 'Show Lord Lucian and Lady Arabella into the
drawing-room, Reynolds,' she instructed, before turning
to Darius. 'If you will excuse me…?'

Much as Grace knew it would be awkward to face
Lucian again after the intimacies of yesterday evening,
it would nevertheless be a relief to have respite from the
obvious tension between the two Wynter brothers.
Besides, no doubt Arabella's presence would help ease
the awkwardness of Grace's initial meeting with Lucian.

'Yes, of course.' Darius's scowl was darker than ever.

Grace curtseyed before escaping the room, pausing
in the hallway to allow a heavy sigh to escape her. She
already knew that the next few days were going to be
difficult, but they would be made even more so if Darius
and Francis remained at loggerheads.

She gave a shake of her head, knowing that she could
not deal with that now, and that Lucian and Arabella
awaited her in the drawing room.

'Arabella!' She moved gracefully across the room to
greet the younger woman, and Arabella reached out to
grasp Grace's hands in her own before kissing her
warmly on the cheek.

Grace was completely aware of Lucian as Arabella offered her words of comfort. He stood broodingly silent beside the fireplace, his dark hair falling over his brow, his lids lowered over enigmatic dark eyes, his expression one of sculptured hardness. His appearance was immaculate in black coat and grey breeches, the snowy white linen of his shirt completely unadorned.

Very much like the shirt Grace had stripped from him the evening before…

'Lord Lucian.' She turned to give him a brief curtsey, her lashes lowered. 'It is very kind of you both to respond so quickly to my note.'

Lucian frowned darkly at Grace's distant behaviour. 'I told you I would come if you had need of me…'

'So you did.' She gave an acknowledging inclination of her head as she avoided so much as looking at him.

It incited conflicting emotions inside Lucian. He had not wanted to be alone with Grace this morning—the clarity of his dreams the previous night, of his possessing Grace fully, dictated that in the circumstances it would not be a wise move on his part. But recognising that Grace did not wish to be alone with him either contrarily made Lucian wish he had not, after all, brought Arabella with him. He so wanted to take Grace into his arms and shake her out of this distant behaviour towards him by kissing her senseless!

Grace indicated for them both to be seated—an invitation Lucian did not take up as he continued to stand beside the fireplace, looking down at her frowningly. She looked pale and fragile this morning, the dark shadows beneath her eyes indicative of her lack of sleep, but at the same time she was possessed of a delicate courage that would not allow her to break down.

'I believe Lord Darius—the Duke…' She gave a pained frown at the necessity of using Darius's new title. 'I believe he is making arrangements for us all to return to Winton Hall as soon as possible.'

Arabella, seated beside Grace on the sofa and retaining possession of one of her hands, was the one to answer. 'You are retiring to the country?'

Grace nodded. 'It is my aunt's wish that my uncle be buried in Worcestershire.'

Arabella looked up at Lucian. 'You will accompany Grace, of course?'

It was a statement rather than a question. One that Lucian knew he should have been expecting. But he had not. Of course, as Grace's betrothed he would be expected to accompany the Wynter family back to their home in Worcestershire—to be at Grace's side at the funeral, and to remain there for as long as she wished him to do so.

With those dreams of possessing Grace fully still so clear in his mind, Lucian knew it would not be wise to spend so much time in Grace's company until he had those wild images back under his control. But fate, it seemed, was conspiring against him…

The fact that Grace had seen dismay flicker briefly on Lucian's austere features before he had a chance to mask the emotion was indicative of just how strongly opposed he was to Arabella's suggestion; Lucian, more than any other man Grace had ever known, usually had the ability to hide his inner emotions behind a cynical façade.

Her smile was tight. 'I am sure that will not be necessary—'

'On the contrary, as your betrothed it is *very* necessary that I accompany you to Winton Hall.' Lucian's tone brooked no argument.

Grace shook her head. 'I am sure that you would much rather remain in London enjoying the—the entertainments here than be forced to endure the boredom of Worcestershire.' Her gaze was challenging as it met Lucian's for the first time since his arrival.

Those dark eyes gleamed with mocking amusement. 'Even under such tragic circumstances as these undoubtedly are, I am sure I could never be bored in your company, Grace.'

Her eyes glittered with answering anger. 'Perhaps I find no such comfort in your company, My Lord!'

'Nevertheless, I am afraid that for propriety's sake you must endure it.' Lucian looked bored by the conversation.

For propriety's sake.

Once again Grace's life was to be dictated by what Society expected, demanded, rather than what she or Lucian wanted for themselves!

Especially Lucian.

For her own part Grace could not imagine spending days, possibly weeks, without sight or conversation with Lucian. If only Lucian had not made it so obvious that he found the idea much less than appealing!

'Come, Grace, we must not continue to embarrass Arabella with our lovers' quarrel.' The glitter in Lucian's gaze warned Grace that he had ceased to be amused.

'Oh, I am not in the least embarrassed,' Arabella assured them brightly. 'On the contrary, I find it most illuminating.'

'Might I enquire in what way?' Lucian rasped frowningly.

Arabella shrugged. 'This last year I have had the chance to observe Hawk and Jane as they fell in love— and now you and Grace.' Her eyes sparkled mischievously. 'It is all so much more fun than I had imagined.'

Lucian raised derisive brows. 'For whom?'

'Oh, for the observer, naturally.' Arabella chuckled. 'It does not look at all an enjoyable experience for the two people involved!'

Grace could find no argument with *that* sentiment!

Not that Lucian was in love with her, of course. But she was in love with him. Deeply. Irrevocably. And apart from those occasions when Lucian took her in his arms, when she seemed to lose all sense of propriety let alone denial, Grace had not found it to be in the least an enjoyable experience!

Perhaps if Lucian could have loved her in return it would have been different. As it was, Grace could only take what measures she could to hide her feelings for him. Not something she was having too much success at when she melted into his arms every time they were alone together!

Arabella stood up, a smile playing about her lips. 'I believe it may be time for me to take another turn about the rose garden…'

'No—'

'Do not—'

Grace and Lucian both broke off their disapproval of this suggestion to frown at each other—Grace warily, Lucian impatiently.

'There is no need for you to go anywhere, Arabella,' Lucian finally rasped irritably. 'I am sure that whatever argument Grace believes she has with me this morning can wait until after I have spoken to Darius concerning our travel arrangements,' he added derisively.

'But not, I presume, in my presence?' Arabella murmured disappointedly.

'You presume correctly.' Lucian nodded curtly. 'If you will excuse me, ladies?' He gave a terse bow before striding from the room.

'Interesting,' Arabella murmured curiously, before turning to give Grace an approving smile. 'I do believe you have my brave and fearless brother running from the enemy. Oh, the enemy is not you, Grace,' she assured her, as she saw Grace's dismayed expression. 'You are merely the cause of the battle…'

Grace gave a puzzled shake of her head. 'You are talking in riddles, Arabella.'

'I am, am I not?' Arabella smiled mischievously. 'And it is such an intriguing riddle. How it makes me wish you were not both going to disappear into the wilds of Worcestershire!' she added wistfully.

'Worcestershire is hardly wild, Arabella,' Grace said dryly, her expression brightening as she was struck with sudden inspiration. 'You could always come with us! *Do* say you will come, Arabella!' she pressed eagerly, when the younger woman looked taken aback by the suggestion.

Arabella stepped away from her, moving to stand in front of the window as she gave the invitation some thought.

It was an invitation Grace knew she had made only because Arabella's presence, so practical and yet so teasing, would help to ease the growing tension between herself and Lucian. Which was hardly being fair to Arabella…

'I should not have asked.' Grace gave Arabella a rueful smile as the younger woman turned curiously back to face her. 'It was wrong of me to suggest you leave London when the Season has only just begun!'

'My Aunt Agatha would probably have an apoplexy,' Arabella acknowledged dryly. 'She has such high hopes of marrying me off this Season!'

Grace raised a dark brow. 'And is that your wish, too?'

Arabella's mouth firmed stubbornly. 'I have no expectations of marrying at all.'

'Not at all…?' Grace was stunned. Arabella was only nineteen, all that was grace and beauty, and her dowry as the sister of a duke must be immense.

Arabella gave a softly derisive laugh. 'Do not look so surprised, darling Grace. I grew up with three older brothers who are bold, arrogant and handsome. I adore each and every one of them. So much so that I have no hopes of ever finding a man who would compare to any one of them!'

Grace found she had no argument to make against that last statement. How could she have when she had never met—and knew she never would—any man to compare with Lucian…?

Chapter Twelve

'I am sure that no one would find reason to object if you were to suggest returning to London now,' Grace assured him softly as she walked beside Lucian, following the path that circled the lake at Winton Hall. 'Uncle George has been buried in the family crypt. My aunt is making plans to move into the Dower House.' She shrugged. 'There is nothing more you can do here.'

Lucian frowned darkly. The fact that he had suggested this walk in order that they might be alone, so that he might tell Grace of his decision to make his departure tomorrow morning, did not signify in the face of her easy dismissal of him.

There had been little opportunity for them to talk at all this last week, let alone in private. With Arabella politely declining to accompany them, the journey from London had been a silent one. The Duchess, beside herself with grief, had leaned heavily upon the quiet strength of Grace's company. The same strength that

Grace had employed in dealing with the more subdued grief of the servants at Winton Hall.

The Duchess had collapsed completely after the funeral service four days ago, leaving Grace to act as dignified hostess to the family and friends who had come from miles around to attend the final leavetaking of a man who had obviously been much loved and respected. Lucian's brother Hawk had even put in a brief appearance.

Hawk had been his usual haughty self, of course. One glance down his long, aristocratic nose enough to keep the other funeral guests firmly at bay as he stood talking with Lucian and Grace. Grace had been slightly in awe of the autocratically arrogant Duke of Stourbridge, although she had kept that emotion firmly under control as Hawk had put her at her ease by talking of her father's paintings that hung in Mulberry Hall. Only Lucian, it seemed, had been initially unaware of exactly who Grace's father had been!

'I approve.' That had been Hawk's only—telling—comment when Lucian walked with him to the ducal carriage some half an hour later.

Lucian's brows had risen. 'I do not remember asking for your approval.'

Hawk had climbed agilely into the coach. 'You have it anyway. Bring her to Mulberry Hall as soon as you are able to get away.' He had nodded haughtily for the groom to close the door, effectively putting an end to the conversation.

Hawk, the lofty Duke of Stourbridge, approved of

Grace. Arabella approved of Grace. Sebastian definitely approved of her. Only Lucian, it seemed, was in total confusion concerning how he felt about her. Still.

Oh, he had no doubt that Grace had all the attributes to make any man a suitable wife. She was beautiful. She was charming. She was gracious.

She was also headstrong, extremely opinionated, and given to impulsive behaviour. In short, Grace was nothing at all like the quiet, undemanding woman Lucian had thought would make him a suitable wife!

There was also the added disquiet that Lucian's nightly dreams now consisted solely of *her.* Of caressing her. Of arousing her. Of possessing her! Dreams that were indeed more disturbing than those nightmares of battle and death!

'Are you so sure of that…?' Lucian looked down at Grace enigmatically now, as he came to an abrupt halt on the pathway.

'So sure of what?' Grace felt a jolt of uneasiness as she looked up into his dark gaze.

There had been so much to do this last week that it had not been too difficult to avoid being alone in Lucian's company, but Grace was now suddenly aware of how very alone they were on this pathway that meandered through the woods on the side of the lake farthest from Winton Hall.

And she was aware of how handsome Lucian looked, in dark brown superfine, cream breeches and a waistcoat over snowy-white linen, with a small diamond pin in the centre of his meticulously tied cravat. Rakishly handsome, she corrected self-derisively as she felt a familiar fluttering sensation at her breast.

He quirked one dark brow. 'That there is nothing left for me to do here?'

Grace's uneasiness grew as she recognised the intimacy of his tone. They were too alone here. Too far from the house. Too far from other people…

She gave a shake of her head. 'I am, of course, grateful for the help you have given me this last week…'

She had appreciated Lucian's skill in diverting the irritating Francis from annoying Darius too badly. Had admired Lucian's gentle concern for her aunt's welfare, and been fully aware that he had quietly ensured Grace was given some time each day in which to be free of the roiling emotions that now existed beneath the polite veneer of the Wynter family.

Grace had been able to appreciate all of those things while at the same time being completely aware of Lucian's avoidance of her company…

He gave a mocking smile now. 'That statement sounds as if a "but" should follow…?'

Grace nodded. 'But now it is time for you to return to your own life.'

He raised dark brows. 'I had believed my betrothed to be a *part* of my life…'

'Lucian—'

'Grace.' He looked down at her haughtily.

She gave a pained frown. 'We both know that our betrothal is bogus—something that we have been forced to continue to endure for my aunt's sake. But there is absolutely no reason for you to remain here any longer.'

'In a word, you are dismissing me?'

Grace could hear the underlying anger in Lucian's tone now—could see that same emotion in the hard glitter of his eyes. 'Of course I am not dismissing you. I am merely allowing you—I am merely expressing the wish—You know exactly what I am trying to say, Lucian!' she concluded impatiently, as that glitter took on a dangerous sheen.

A threatened danger that only increased Grace's awareness of how alone they were...

Lucian gave a terse inclination of his head. 'I believe you are telling me that I have served my purpose and now I may leave.'

'I do not—I did not— Oh, it is impossible to talk to you when you are in this mood!' Grace cheeks became flushed with temper.

Lucian had always hated the colours of mourning, the drab black and grey reminding him too much of the death of his own parents in a carriage accident eleven years ago.

But Grace's black silk gown, high-waisted, with its neckline clinging to the swell of her breasts, somehow looked sensuously alluring on her rather than mournful. Her skin had a translucent sheen, and her eyes—those expressive grey eyes—looked even larger and more unfathomable. The fullness of her lips was a deep, enticing red, and the smooth column of her throat a delicate invitation...

Lucian's gaze remained fixed on her lips. 'What mood is that, Grace...?'

She made an impatient movement. 'You are deliberately misunderstanding me. Deliberately provoking me!'

The things Lucian had dreamt last night of doing
with and to this woman were more than enough provocation for any man!

It had been barely daylight when Lucian had awoken
with the taste of Grace upon his lips. The feel of her
silken skin beneath his hands. The burning of her flesh
pressed against his.

His body had been hard with arousal, aching, throbbing with the need to plunge into the same silken wetness
he had caressed and stroked to completion a week ago.
An impossibility of need that had resulted in his coming
out into the grounds of Winton Hall and diving into the
cold, numbing waters of the lake they now walked beside!

To no real avail, Lucian acknowledged self-derisively. Just looking at Grace now had brought a return
of that throbbing coursing through his body, and the
aching of his thighs was even stronger than it had been
earlier this morning.

'What of your own provocation towards me, Grace?'

Grace looked up at Lucian uncertainly. 'I was
merely offering you the opportunity, the excuse to take
your leave…' She trailed off, her uncertainty increasing as the dark intensity of Lucian's gaze remained
fixed upon her mouth.

Something blazed in those dark depths and Grace
nervously moistened suddenly dry lips with the tip of
her tongue, her breath catching and holding in her throat
as she found it impossible to look away from the dark

arrogance of Lucian's face—as memories of the last time the two of them had been alone together caused the colour to flare hotly in her cheeks.

Even the trees about them seemed to still, the birds to fall silent. Not a sound was to be heard now but their own breathing—Grace's soft and uneven, Lucian's barely discernible to her, as she realised that the strange whooshing noise in her ears was the sound of her own blood coursing through her veins.

She gave an abrupt, desperate shake of her head. 'Lucian, we cannot—'

'I *have* to, Grace!' he groaned, even as he took her into his arms and crushed her body against his. 'Can you not feel how much I have to?' he encouraged huskily.

Oh, yes, Grace could feel how much he wanted her. How could she not, when Lucian's arousal was pressed so intimately against her? When an answering heat throbbed between her own thighs?

Grace made one last attempt at sanity. 'We cannot be private here, Lucian. There are the estate workers. The gardeners. Anyone could come along and find us here together!'

His face had darkened. 'Are those your only reasons for refusing me, Grace?'

'I am not refusing you,' she protested heatedly, achingly. 'How can you think that when only a week ago I—I asked you to show me—to teach me how to—' She broke off, her cheeks burning at the memory of how she had pleaded with Lucian to show her how to give him the pleasure he had given her.

Lucian's lips were against her throat, hot and demanding as he tasted every inch of its creamy length. His tongue was seeking out the sensitive hollow at its base, sending quivers of pleasure through Grace's already aroused body.

'I do not intend to say no this time, Grace,' he promised gruffly, his breath warm against her skin. 'You shall have all of me. As I shall have all of you…'

'Hello, there!'

Grace sprang away from Lucian as if burnt, her cheeks paling as she gave him one last stricken glance before turning to straighten her hair. She watched Francis Wynter stroll down the pathway towards them with long easy strides, a relaxed smile curving his lips as he neared them.

To Grace's surprise, once Francis had recovered from the obvious shock he had experienced at the death of his eldest brother he had become passably pleasant to her, and gently kind to the Duchess—even going so far as to apologise to Grace and Lucian for the discomfort he had caused them in London. His manner towards Darius was a different matter, of course, but that strained relationship seemed to have survived from childhood, with no hope of it ever changing.

'Grace—St Claire,' Francis greeted them lightly. 'Beautiful day, is it not?' He looked almost handsome with his hair lightly ruffled by the breeze. 'I endeavour to walk this pathway about the lake every day when I am staying at Winton Hall. Of course you will remember the way we all played here as boys, St Claire..?'

Lucian remembered the way he and Simon had played, and occasionally Darius too, if he happened to be home from school, running off into these woods in order to escape from Francis's complaints that they never allowed him to join in their games. Justifiable complaints, obviously, but Francis really had been a whining little brat of a boy.

Lucian found him no less irritating as an adult, and his interruption just now was no more welcome than his company had been all those years ago!

Timely, but still unwelcome.

Grace looked less than composed, Lucian noted frowningly, her cheeks flushed and a slightly hunted look in her eyes as she shot him a censorious glance.

'I remember throwing you in the lake a few times,' he answered the younger man tersely.

Francis frowned his consternation for several seconds before his brow cleared. 'I am sure it was just boyish high-jinks,' he confided indulgently.

'And I thought it was our way of getting rid of you,' Lucian drawled hardly, not particularly liking or approving of the way Francis was now standing within touching distance of Grace.

'I probably was a bit of a pest.' Francis nodded, his expression inscrutable as his gaze met Lucian's. 'Perhaps we might enjoy the rest of our walk together…?' he prompted lightly, and he reached out to lift Grace's hand and tuck it into the crook of his arm.

Lucian's eyes became glittering slits as he observed the familiarity. Admittedly, the other man had apologised to them both for anything he might have said to his friends in London, which might unfortunately have become public knowledge, and as such caused them embarrassment, but that did not mean Lucian had forgotten the incident. Or that he now welcomed Francis's attentions to Grace.

'Grace and I were about to return to the house.' Lucian looked coldly at the younger man. 'You are welcome to join us there if you so wish…?'

It was the first Grace had heard of their intention to return to Winton Hall. But perhaps in the circumstances it might be better if they did so. She certainly had no interest in continuing their walk with Francis present, and continuing in the way they had been was also out of the question…

Goodness knew what would have happened if Francis had not come along and interrupted them!

'I am more than willing to act as Grace's escort if *you* wish to return to the house, St Claire.' Francis looked at her enquiringly.

'I really should go back, too.' Grace freed her hand from the crook of Francis's arm and stepped away from him. 'Aunt Margaret intends packing some of her things today, and she may have need of me.'

'Of course.' Francis gave an understanding nod of his head. 'It really is shabby of Darius to move her into the Dower House with such unseemly haste,' he added disapprovingly.

Grace looked stricken. 'Oh, I do not think that Lord Darius—the Duke—' she corrected herself flusteredly '—I do not think he has encouraged my aunt in the move.'

'Your loyalty does you credit, Grace,' Francis approved with a return of his usual pomposity. 'Nevertheless, I fear Darius alone is responsible for making Margaret feel something of an intruder in the house she has called home for thirty years or more.'

'And *your* disloyalty on the subject does you no credit whatsoever, Francis,' Lucian rasped harshly, his expression one of contempt as he looked at the younger man. 'I have heard with my own ears Darius's efforts to persuade the Duchess into delaying her move to the Dower House for several more weeks at least.'

'Well, of course you have,' Francis acknowledged condescendingly. 'There has already been enough gossip concerning Darius in recent months, without his adding to it by behaving unchivalrously to our sister-in-law in the presence of the brother of the powerful Duke of Stourbridge. What takes place in private is a different matter, however…' he added sadly.

Lucian's hands clenched into fists at his sides as he resisted the impulse to punch the younger man on the nose! Darius was his friend, damn it, gossip or not—had not Arabella made the same musings to Lucian only a week ago concerning Darius's recent good fortune? Lucian could not stand silently by and listen to Francis as he maligned his own brother!

Lucian's gaze was icy. 'You will explain that last remark, Wynter.'

Francis gave an unconcerned shrug. 'I am sure if you

were to ask Margaret she would be unable to deny that privately Darius has made his feelings concerning her removal to the Dower House more than clear.'

Lucian's mouth thinned frustratedly. The Duchess had suffered enough this last week, with the sudden and unexpected death of her husband; Lucian certainly had no intention of adding to her distress by posing any questions to her concerning the reasons for her insistence in removing herself to the Dower House so speedily.

'I believe you are being decidedly indiscreet in discussing this matter at all, Francis,' he rasped impatiently. 'I strongly advise you against repeating any more of this malicious gossip in either my own or Grace's hearing! Despite your apology, you have learnt nothing, it seems, after your earlier indiscretion in gossiping about Grace and myself!'

Grace had been stunned by Francis's accusations against his brother. Initially... But on further reflection she could not help but wonder if there were not some truth in what Francis said concerning the reason for her aunt's decision to decamp to the Dower House only a week after the death of her husband. It was precipitate, to say the least, as Grace had pointed out to her aunt only yesterday. But the Duchess remained adamant in her decision to leave by the end of the week.

Because Darius had all but asked her to go...?

'In that case...' Francis bowed stiffly. 'Grace. St Claire.' He strode off in the opposite direction from the one they would be taking back to the house, his back rigid as he obviously remained offended by Lucian's reprimand.

Grace looked up at Lucian from beneath lowered lashes, sure that if he ever looked at *her* with the icy disdain he had just shown Francis Wynter she would quiver in her slippers!

'Lucian…?' she prompted softly, when he continued to stare after the other man with narrowed eyes.

Lucian drew in a harshly controlling breath before turning back to Grace. 'It is totally beyond my comprehension why someone has not run that man through before now!' he rasped disgustedly as they began to stroll back towards the house.

Grace gave a rueful smile. 'And I had such high hopes that his pleasantness of this last week might continue!'

Lucian's mouth thinned. 'A leopard does not change its spots, Grace,' he warned her tersely. 'Although I believe in Francis Wynter's case that may be insulting the leopard!'

'You are probably right.' Grace nodded, her curls gleaming darkly from beneath her bonnet as the two of them walked out of the woods and into the sunshine. 'You do not think that there is any truth in what Francis said?'

That was what bothered Lucian the most about his conversation with Francis Wynter—his own fear that the younger man's accusations might have some basis in fact!

There was no doubting that the Darius in whose company Lucian had spent this last week was not the same man Lucian had known since boyhood. Darius had never been a man to suffer fools gladly, which was one of the things Lucian and he had in common, but this last year had given the other man a sharper edge to his manner, and a cynicism that was all but impenetrable, making it impossible to discern what Darius was thinking or feeling at any given time.

The truth of the matter was that Lucian no longer had any idea what Darius might or might not be capable of!

He frowned darkly. 'I make a habit of never listening to idle gossip, Grace. Especially when it is spoken by one such as Francis Wynter!'

Grace's cheeks warmed as she felt herself reprimanded. It was a reproof she did not feel was merited when she was only intent upon seeking the truth. It really would be too awful if, as Francis had implied, Darius *were* privately being unkind to her Aunt Margaret.

'I forbid you to question your aunt on the subject,' Lucian added coldly.

'You forbid me…?' Grace repeated softly, the colour in her cheeks caused by anger now.

Lucian's face was all hard angles as he looked down the length of his aristocratic nose at her. 'It would serve no purpose even if you were to learn that it *is* Darius's wish for your aunt to remove herself to the Dower House. He is perfectly within his rights.'

'It would serve the purpose of telling me that he is a cold-hearted monster!' Grace contradicted indignantly.

'Grace, I do not intend arguing with you on this matter—'

'Good—because I have no intention of arguing with

you, either.' She increased her pace so that she drew ahead of him on the pathway. 'I shall do exactly as I please. Take your hand off me, Lucian!' she warned softly as she found her progress suddenly impeded.

Lucian gave a frustrated sigh at her obvious anger. The two of them had spent little enough time together this past week as it was; for them to argue the very first time they were alone together was unsupportable. 'Perhaps if I were to *request* that you do not pursue the subject with your aunt…'

'It is too late for requests, My Lord,' Grace assured him with false sweetness. 'As I said, I shall do exactly as I please—'

Lucian's impatient snort cut across her stubbornness. 'Your father should have put you over his knee more often when you were a child.'

'My father was everything good and kind.' Her tone implied that *he* was not. 'The mere idea of physical retribution upon his own child would have been completely abhorrent to him,' she continued stonily. 'And if he were alive now he would thrash you within an inch of your life for even suggesting such a thing!'

No matter how she might mock the sentiment, Grace really was incredibly, enticing beautiful when she was angry, Lucian acknowledged achingly. Although certainly not in the mood to entertain resuming their earlier intimacy!

He gave a shake of his head. 'I was not suggesting that I was considering putting you over my own knee, Grace—'

'Perhaps that is as well, My Lord—you would be made very sorry if you even attempted such a thing!' Her eyes sparkled challengingly, her clenched fists at her sides a warning of her intention of defending herself if necessary.

Lucian let out a frustrated sigh. Could he have *no* conversation with Grace without them either arguing or making love? If they did have to do one or other of those two things, Lucian would so much rather it was the latter!

But it was impossible not to admire Grace's obvious intent to bring about physical retribution upon him if he should so much as attempt to put her across his own knee and smack that enticing part of her anatomy. The mere idea of it was enough to arouse him all over again…!

Oh, not in the context of physical abuse, or any intention of actually hurting Grace. No, Lucian had physical arousal more in mind—both Grace's and his own.

Grace would look so very desirable draped across his knee, her beautiful face flushed and aroused as he dealt a few gentle slaps to her shapely bottom. Especially if she were wearing no clothes at the time, her bottom bared and her breasts thrusting forward, her body warming in arousal— Damn it, if he did not soon fully make love to Grace he was going to go quietly insane!

'Grace, the last person to challenge me in such a way spent the next week in his bed, nursing a couple of broken ribs and a very bruised jaw!'

Grace eyed him uncertainly, knowing by the coldness

of Lucian's narrowed gaze and the tight clenching of his jaw that she had pushed his patience to the limit of its endurance. She also knew that she was now arguing with him for argument's sake…

Not that she wasn't angry with him for daring to forbid her to do anything—because she most certainly was. But Grace was very aware that a few short minutes ago she had once again been in Lucian's arms. Willingly. That but for Francis Wynter's interruption she might even now be lying on the soft brown soil beneath the trees, doing much more than allowing him to kiss her. His description of placing her across his knee while he administered smacks to her bottom had ignited a warmth between her thighs that she had no control over.

It would not do. In view of the fact that it was still her intention to end their betrothal at the earliest opportunity, it really would not do!

Her mouth curled disdainfully. 'How typical of a man to think that he can settle all disagreements with one form of physical retribution or another.'

'I guarantee, Grace, that you would thoroughly enjoy the sort of physical retribution I would bring to bear on *you!*' The leashed power of Lucian's tensed body was almost tangible as he looked down at her from between narrowed lids.

Grace's chin rose defensively. 'And how typical of a man, also, to assume that a woman *could* be subdued by such idle threats as those!'

'Oh, they are not idle threats, Grace.' His voice was

silkily soft—dangerously so. 'I do assure you, that the retribution I have in mind will very quickly become a promise of intent if you do not cease challenging my every word and action.'

Grace continued to face him defiantly. 'I do not believe you would take me by force, Lucian.'

Lucian's tension relaxed slightly, and he allowed a mocking smile to curve those sculptured lips. 'You have not led me to believe it would be by force, Grace…'

No, she had not. The opposite, in fact…

A fact Lucian, as a gentleman, should not have voiced! 'I am not one of your tavern wenches or camp followers to be spoken to in this familiar manner,' she told him haughtily.

Dark brows rose over cold, dark eyes as he once again spoke in that softly dangerous tone. 'One of my "tavern wenches" and "camp followers"…?'

Grace gave a disdainful snort. 'Do not even attempt to tell me that you have not known your fair share of them, My Lord!'

Yes, Lucian had 'known' tavern wenches—along with some of the more desirable actresses, and also several married ladies of the ton. But Major Lord Lucian St Claire had most definitely drawn the line at bedding camp followers. As a young unmarried lady of only twenty years Grace should not even *know* of such things, let alone talk of them!

'I believe this conversation to be well and truly over, Grace,' he told her haughtily.

'I believe you are right, My Lord.' Her manner was

scathing as she gave a brief, dismissive curtsey before turning and walking away.

It wasn't until several minutes later, when Grace had unhurriedly covered the distance to the house and disappeared inside with a final angry twitch of her skirts, that Lucian realised he had not, after all, informed Grace of his decision to take his leave in the morning…

Chapter Thirteen

Dinner that evening was a dismal affair. Oh, the food was superb—as usual. And the Winton Hall butler, Westlake, ensured with his presence that the meal was served with such quiet efficiency that one course followed another with ease. It was the five people seated around the table in the small family dining room who made the meal so inharmonious.

Darius sat at the head of the table, of course—as was his right. The Duchess, delicately dignified in black, sat at the opposite end. Grace was seated to Darius's left, with Lucian at her side and Francis opposite. Hardly a word was spoken by any of them, except a brief comment by Francis on the weather. A comment that only Darius acknowledged, and then just with a grunt.

Grace still remembered the warm arousal brought about by her earlier conversation with Lucian too clearly to feel comfortable in his presence. Lucian seemed disinclined to converse with her, either—

perhaps because he did not want to give Grace the opportunity to introduce the subject of her aunt's move to the Dower House? If he thought *that* would keep her silent on the subject, he was mistaken!

Although Grace wisely did not speak until she and her aunt stood up to leave at the end of the meal, so that the men might be left to enjoy their cigars and brandy. 'Might I have a few minutes of your time tomorrow, Your Grace?' She could feel the intensity of Lucian's dark gaze fixed upon the back she kept firmly turned towards him.

Darius stirred himself, that devil/angel face politely enquiring as he looked up at Grace. 'But of course, my dear. I will be in my—the study most of the morning.' He looked irritated by the slip, a dark scowl marring his brow as he turned to his sister-in-law. 'I am sorry, Margaret.'

The Duchess attempted a dignified smile, the effort marred by the fact that her mouth trembled slightly and her eyes filled with tears. 'It *is* your study now, Darius.'

'Yes, but—damn it!' Darius's scowl deepened. 'Excuse me, ladies.' He gave a tight smile. 'I am afraid I find this situation intolerable.'

'I believe we all do, Darius.' The Duchess gave a gracious inclination of her head as she regained her composure. 'If you will all excuse me? I believe I will retire for the night.'

Grace's heart ached as her gaze followed her aunt's departure from the dining room. The Duchess had somehow become shrunken this past week, a shadow of her former self. Her step was no longer light and youthful, and her face looked every one of her forty-eight years.

Grace's eyes sparkled with anger as she turned back to Darius. 'Do you *mean* to be cruel, Your Grace?'

Darius looked taken aback by the attack—a feeling he quickly masked, his handsome face appearing as if carved from stone, and that cobalt-blue gaze meeting hers coldly. 'You are overstepping the line, Grace.'

'Am I?' Twin spots of colour had appeared in Grace's cheeks. 'My aunt has been widowed but a week, and yet you—'

'I believe I will forgo the brandy and instead retire with Grace to the drawing room.' Lucian stood up as he spoke, his hand moving beneath Grace's elbow as he drew her to his side, not in the least gently.

Darius looked up at his boyhood friend frowningly, and a silent exchange passed between the two men before he turned back to Grace, his expression unrelentingly hard. 'I have almost forgotten this last week that the two of you are betrothed.' He gave a terse inclination of his head. 'You have my permission to retire to the drawing room with Lord Lucian, Grace.'

'Come along, Grace.' Lucian didn't allow time for her to voice the comment he could see hovering on her lips as he strode forcefully from the room dragging Grace with him. He turned to her impatiently once they were outside in the hallway. 'You are in danger of more than overstepping the line, Grace!'

She looked unrepentant. 'You—'

'This is not about *me*, Grace.' A nerve pulsed in his

tightly clenched jaw as he glared down at her. 'Nor is it about you. Do you really believe that your aunt would approve of your causing a scene on her behalf at the dinner table?'

Grace continued to look rebellious for several more seconds before her gaze dropped. 'That was unfair, Lucian.'

'If you dare to attack Darius in that way a second time you might find that he can be more than unfair!' Lucian could not allow Grace to take the step she seemed so hell-bent on taking. 'Whether you like it or not, Grace, this is now *his* home, and you are only in it by his leave! Carry on the way you are going and he may decide to toss you out into the gutter.'

'I have my own home in Cornwall—'

Lucian shook his head. 'You have property and money that has been put in trust. Until such time as you marry. But until that time they both remain in Darius's control!' Now it was Lucian who was being deliberately cruel. For Grace's own sake. She simply could not go around repeating accusations that were merely gossip and hearsay.

Grace's face paled as she realised the truth of his words. She *was* here by Darius's leave. They all were. 'I shall be moving into the Dower House with my aunt in several days—'

'Only if Darius allows it. You are *his* ward, Grace. His to bid either go or stay,' Lucian added hardly. Grace gave him a startled look. 'Perhaps the prospect of marrying me does not now seem like such a distasteful one after all?' He eyed her mockingly.

The prospect of marrying Lucian was not distasteful to Grace at all. The prospect of marrying a Lucian who did not love her as she loved him *was,* however…

She met his gaze unblinkingly. 'Exchange one despot for another? Is that what you mean?'

Lucian's mouth tightened. 'Grace, you are seriously in danger of receiving that beating we discussed earlier!'

Her expression was scornful. 'I should like to see you try!'

Lucian was tempted. Very tempted. But the memory of his earlier imaginings told him he would not be able to stop himself from making love to Grace once he had administered that smack to her bottom. Always supposing she had not already totally unmanned him for inflicting such indignity upon her person!

'No, Grace, you would not,' he bit out coldly. 'I suggest, before you go any further with this, that you consider your aunt's feelings in the matter.'

'It is of my aunt that I am thinking.'

'The Duchess, if you have not noticed, is resigned to her change in circumstances. You, however—' Lucian broke off as the sound of raised voices could be heard coming from the dining room.

No—only one raised voice.

Francis's.

Darius's voice was a low murmur in comparison.

Lucian couldn't hear what was being said between the two brothers, only the tone of their voices told him that the exchange was not a pleasant one.

He shook his head. Without the steadying influence of George Wynter, the deceased Duke of Carlyne, all veneer of civility seemed to be crumbling from the Wynter family.

'There,' Grace said with satisfaction. 'Can you not see now that Darius—?'

'He is now the Duke of Carlyne to you, Grace. To everyone. With all of the power and privilege his title engenders.'

'But—'

'He is the Duke of Carlyne, Grace!'

Her mouth firmed stubbornly. 'Your own brother is also a duke, but I cannot believe that he would resort to bullying and shouting in order to have his own way!'

Lucian gave a rueful smile. 'Hawk has never needed to raise his voice in order to have his every instruction obeyed. His manner simply does not allow for anything else!'

Recalling her own brief meeting with the haughty and aristocratic Duke of Stourbridge, Grace could well believe that. 'But—'

'Grace, *all* brothers have disagreements from time to time,' Lucian reasoned impatiently.

'Do you argue with your brothers?'

'I have told you—Hawk has never seen reason for argument when in the end he will have his own way. Sebastian has always been such a charming rogue that he does exactly as he pleases. But as brothers we do disagree. Constantly. Grace, we simply cannot continue to stand out here in the hallway eavesdropping!' Lucian lost all patience as she looked no less stubbornly determined. 'We will retire to the drawing room as I suggested.'

'As Darius has *permitted* us to do?' The scorn could be heard in Grace's voice. 'I think not, Lucian!' Her chin rose determinedly. '*I* am going to my bedchamber. *You* may do as the Duke bids, if that is your wish!' She turned on her heel, her head held high as she walked down the hallway to where the main staircase was situated.

Lucian was torn. As he saw it, he had two choices. He could follow Grace and demand that she apologise for the slight she had just cast upon his manhood. Perhaps not the wisest choice when he had found there seemed only one way of subduing her outspokenness…? No, unpalatable as it was, Lucian knew he would be better advised to go with the second choice—that of returning to the dining room and stopping the two Wynter brothers from killing each other!

Before he could do that, however, the door opened and a red-faced Francis Wynter stormed out of the room. His eyes widened accusingly as he saw Lucian standing there, obviously having overheard the heated exchange, if not the content of it. He gave Lucian a resentful glare.

'I am sure you will not be surprised to learn that I have also been instructed to vacate Winton Hall by the end of the week! I expect that Grace will be next,' he sneered. 'Unless, of course, Darius deduces that Grace's property and fortune would be an advantageous addition to the Duke of Carlyne's estates, and so decides to marry her himself!' he added maliciously.

Lucian recoiled as if with the force of a blow. Darius marry Grace? Never! Not only would Grace not agree to it, Lucian would not allow it.

'Lucian, would you come in here, please?' Darius called wearily.

'His Grace commands!' Francis snapped scathingly, before turning on his heel and stomping off.

Lucian frowned and continued to stand in the hallway, knowing that, intolerable as this situation was, there could now be no question of his leaving tomorrow or at any other time—until he had seen Grace safely settled with her aunt in the Dower House.

'Lucian…?'

Lucian's mouth firmed as Darius heavily repeated his request for Lucian to rejoin him in the dining room. No matter what Grace or Francis might imply to the contrary, Lucian was not accustomed to being summoned anywhere. Not only did he make a point of never doing as Hawk commanded, but he had also been a major in the army, in command of his own regiment. As such he was used to being the one giving the orders rather than obeying them.

'Would you please do me the honour of joining me for a brandy, Lucian…?' Darius did not call out the invitation this time, but instead came to stand in the open doorway, those cobalt-blue eyes bleak, lines etched beside his nose and mouth. 'I am much in need of the company of a friend right now.' He gave a rueful grimace.

The two men had been friends a long time—not

close friends, as Lucian and Simon had been, but friends nonetheless…

'Very well.' Lucian gave a terse inclination of his head as he stepped into the dining room. 'What the hell is going on, Darius?' He frowned darkly at the other man as he watched Darius pouring large measures of brandy into two glasses.

Darius gave a weary shake of his head as he handed one of the glasses to Lucian. 'I cannot say.'

'Cannot or will not?'

'Will not.' Darius scowled. 'It is—a family matter.'

Lucian raised dark brows. 'And does this "family matter" have something to do with the death of your brother and your treatment of your sister-in-law?'

Darius had stiffened, his eyes having gone icy cold. 'I invited you in here as a friend, Lucian, not as my inquisitor!'

Lucian threw the brandy to the back of his throat and swallowed before answering the older man. 'I am not sure that I know you any more, Darius…'

'You do not know me, or you do not *want* to know me?'

'Do not twist my words to suit yourself, Darius!'

The older man's mouth twisted humourlessly. 'What is it you are asking me, Lucian? I advise you to think carefully before answering,' he added softly. 'First consider what you would do with the truth once you have it.'

Lucian frowned. 'No man is above the truth, Darius.'

'No?' Darius strolled over to refill his glass from the decanter. 'You do not believe that sometimes it is necessary to conceal the truth for the protection of others?'

Lucian eyed the other man frustratedly. 'For example?'

Darius gave a hard, dismissive laugh. 'Oh, no, Lucian. This is *your* conversation!'

'In that case, I believe it to be over.' Lucian slammed his empty glass down on the dining table. 'Grace wishes to move into the Dower House with her aunt when she leaves. I trust she has your permission to do so?'

Darius looked suddenly weary again. 'Lucian, despite what Francis may have implied to the contrary, I assure you I have no plans concerning Grace's future that conflict with your own.'

'Perhaps that is as well.' He nodded tersely as he strode towards the door.

'Perhaps.' The other man sighed. 'I wish—'

Lucian turned sharply. 'Yes…?'

Darius gave an abrupt shake of his head. 'Wishing cannot change what already is. One can only live with it.'

'And can you live with it, Darius?' Lucian frowned. His mouth tightened. 'I have no choice.'

'Everyone has a choice, Darius.'

'I thought that too, until very recently, but events have proved me wrong.'

Lucian gave the older man one last searching glance before leaving, knowing that the two of them had said much more in this conversation than their actual words had conveyed…

'It is very kind of you to take so much trouble on my aunt's behalf.' Grace looked at Lucian the following morning, as he helped her to instruct the small army of servants that had been brought over from Winton Hall in order to ready the Dower House for the Duchess's occupancy.

He quirked derisive brows. 'You do not think I can be kind, Grace…?'

'Oh, I know that you can.' She laughed softly. 'But it is not one of your most noticeable traits!'

'Now you have wounded me, Grace!'

Grace decided to ignore his mockery. 'After our conversation yesterday I did not expect you to be quite so accommodating concerning my wish to move into the Dower House.'

Lucian sobered. 'I believe I said that Darius was the one who must give his permission.'

'Which you say he has now done?'

'Yes.'

Grace gave him a searching glance, sensing there was more behind the terseness of Lucian's statement than he was willing to share with her. 'When did he give his permission?'

Lucian delayed answering her while she directed one of the maids to the bedroom the Duchess had already chosen as her own. 'Darius and I had occasion to speak together after you had retired to bed last night.'

Grace turned to him sharply. 'Indeed? And did you engineer that occasion so that I did not attempt to speak to Darius this morning?' She was perfectly aware that by encouraging her to begin organising the Dower House for the Duchess's habitation Lucian had taken her away from Winton Hall for the morning. And consequently from her meeting with Darius, too.

Lucian raised taunting brows, looking this morning every inch the haughty member of the ton that he undoubtedly was. 'Charming as I find you, my dear Grace, I do assure you that I converse with others on topics other than you!'

He had meant to deal her a set-down, and he succeeded. Grace felt the warm blush that now coloured her cheeks. 'Nevertheless, it appears that you and Darius *did* discuss me yesterday evening…?'

'It was hardly a discussion.'

'Then what was it?'

Lucian eyed her impatiently. 'I suggest we retire to the garden and indulge ourselves with the picnic Cook has sent over for our lunch.'

He pointedly held the front door open, very aware, even if Grace was not, that several of the maids were working within listening distance of their conversation.

The carriage stood outside, where they had left it earlier, and Lucian collected the picnic basket and a blanket from inside it before heading for the garden at the side of the small manor house where the Duchess of Carlyne was to live. Grace was at his side as he chose a spot beneath the dappled shade of a willow before laying the blanket down on the grass to sprawl his length upon it.

'I am waiting for you to do the honours, my dear.' He looked up at Grace as she made no move to join him, instead reaching up to remove the deep grey bonnet that matched her mourning gown before shaking her dark curls free.

She remained standing. 'And *I* am still waiting for an answer to my question.'

This young woman could give Arabella lessons in stubbornness! 'Maybe if you were to feed me first…?'

Grace gave a rueful laugh. 'You cannot possibly be hungry again so soon after that huge breakfast!'

Lucian *had* eaten a large breakfast earlier—mainly because neither he nor anyone else at the dinner table the previous evening had eaten much of the meal that had been set before them. The surrounding tension had not been conducive to a healthy appetite. Not so this morning, when only he and Grace had made an appearance in the breakfast room.

'That was hours ago,' he dismissed dryly. 'Grace, has no one ever told you that the way to a man's heart is through his stomach?' He lay back on the blanket to look up at her, his arms folded behind his head to act as a pillow.

'I have never claimed an interest in your heart, My Lord!' she came back starchily, but she nonetheless joined him on the blanket to begin taking meats, cheeses, bread and fruit from the basket.

Lucian picked up a green apple and took a crisp bite out of it. 'It is the way to soothing a man's temper, too.'

Grace arched dark brows. 'Surely you do not have a temper, My Lord?'

He gave an appreciative grin. 'In the same way that you do not, perhaps?'

She gave a gracious inclination of her head. 'Then you must be the most amiable of men!'

Lucian threw back his head and gave a shout of laughter, suddenly arrested by the sound as he realised he'd not had occasion for such amusement in a very long time. Years, in fact.

Grace had given him laughter rather than the cynical amusement he had become accustomed to feeling…

She had given him much more than that, of course. But Lucian veered away from dwelling too deeply on his emotions.

'Oh, definitely the most amiable of men,' he agreed mockingly.

Grace was disappointed to see the return of his usual mockery.

Lucian had looked so boyish when he'd laughed so spontaneously. So handsome, so—so—Perhaps she should not think of how her heart had swelled with love for him as she had watched the laughter light up his eyes, or how kissable were his lips when relaxed into that amused smile!

'We were talking of Darius, I believe?' she prompted firmly.

If Grace had hoped to disconcert Lucian by her doggedness then she was to be disappointed, as he gave an unconcerned shrug. 'I merely asked him if he had any objections to your living here with your aunt. He did not.'

Grace's brow creased with frustration. 'No doubt you gave him the impression that that was the subject I wished to discuss with him this morning?'

'No doubt.' He offered no apology for having done so.

'You did not question his haste in removing my aunt from Winton Hall?'

'I did not. Neither shall I.' Lucian's mouth had thinned. 'And neither shall you,' he added firmly, as he reached for a chicken leg and bit into it with even white teeth.

Grace picked up a strawberry and nibbled on it distractedly. 'I am sure your arrogance is commendable, Lucian—'

'You are sure of no such thing!' Lucian dismissed laughingly, reaching out to take the strawberry from Grace's fingers and feed it to her himself.

He might never before have considered the eating of fruit erotic, Lucian acknowledged, but he suddenly found himself mesmerised by the way Grace placed her lips about the strawberry before biting down on it with her small, pearly white teeth, and then licked the juice from those lips with her tiny pink tongue. He could think of nothing he would like more than for those red lips to be about *him,* or for that tiny pink tongue to lick and taste *him* as it was the strawberry.

Dear God, was there nothing this woman did that did not lead him into thinking of making love to and with her?

It appeared not. And Lucian found himself becoming even more aroused as he tempted Grace with a second strawberry.

Grace was aware of the heat in Lucian's gaze as he watched her enjoying the sweet juices of the fruit. She did not know quite what was causing it, but was too caught up in the sudden expectant tension between them to question it too deeply. She was prepared merely to enjoy the moment, and her gaze was languorous as she raised it to meet his.

'May I…?' She picked up another strawberry and offered to do the same for him.

'Please,' he rasped in acquiescence, lying back upon the blanket so that Grace had to lean over him. He made no effort to bite into the fruit but instead tasted it with his tongue, slowly, lasciviously, even as his gaze continued to hold hers captive. 'Do you know what I am thinking at this moment, Grace? What I am imagining…?' he murmured huskily.

Grace could only shake her head in reply, the breath caught in her throat making it impossible for her to speak.

Lucian deliberately laved the strawberry once more with the tip of his tongue. 'I am imagining this is you, Grace. Your breast. The lovely dusky nipple—' He broke off as she gave a strangled gasp. 'This is what I did to you that night, Grace. Remember?' His licked the fruit once more.

Of course Grace remembered. How could she ever forget?

'Imagine this is you, Grace.' Lucian's voice was low, mesmerising, and Grace's gaze was caught and held by the way he drew the strawberry into his mouth and sucked the juices. 'Feel it, Grace.' He traced his tongue delicately over the pointed tip. 'Feel it!' he groaned as he once more sucked that juicy red tip into his mouth.

Grace did feel it. Her breasts swelled, their nipples

hard and thrusting against the soft material of her shift, and a heat between her thighs dampened her. She felt herself swelling there too, and that heat became a throbbing ache as she continued to watch Lucian suckle on the strawberry.

How did he do this? How did Lucian arouse her so when he was not even touching her?

Grace had no answers. Knew only that the aching heat between her thighs was growing, burning, demanding release. A release that she knew Lucian could give her. That Grace wanted him to give her.

She drew in a ragged breath. 'Lucian—'

'Miss Grace! Miss Grace!'

Grace awoke as if from a dream to turn her gaze sharply from Lucian's. A maid was hurrying across the grass towards them, and one glance at the anxious expression on the young girl's face was enough to tell Grace that something was wrong.

Very wrong!

Chapter Fourteen

'I think it best if you regain control of your imagination now, Grace,' Lucian drawled deliberately as he rose economically to his feet.

One look at how suddenly pale Grace had become was enough to tell him how alarmed she was by the maid's apparent anxiety. And the unappreciative glare Grace shot in his direction before she turned to address her attention to the young maid told him that though Grace did not appreciate his mockery, it had nevertheless succeeded in calming her.

It was a pity they had been interrupted when Lucian had so been enjoying himself—the more so because he had been able to witness Grace's arousal. Her eyes had been languorous, her lips parted; there had been a delicate flush to her cheeks and down her throat, the swell of her breasts quickly rising and falling as her arousal grew.

'Calm yourself, Rose, and tell us what has happened

to upset you.' Lucian could never remember having seen the plump maid before, but obviously Grace recognised her and spoke briskly.

'You're to come back to the house immediately, miss—'

'That does not tell us what has happened, Rose.' Grace gave her a reproving look.

'No, miss. I mean, yes, miss. There's been an accident, miss.' The young girl's excitement began to rise once again.

'What sort of accident?' Lucian decided to take charge when he saw the way Grace's hand moved convulsively to her throat, even as her pallor increased.

The maid blinked. 'I don't know, sir—My Lord,' she corrected hastily. 'I was only told to fetch Miss Hetherington because there's been an accident—'

'Who instructed you to come for Miss Hetherington?' Lucian frowned his increasing impatience with this garbled account.

'The Duke, sir. I mean His Grace, Your Lordship.' A Welsh lilt could be heard in the girl's voice now. Not surprising when they were only thirty miles or so from the Welsh border. 'You're wanted back at the house immediately, Miss Hetherington,' she repeated breathlessly.

'Rose, I want you to remain here and put these things back into the basket while I drive Miss Hetherington back to the house in the carriage.' Lucian took a firm hold of Grace's arm, knowing how disturbed she was by the maid's news when she made none of her usual objections to his taking charge.

Grace's thoughts were racing as she almost ran to keep up with Lucian's strides back to the carriage. An accident, Rose had said. But what sort of an accident? And involving whom...?

Obviously not Darius, or he would not have sent the message. Or would he? The accident might not have been serious enough to render him incapable of issuing instructions—Grace believed Lucian would have to be rendered unconscious to prevent *him* from issuing orders!

'For God's sake, do as I advised and give your imagination a rest, Grace!' Lucian was grim-faced as he helped her up into the carriage.

Grace glared down at him. 'I did not imagine Rose's distress.'

Lucian moved round to climb in at the other side of the carriage and take up the reins himself. 'I believe I detected excitement in her manner rather than distress.'

Grace had also noted the almost feverish glint in the young maid's eyes, and the flush to her cheeks. 'Rose's demeanour does not change the fact that Darius's instruction was for me to return immediately.'

'No.'

'No?' Grace arched surprised brows at his ready agreement.

Lucian gave an acknowledging inclination of his head even as he concentrated on driving the matched greys back to Winton Hall. There was a track from the Dower House that meandered its way through the grounds back to the main house, but it was deeply rutted and seldom used, so it was quicker and easier to travel by the road that encircled the Carlyne estate.

Much as Lucian might tell Grace to cease her imaginings, in reality he liked the sound of this latest upset in the Wynter household no more than she. The family seemed beset by accidents these last few months. Firstly Darius's wife had fallen from her horse while hunting and broken her neck. Then there had been the loose wheel on the carriage as the Duke and Duchess drove to London with Grace for the Season—an occurrence that could have had much more serious repercussions if the wheel had actually come off. That was something that Grace did not seem to have noted as yet, but she would surely do so if she once sat down and considered the matter. Finally there had been the Duke's sudden heart seizure, within days of the family's arrival in London.

Admittedly, the latter could not be called an accident, but Arabella had been right when she'd pointed out to Lucian that the gossips would only see the larger picture rather than the minutiae. Another 'accident' in the Wynter family would be certain to create yet more gossip, if not an actual scandal.

Lucian didn't know whether to be relieved or otherwise when the first person he saw as he and Grace entered Winton Hall a few minutes later was Darius Wynter. The new Duke was standing to one side of the entrance hall, conversing quietly with a man whose mode of dress indicated he might be one of the gardeners.

Darius dismissed the man, before striding over to greet them, his expression unsmiling as he took Grace's hand in his. 'There is no need to look so alarmed, Grace,' he soothed. 'The physician has been sent for.'

'Aunt Margaret?' Instead of calming her, Darius's clipped manner only seemed to have alarmed Grace more and she snatched her hand from his. 'What have you done to Aunt Margaret?'

Darius's face tightened. 'There is no need for hysteria, Grace.'

'Grace is not a lady given to hysteria.' Lucian thought it best to steer Darius away from making the same mistake he once had, his cheek twitching in memory of Grace's reins striking against it.

Darius shot Lucian a frowning glance. 'All evidence to the contrary,' he drawled. 'I suppose that silly maid made a drama out of the incident?'

Lucian reached out to take a firm hold of Grace's arm as he sensed her growing temper with Darius's lack of explanation. 'We will have more of an idea of that when we know what comprises the accident.'

'Is it Aunt Margaret?' Grace could contain her emotions no longer and she glared up at Darius. 'Tell me what has happened to her!'

'Nothing has happened to her.'

'Rose said there had been an accident—'

'Rose, I presume, is the maid?' Darius dismissed hardly. 'This morning's accident did not involve Margaret, Grace.'

She frowned her consternation. 'Then who—?'

'Francis.' Darius's expression was bleak. 'Francis is the one who has met with an accident. Margaret is up in his room with him now, waiting for the physician to arrive— Where are you going, Grace?' he demanded, as Grace turned and bolted for the stairs.

Grace didn't even bother to answer him as she raised the skirt of her gown in order to run up the stairs to Francis's room, obviously not trusting herself to say anything further until she had learnt more of Francis's condition.

'Darius…?' Lucian's gaze was narrowed on the other man.

Darius seemed to gather his thoughts together with an effort as he turned back to Lucian, his expression grimmer than ever. 'Will you come to the library with me? There is something I need to discuss with you.'

Lucian arched dark brows. 'I trust you are going to be more confiding than you were yesterday evening?'

The other man drew in a sharp breath. 'I believe I will have to be,' he finally admitted with a sigh.

Lucian gave one last glance up the wide staircase as he turned to follow Darius to the library, hoping that Grace would have her emotions back under control by the time she returned from Francis's room; she really was not a woman given to hysteria, but temper was another matter entirely…

'Francis was attacked as he walked through the same woods where we met up with him yesterday.' Grace looked across the dinner table at Lucian as they dined alone together. The Duchess had remained in her room, and Darius had sent his apologies also.

Grace had dismissed the servants once tea and brandy had been served, seeing no reason why she need retire to the drawing room with only the two of them present. Besides, there had been no opportunity for the two of them to talk alone together since their return from the Dower House, and Grace very badly needed to discuss this attack on Francis.

'So I believe.' Lucian's tone was non-committal. He looked very fine in his evening clothes as he relaxed back in his chair.

Too relaxed, in Grace's opinion. 'Hardly an accident—would you not agree?'

He gave a dismissive shrug. 'That, surely, is a matter of opinion?'

Grace frowned. 'From all accounts Francis was struck on the side of the head. I hardly think the branch responsible sprang from the ground of its own volition and struck him!'

'I hardly think so, either.' Lucian gave a derisive smile. 'But it could have fallen from the tree on which it grew, could it not…?'

'You—But—You are of the opinion that on this beautiful sunny day, a day with not a breath of wind, a tree decided to choose the very moment when Francis walked beneath it to shed one of its branches?' Grace's scorn with that explanation was obvious as she looked at him scathingly.

Put like that, Lucian could see the explanation did sound rather lame. But the truth was even more unbelievable…

Lucian's conversation with Darius in the library that morning had indeed been of a more confiding nature than previously. Confiding *and* confidential. A point Darius had been at great pains to point out before their conversation began. So much so that Darius had extracted a promise from Lucian that he would not share the information with anyone. That included Grace... something that Lucian already knew was going to cause problems between them.

Perhaps if he had known what Darius was going to tell him he would not have given his promise to the other man, but being a man of his word, Lucian had no intention of breaking it once it had been given.

'It is one explanation, yes.' He gave an inclination of his head.

'A ridiculous one!' Grace's face was flushed as she stood up to restlessly pace the room, her dark curls bouncing enticingly about her heart-shaped face, the dark grey ribbon threaded through them an exact match in colour for her silk gown. 'It is the one Darius gave you this morning after I left the two of you together, is it not? You cannot seriously believe such a tale?' she scorned, with an incredulous shake of her head.

Lucian raised dark brows. 'Perhaps you would allow me to answer your first question before berating me with another?'

She gave a disgusted snort. 'Answer, then!'

Lucian drew in a controlling breath. 'There is absolutely no evidence to support Francis having been attacked by anyone—'

'The lump on the side of his head the size of a pigeon's egg does not count, I suppose?'

He shrugged. 'It proves that he was struck with something—we will accept that it was the branch,' he conceded, as he saw the light of rebellion in Grace's eyes. 'Whether or not anyone actually wielded the branch is another matter entirely.'

'The next thing you will be telling me is that Francis struck *himself* on the side of the head!'

Lucian's mouth tightened. 'No, Grace, I will not be telling you that.'

'That is something, I suppose.' Her skirts moved about the slender length of her legs as she continued to pace. 'Lucian, I know that you and Darius have been friends for some years—' her tone had softened, become reasoning '—but surely you must see that this explanation is the one he wishes people to believe rather than the truth?'

Lucian took a swallow of his brandy before answering her. 'I do not remember saying that Darius *had* given that as an explanation for Francis's injury…'

Grace gave an impatient shake of her head. 'What explanation *did* he give, then?' She had thought she could at least rely on Lucian to see that all was not right here—to accept the possibility that Darius Wynter might—just might—be behind this attack on Francis. After all, once Darius had safely disposed of the Duchess, by moving her to the Dower House, all that remained was to rid himself of Francis. Not literally, of course. But a scare like this morning's might be enough to encourage Francis to leave Winton Hall.

It was the only explanation that had made any sense to Grace as she had allowed her thoughts free rein during the afternoon spent with her aunt in her private sitting room.

Francis was too candid in his remarks concerning Darius.

The two brothers had argued yet again after dinner yesterday evening. And this morning Francis had been attacked. Could Lucian really see no connection between those two events…?

Lucian gave her a quelling glance. 'One does not go around demanding explanations from a duke, Grace.'

'*You* may not,' Grace acknowledged impatiently. '*I* certainly shall—'

'No, Grace, you will not. You *will not*,' Lucian repeated firmly as Grace's eyes widened indignantly. 'Darius is now in possession of an ancient and noble title.'

'But he may have behaved ignobly.'

Lucian stood up. 'Such conjecture is for gossips and scandalmongers, Grace. Of which, I sincerely hope, you are not one.'

Her cheeks became flushed at the rebuke. 'I am talking privately with you on this matter, Lucian.'

He gave a haughty inclination of his head. 'I suggest you see that it remains that way.'

'How can you just stand idly by and allow these atrocities to continue? I had believed you to be a man of conviction. Of *action!*' Grace gave a frustrated shake of her head.

Lucian's mouth twisted derisively. 'But that is the whole point, Grace—I remain utterly unconvinced concerning the claims you are making against Darius. Neither is it my intention to remain here any longer, as you say, "idly standing by",' he added softly.

Grace stopped her pacing long enough to give him a searching glance. 'I do not understand…'

'I received word from Hawk this afternoon that my nephew, the new Marquess of Mulberry, was born yesterday evening.'

'But that's wonderful news!' Grace cheeks were suffused with pleased colour, her eyes sparkling with pleasure. 'Your brother must be so pleased. I trust the Duchess and the Marquess are both well?'

Lucian wondered if he would ever understand women. This woman in particular. Seconds ago Grace had been berating him concerning his lack of action where Darius was concerned, and now her whole attention was centred on the birth of his nephew.

'They are,' he confirmed dryly. 'In the circumstances, it is my intention to travel to Mulberry Hall in Gloucestershire tomorrow, so that I might offer Hawk and Jane my congratulations in person.'

'How exciting!' Grace glowed with pleasure. 'But of course you must go.'

'We shall both go, Grace,' Lucian informed her softly.

She looked confused. 'Both…?'

He nodded. 'Darius has given his permission for you and your maid to accompany me.'

'Darius has?' Grace's pleasure faded as her face became tight with suspicion. 'But I cannot leave here now!'

'Why not?'

'Because—there is my aunt to consider. I could not possibly leave her here alone.'

'I believe, now we have helped make the Dower House fit for residence, it is your aunt's intention to move there tomorrow.'

'Even more reason why I cannot leave now.'

'You will accompany me to Mulberry Hall tomorrow, Grace.' Lucian's tone brooked no further argument on the subject.

It was a warning Grace chose not to heed. 'I will do no such thing. I am pleased for your brother and his Duchess, and of course you must visit when you are already so close, but *my* responsibility lies here. With my aunt.'

'The Duchess of Carlyne has already given her own permission for you to accompany me tomorrow.'

Grace faltered, her gaze searching Lucian's face. 'I will not leave her here alone,' she repeated stubbornly.

Lucian's mouth curved derisively. 'What do you think is going to happen in your absence, Grace? Do you imagine that Darius is going to grasp the opportunity to dispose permanently of the Duchess and Francis?'

Put like that, it did sound slightly ridiculous, Grace allowed irritably. Her chin rose defensively. 'I hardly think this subject merits your mockery, Lucian.'

He snorted. 'I hardly think it a subject I can take seriously, either.'

Grace shook her head. 'That is because you are blinded to the truth by the bonds of friendship.'

'The only thing blinding me at the moment, Grace, is the thought of being alone in a carriage with you for several hours!'

Her breath caught in her throat as she realised how close Lucian was now standing—so close she could almost feel the heat of his gaze upon her face. 'My maid will be present,' she reminded him huskily.

He nodded. 'And I am sure that she will enjoy riding outside with the groom.'

Grace swallowed as she thought of those hours she might spend alone with Lucian in a carriage. Kissing him. Touching him. Having him kiss and touch her in return. Having his words of this morning become a reality. The whole idea of it was so tempting…

She was aware that this time the shaking of her head lacked conviction. 'My aunt needs me…'

'*I* need you more, Grace.' Lucian found using this deliberate seduction of Grace as a means of distracting her attention distasteful. Not insincere—never that—just distasteful.

But what other choice did he have? He and Darius had decided that it would be better if Grace did not remain here for the next few days. It would be better if the Duchess were not here, either, but her removal tomorrow to the Dower House would serve equally well. The delivery of Hawk's letter this afternoon telling Lucian of his nephew's birth could not have arrived more opportunely, giving Lucian the perfect excuse to take his leave and to take Grace with him.

Her eyes were huge luminous pools as she looked

up at him—so deep a grey Lucian felt he might drown in them. He reached up to curve one hand about her cheek, running his thumb lightly over the full pout of her lips, parting them. Her breath was a warm caress against his skin.

'Please say you will come with me tomorrow, Grace.'

Lucian's hand was warm against her face, his thumb a sensual caress. Grace's body was suffused with heat as he dipped that thumb suggestively between her lips. It was a temptation Grace could not resist as her tongue stroked lightly against the intrusion, her breathing light and uneven as the bodice of her gown suddenly felt constricted against her breasts.

Her lips remained parted as Lucian removed his thumb to replace it with his own lips, claiming hers in a long, exploratory kiss that rendered Grace weak at the knees, clinging to the broadness of his shoulders when he finally raised his head to look down at her with smouldering dark eyes.

'Say you will, Grace,' he encouraged throatily.

Grace could no longer think straight, let alone recall the reasons for her objections to his suggestion.

'Just think of it, Grace,' Lucian prompted softly. 'All those hours alone in the carriage in which to indulge our every fantasy.'

Her cheeks coloured heatedly. 'I doubt that a carriage is the place for—for such activities, My Lord.'

His grin was wolfish. 'You can have no idea how perfect a place it is, Grace!'

She blinked. 'It is…?'

Lucian nodded, his smile teasing. 'Remember I once described to you how I imagined having you sit astride me…?'

Of course Grace remembered! Achingly. Shockingly.!

Lucian saw the answer to his question in her modestly lowered lashes and the delicate blush that appeared in her cheeks. 'In a carriage there is no need for you to ride me, Grace, merely to take me inside you. The movement of the vehicle will do the rest for us. Very slowly. But equally as satisfactory.'

Her throat moved convulsively. 'You are— That is— I do not know what to say!' She looked flustered as she stepped away from him, desperately trying to recapture her scattered wits.

'You only have to say yes, Grace, and our lovemaking can become a reality,' Lucian pressed huskily.

She looked up at him frowningly, more tempted than she could say. And yet… 'No,' she said firmly. 'I really cannot abandon my aunt in this way when she is grieving so. It would be unfeeling of me to do so,' she added stubbornly, when she could see Lucian was about to argue with her. 'My mind is made up, Lucian.'

He looked less than pleased at her obvious determination. 'In that case I too must stay.'

'That is completely unnecessary.' Grace gave him a reproving frown. 'Your brother and sister-in-law will be expecting you home to meet your new nephew.'

'Then they will have to expect,' Lucian announced arrogantly.

Damn it, he had almost had her agreement. He was *sure* that he had. Then at the last minute, the very last minute, her indomitable will had taken a stand. Not that Lucian didn't admire her strength of will. In fact, it was one of the things he was coming to most admire about Grace. Her loyalty and devotion to her aunt were also qualities he could not fault.

Grace gave a puzzled shake of her head. 'I do not understand. Have you not already sent word informing your brother of your imminent arrival?'

Damn it, he had. Well, he would just have to send another note explaining his delay.

'Of *our* imminent arrival,' Lucian corrected dourly. 'Which means they are expecting me to arrive with my betrothed.'

'I have told you—'

'I have no choice but to respect your decision, Grace.' He gave a terse inclination of his head. 'In the circumstances, I refuse to go to Mulberry Hall until you can accompany me,' he said as she continued to frown.

Grace understood the situation even less now. Oh, she would miss Lucian if he were to leave tomorrow for his brother's home in Gloucestershire—she had absolutely no doubt about that. Lucian had become such a part of her life these last weeks—this last week especially—with his kindness towards both her aunt and herself. But she accepted that he had other responsibilities, other pulls upon his time. Surely the birth of his nephew, the new little Marquess of Mulberry, was one of those times…?

'What is it you are not telling me, Lucian?' she prompted shrewdly.

His brows rose. 'You doubt my reluctance to be apart from you?'

He meant to silence her with a return of his arrogant haughtiness, Grace guessed. He only succeeded in arousing her suspicions anew. 'You are keeping something from me, Lucian,' she stated wryly.

Damn it. Was ever a woman so—so infuriating? Lucian wondered frustratedly. So stubborn. So *adorable*...

Lucian drew in a controlling breath. 'The things you do not yet know, Grace—the things you have yet to experience—are far and beyond anything I might have to tell you.'

Those grey eyes narrowed. But not with anger, as Lucian had hoped. Had depended upon. No, Grace now looked upon him with open suspicion. A suspicion he dared not, could not, satisfy.

He nodded stiffly. 'If you will excuse me, I will go and talk to your aunt now about my accompanying the two of you to the Dower House.'

An unusual arrangement, Lucian acknowledged silently. A single man staying under the same roof as two single ladies. But when one of those ladies was the man's betrothed, excusable, perhaps. And necessary, now that Grace refused to accompany him to Mulberry Hall!

Grace's mouth twisted ruefully. 'The answer to that is already a foregone conclusion, My Lord, when my aunt so obviously adores you!'

Lucian's expression softened. 'Her fondness is reciprocated.'

In the case of her aunt, yes, Grace accepted. She still had absolutely no idea what Lucian felt towards *her.* Apart from the fact that he wished to make love to her, of course. He had left her in no doubt concerning that!

He straightened. 'I really must go, Grace. I have a letter to write to my brother, amongst other things.'

'Our conversation is not over, Lucian.'

'For the moment, Grace, yes, it is.' He crossed the room in long strides before turning in the doorway to look at her. 'I would prefer that you not discuss this with anyone else, Grace.'

She bristled at the rebuke she heard in his tone. 'I am not one given to gossip, Lucian.'

He smiled humourlessly. 'Then I must be grateful for small mercies!' came his parting shot.

Grace stared after him, totally sure from Lucian's behaviour that he was keeping something from her.

But she was just as aware, from the hardness of his gaze and the stubborn set of his sculptured lips before he turned to leave, that for the moment she would have to settle for that knowledge alone.

Which in no way would prevent Grace from trying to find out the truth for herself…

Chapter Fifteen

To Grace's surprise—and Lucian's, she felt sure—
Lord Sebastian St Claire arrived at the Dower House
three days later, on his way back to London after a visit
to Mulberry Hall to welcome his new nephew into the
family. He had come, he said, to offer the Duchess his
belated condolences on her recent loss.

Grace didn't care what Lord Sebastian's reason was
for being there; she was simply grateful that his mischievous smile and wicked sense of humour helped to
lift her aunt's spirits and consequently her own. Lucian
had been decidedly terse in her company these last three
days, and as there had been no further occasion for
Grace to talk with him alone—deliberately so?—she
found the arrival of the younger St Claire brother a
much needed diversion.

His glowing description of the baby Marquess of
Mulberry, his life newly begun, was exactly what the
Duchess needed to bring a soft glow to her eyes and

the warmth back to her cheeks after so many days of bleak despair.

Lucian's mocking glance remained on his brother throughout, confirming Grace's suspicion that Lord Sebastian's interests did not normally include young babies. Even one who was his nephew!

A fact that was confirmed once the Duchess had retired to her rooms so that she might rest before joining them for dinner. 'Since when have you had such a liking for small humans, Sebastian?' Lucian mocked as he stood across the room beside the unlit fireplace.

Sebastian looked unabashed as he sprawled in one of the armchairs. 'Hawk is most displeased that you have not yet arrived to show your adulation of the infant!'

Lucian shook his head. 'I sent a note explaining the reasons for my delay.'

His brother gave a derisive snort. 'From the look on Hawk's face when he read the contents of that note, your reasons were not a sufficient excuse—in his eyes!—for your tardiness.'

No, they would not have been, Lucian acknowledged frowningly. But he had given his word to Darius, and that promise applied to his family as much as it did to Grace. 'I am sure that my presence will not be missed in the adoring throng that no doubt abounds about our new nephew!'

His brother nodded morosely. 'Arabella and Aunt Agatha arrived yesterday.'

Lucian chuckled softly. 'Resulting in too much

female clucking for you to suffer a moment longer, I suspect!'

'You suspect correctly.' Sebastian grinned. 'You are very quiet, Grace.' He turned his attention to her as she sat in the window alcove. 'I trust that neither you nor your aunt are offended by my having arrived here un-invited? Lucian is right; a man can only stand so much adoration of one tiny infant!' He grimaced with feeling.

'I am sure my aunt is not in the least offended,' she at once assured him graciously. 'For myself, I am grateful that you have been able to lift her spirits in a way that Lord Lucian and I have sadly been unable to do.'

Lucian's brows rose as his young brother shot him a challenging glance. 'Sebastian has always been able to charm ladies older than himself,' he drawled mock-ingly. 'It is ladies of a marriageable age that continue to elude him.'

'Thank God!' Sebastian gave a shudder. 'Oh. I am so sorry, Miss Hetherington.' He grimaced. 'I should not have spoken so—candidly in your presence.'

'Please do not give it another thought.' Grace chuckled softly, having been enjoying the exchange between the two brothers. 'I was obviously somewhat remiss in my remarks concerning the male members of the ton the evening we first met, Lucian.' She looked challengingly at him from beneath lowered lashes.

Lucian's expression was wary as he easily recalled that conversation. He recalled every conversation he had ever had with Grace! 'In what way remiss, Grace…?'

She gave an inclination of her head, laughter gleaming in those deep grey eyes. 'There is obviously a fourth category of men in Society that I failed to mention. Those men who would far rather suffer the fires of damnation than marry at all!' She stood up, seeming not to notice Sebastian's splutter of laughter at her remark, her expression wholly innocent.

Lucian knew better. Knew Grace better. She really was the most outspoken minx he had ever met! And he admired—Lucian abruptly broke off that particular thought, his mouth tightening. 'Then it is fortunate that I am not amongst that number!' he rasped harshly.

Grace's laughter faded, and her eyes took on an icy glitter as she obviously heard the *for you* that Lucian had omitted from that sentence.

What was wrong with him? Lucian wondered slightly dazedly. Admittedly these last few days had been a strain, but was that any reason to take his temper out on Grace?

In truth, he had not been in a temper until Sebastian arrived. Could it be that he resented the easy banter that Grace and Sebastian enjoyed? Could it be that he was actually jealous of that camaraderie?

Ridiculous. Grace treated Sebastian with the easy affection she would show towards the younger brother she had never had—was no more interested in Sebastian in a romantic way than he was in her. An easy affection that never had, and never would exist between the two of them! Their emotions, whenever they were together, were far too strong, too intense, ever to be called anything as anaemic as affection.

'We are not married yet, My Lord.' Grace answered in a chilling voice. 'Now, if you gentlemen will excuse me? I believe I will follow my aunt's example and retire to my room for a few hours before dinner.' She didn't wait for a reply, but swept from the room, her head held regally high.

Lucian scowled darkly as he watched her departure through narrowed lids. The situation between himself and Grace was becoming intolerable. Enough for him to break his word and confide in her? No, he accepted wearily. That he simply could not do.

'I believe, dear brother, that you may well have met your match.' Sebastian's appreciative murmur interrupted Lucian's troubled thoughts.

He turned to look at his brother with cold eyes. 'Then it is as well that I am the one betrothed to marry her, is it not?'

Sebastian held up supplicating hands. 'Calm your temper, Lucian,' he taunted. 'Grace is very beautiful. Very accomplished. But I believe I like the idea of her for my sister-in-law far better than as my wife. If only for the pleasure of watching the effect she has upon my taciturn older brother.'

Lucian's mouth thinned. 'And what effect would that be…?' His voice was deceptively soft.

The deception did not fool Sebastian for a single moment, and his smile was taunting as he stood up. 'Only you can know that, Lucian.' He studiously straightened the lace at his cuffs. 'Although I will say…' he looked up, his gaze very direct '…that I approve of the changes I see in you. You have been away from us for far too long, brother,' he added huskily.

Lucian's brow darkened. 'It is two years since I resigned my commission and returned to London.'

Sebastian's smile was rueful. 'In body, perhaps. In mind and spirit…?' He shook his head. 'But you are back with us now, Lucian, and if nothing else I will always be grateful to Grace for being the means of that return.'

'I have no idea what you are talking about.' But he did. He *did!*

His brother gave him a long, searching glance. 'As you please, Lucian.' He nodded abruptly. 'Perhaps you would like to confide in *me* the reason you have remained here, incurring Hawk's disapproval by not travelling to Mulberry Hall to pay homage to your new nephew?'

Lucian was thrown momentarily by Sebastian's abrupt change of subject, instantly realising that he had underestimated his younger brother's intelligence. The ton could perhaps be forgiven for making that mistake, when Sebastian chose to show them only the frivolous side of his nature, but Lucian, knowing his brother rather better than that, should not have dropped his guard in that way.

He forced the tension from his shoulders, forced a lazy smile upon his lips. 'I would far rather that you told me which lady's attentions you were so hastily retreating from when you hurried so promptly to Mulberry Hall.'

Sebastian looked at him frowningly for several seconds. Whatever he read in Lucian's expression caused him to shrug off pursuing his earlier question, and instead he grinned widely. 'That would be very ungentlemanly of me!'

Lucian smiled mockingly. 'I do not remember that ever bothering you in the past.'

'Perhaps the example of your own and Hawk's happiness has made a reformed character of me?'

Lucian gave a disbelieving snort. 'That is more likely to have been the cause of your hasty withdrawal from Society!'

'Well, there is this certain Countess—'

'Good Lord, I hope you do not refer to the Countess of Morefield?' Lucian deliberately referred to a widowed lady of their acquaintance, whose bedchamber they had vied to occupy the previous year, completely unaware of the fact that their arrogantly haughty older brother had already beaten them both to it!

'Certainly not.' Sebastian grimaced in horror. 'No, this is quite another Countess. I tell you, Lucian, I have never seen anyone as lovely as she. She is…'

Sebastian's conversation was diverted to Lucian's satisfaction, and Lucian allowed his thoughts to dwell on Grace and the gulf that seemed to be ever widening between them. It would no doubt continue to widen when he could not be completely truthful with her.

Perhaps once they were married their relationship would be such that omission would cease to be important? And that was as likely, Lucian acknowledged ruefully, as his horse sprouting wings and taking to the air!

* * *

'May I come in?' Grace did not wait for Lucian's reply before entering the small library at the Dower House that he had temporarily taken over for his own use, closing the door behind her before she marched across the room to stand before the desk where Lucian sat, replying to several letters that had been delivered to him earlier that morning. 'I want to know what is going on, Lucian.' Her tone brooked no refusal of her demand.

Grace had not forgiven him yet for his comment yesterday, concerning his betrothal to her, but events had overtaken that annoyance, necessitating in her needing to speak to him.

Lucian's expression was everything that was patient as he looked up at her. Annoyingly so, Grace acknowledged impatiently, as she readied herself for yet more prevarication from him. 'I had reason to go up to Winton Hall this morning.'

'And what reason would that be, Grace?' he prompted, gaze narrowed.

Her mouth tightened. 'I called to enquire after Francis's health, of course.'

'Of course,' Lucian drawled as he sat back in his chair. 'A note would have sufficed as well, surely?'

'As it happens, no, it would not,' Grace announced triumphantly. 'Because neither Darius nor Francis were in residence to receive such a note!'

'Indeed?'

Grace glared at him. 'You already knew they were not!'

He shrugged broad shoulders. 'Darius did mention to me that he and Francis might be returning to London in the next few days. It would seem that Francis is recovered enough for Darius to have made good on that intention.'

'Lucian—'

'Grace,' he interrupted mildly, standing up, his height and breadth of shoulder at once dominating the room. 'The movements of your guardian are none of our concern.'

'None of *my* concern, you mean,' Grace guessed easily, her frustration only increasing. 'You *knew* that Darius and Francis were to leave.'

Lucian met her accusing gaze with a calmness that was deceptive. As deceptive as almost his every word had been for the last four days. Damn Darius. And damn Francis. In fact, he damned everyone and everything that was keeping him and Grace at such loggerheads.

He would much rather be making love with Grace than arguing with her. Even if she did look enchantingly beautiful when she was angry. *Especially* as she looked so enchantingly beautiful when she was angry!

He moved with the intention of taking her in his arms. 'Grace—'

'Do not attempt to distract me, Lucian,' she warned, as she took a step away from his reaching hands.

'Do I distract you, Grace?' he encouraged huskily.

'You know that you do.' Her frown was censorious. 'Why have Darius and Francis returned to London?'

Lucian gave a firm shake of his head. 'I am sorry,

Grace, but I have no intention of discussing this matter with you.'

'You are not sorry at all!' She glared. 'In fact, you are the most annoying, most infuriating man I have ever—Let go of me, Lucian!' she instructed fiercely as his arms moved firmly about her. 'I told you I would not be distracted—' Her words came to an abrupt end as Łucian claimed her lips with his own.

It had been too long since he had held her like this, Lucian realised. Far, far too long!

'Lucian…!' Grace groaned weakly as his lips left hers to trail warmly, hotly, down the length of her throat. She could not, would not, allow herself to be distracted from her purpose in coming here. 'No, Lucian.' She pushed against his chest in an effort to move away from him. 'Someone may come in and find us here together like this.' She struggled to maintain the sanity that was fast eluding her.

'To the devil with someone!' he growled low in his throat, and he leant back against the front of the desk to pull Grace in tightly against his thighs.

Hard, aroused thighs that brought a flush to Grace's cheeks. Dear God, how she loved this man, Grace acknowledged as she looked up into the hard beauty of his face. Those brown eyes were warm and compelling, those chiselled lips a temptation she was finding it increasingly difficult to resist.

'My aunt and your brother are only in the sitting room next to this one,' Grace reminded him huskily, having ascertained their whereabouts in her search for Lucian.

Lucian smiled indulgently. 'Then we must be very quiet, must we not?'

To Grace's embarrassment she knew that she was rarely quiet when Lucian made love to her. That her throaty groans and murmurs of pleasure would surely be audible to the couple in the room adjoining this. 'You seek only to distract me, Lucian—'

'I seek only to put an end to this interminable torture of being close to you and yet not able to touch you!' he corrected her hardly, his arms like steel bands as he kept the length of her body moulded against his.

Grace looked up at him wonderingly. Had these last few days, especially this last one of estrangement, really been as torturous for Lucian as they had been for her? The lines of strain beside his eyes and mouth seemed to indicate that they had.

Did that mean that Lucian had feelings for her after all? Or was it just that he desired her? No doubt it was the latter, Grace acknowledged heavily; Lucian had made it more than clear that he did not intend falling in love with any woman, let alone the one who was to become his wife.

This time Grace was firm in her resolve to break free of his restraining arms, and her determination was rewarded when Lucian allowed her to step away from him, his gaze hooded.

'This is perhaps as good an opportunity as any for us to discuss the timing for the ending of our betrothal,' she said.

'Opportunity…?' Lucian echoed softly.

Grace shrugged narrow shoulders. 'My uncle—my uncle's recent death.' Her voice was husky with the pain of that loss. She refused to think yet of the pain she would suffer at the ending of her betrothal to Lucian. Of never seeing him again except as just another member of the ton. But better that, surely, than that Lucian should be tied for all time to a woman he did not and never would love in the way that Grace loved him? 'The wedding obviously cannot now take place for several months at least—possibly the whole year of my aunt's mourning. By which time—'

'Your aunt will have realised that there are to be no repercussions from our impetuous behaviour prior to our betrothal,' Lucian finished gratingly. 'That is your meaning, is it not, Grace?'

'Well…yes. Of course.' She looked slightly flustered. 'By the time my aunt and I return to Society next year, the fact of our own betrothal and its ending will have been forgotten.'

'I somehow doubt that very much, Grace.' Lucian's mouth twisted derisively. 'Neither do I intend discussing this subject any further when emotions are in such turmoil following the Duke of Carlyne's death and—and other events.' He straightened to move back and sit down behind the desk.

'Emotions, Lucian?' Grace raised dark brows. 'I had not believed you to be in possession of any of those.'

Lucian scowled darkly. This was the second time in as many days that accusation had been levelled against him. Not that Sebastian's comment about his reserve had been an accusation as such, more an expression of a regret. But Grace undoubtedly meant it as a criticism.

How could Lucian explain the reasons for his emotional withdrawal since leaving the army without telling her of the nightmares that had haunted him for so long afterwards, and the savage butchery that had created them?

More importantly, he was reluctant to reveal that those horrific images and memories had been driven away completely by dreams of Grace in their stead…!

Lucian did not know himself well enough yet—was not familiar enough with these newfound emotions to share them with anyone. Especially Grace.

He chose to retreat behind mockery. 'I am as surprised to discover their existence as you are, Grace,' he drawled self-derisively. 'Perhaps there is some hope for me after all?'

'Perhaps…'

Grace no longer knew what emotions they were talking about! Sadness at her uncle's death? Sympathy for her aunt's terrible loss? Or something else entirely…?

Lucian nodded tersely. 'If you will allow me to finish dealing with my replies to these letters before luncheon…?'

Grace nodded distractedly as she turned to leave.

'And, Grace…?'

She turned slowly back to face Lucian, her thoughts in turmoil.

What had transpired between the two of them just now? Because something had. Something important.

'Sebastian has informed me of his intention to take

his leave in the morning and return to London. Let us try to make his last evening here with us as pleasant as possible for both him and your aunt, hmm?'

In other words, Lucian did not want any sign of dissension between them to be visible to the Duchess or Lord Sebastian!

Grace wasn't sure there *was* still any dissension between them. There was puzzlement on her part, yes. And reserve on Lucian's. But dissension? No, Grace didn't think so. Both people had to be emotionally engaged for that to exist, and Lucian had once again retreated behind his emotionless mask.

She gave a cool inclination of her head. 'I will try, for their sakes.'

Lucian's smile was tight. 'That is all I ask.'

For the moment, he conceded frowningly once alone. But soon, very soon if Grace continued this talk of ending their betrothal, he would have to confront and question his own feelings on the matter...

Chapter Sixteen

Grace chose to wear a grey silk gown overlaid with grey lace on its short puffed sleeves and bodice for dinner that evening. A simple gold cross that had belonged to her mother was her only jewellery, and her hair was simply styled in loose dark curls that fell from her crown to move tantalisingly against her nape.

Unfortunately Lucian was not in the drawing room to comment on her appearance when she entered it. Only Sebastian was there, to rise from his sprawling position on one of the sofas as he extended her a bow.

'I am sure that it is permitted for your future brother to tell you how exquisite you are looking this evening, Miss Hetherington.' Those brown eyes had darkened in appreciation.

Grace laughed softly. 'You really are the most terrible flirt, My Lord!'

'Terrible?' Sebastian arched dark brows, looking very dashing in dark evening clothes and snowy white

linen. 'I have always believed myself to be exceptionally good at it!'

'You know exactly what I mean.' Grace tapped his
wrist lightly with her fan.

'I do,' he acknowledged with a rueful inclination of
his head. 'I almost envy Lucian, Miss Hetherington. I
have a feeling a man would never be bored with you as
his wife,' he explained.

'You mean that as a compliment, I hope?'

'But of course!'

'Of course.' Grace sank elegantly onto one of the
sofas, still smiling.

Sebastian gave a shake of his head. 'I must say that
I still find the suddenness of your betrothal to my
brother somewhat…interesting.'

'In what way, My Lord?' Grace prompted guard-
edly. 'I am sure that you are as familiar with the gossip
circulating about the two of us amongst the ton as your
sister is?'

'Arabella?' Sebastian grinned affectionately. 'Trust
Arabella to show no hesitation in relating that gossip to
you!'

'Only after someone else had brought it to my attention, I assure you,' Grace returned dryly.

'Lucian?'

Grace's expression was one of cool composure.
'Who it was does not signify, My Lord. All that matters
is that I was already aware of it before Arabella spoke
to me on the subject.'

'On what subject, might I ask?' Lucian rasped as he
entered the drawing room.

'Nothing of any importance.' Grace gave Sebastian a sympathetic smile even as she acknowledged that, although Sebastian might appear dashing in his evening clothes, Lucian looked by far the more elegantly handsome of the two. The more breathtaking of the two…

'Do not look at me in that way.' Sebastian backed away from Lucian's accusing scowl. 'I assure you I did not say or do anything in the least improper before your arrival. Did I, Grace?' He looked at her appealingly.

'You have just done so by addressing her in so familiar a manner.' Lucian placed a possessive hand beneath Grace's elbow.

'Oh, hell—'

'And now you have sworn in her company, too,' Lucian mocked. 'Really, Sebastian, I cannot see *any* woman ever accepting such an ill-mannered rake as you as her husband.'

'Really?' Sebastian looked noticeably cheered rather than nonplussed.

'Undoubtedly,' Lucian reassured him dryly, his mood lightening.

The teasing between the two brothers set the tone for the rest of the evening, with Sebastian even managing to make the subdued Duchess laugh once or twice with his outrageousness. Deliberately so, Grace suspected, in order to conceal the fact that Grace and Lucian, despite their earlier agreement to the contrary, barely addressed a word to each other.

Grace because she was still slightly annoyed with Lucian for not confiding in her. And Lucian because— Well, she had no idea what Lucian's reasons were for his silence towards her. Which was part of the problem, of course. These last few days Grace had simply had no idea *what* Lucian was thinking from one moment to the next.

Instead she concentrated her attention on the interplay between the two brothers. How different was the relationship between Lucian and Sebastian than that of the three Carlyne brothers, Grace acknowledged sadly. She could not imagine the three of *them* ever spending such a pleasant evening together. George had been affable and charming, of course, and well liked by both his brothers. But the relationship between Darius and Francis seemed to consist of contempt on Darius's part and jealousy and dislike on Francis's.

Grace became very still. Had she been looking at this situation in quite the wrong way? Francis *was* jealous of Darius. He had also made no effort to hide his dislike of Darius since the Duke of Carlyne had died—to the point where Francis had expressed that dislike when he talked to Grace and Lucian of Darius's treatment of the Duchess since her husband's death.

Grace gave Lucian a briefly searching glance, knowing that, for all that the two of them disagreed constantly, Lucian was nevertheless a man of honour. A man of integrity. And, no matter how damning the evidence against Darius might appear, Lucian insisted that the other man was innocent of any and all accusations. Whilst at the same time doing very little to hide his contempt of Francis Wynter.

If Darius was innocent, then perhaps that meant—
No...!

What Grace was now thinking simply could not be!
Could it...?

'Is the beef not to your liking, Grace?' her aunt
prompted with concern, obviously noting that Grace
had ceased eating and was simply staring down at the
food on her plate, her cheeks pale. 'I am sure we can ask
Cook to provide something else if it is not. A little
chicken, perhaps?'

'No, the—the beef is perfectly delicious, Aunt,'
Grace hastened to assure her, some colour returning to
her cheeks. 'I was merely— It is just— Is it my imagination, or has it become rather warm in here?'

Her aunt frowned. 'Perhaps if we were to open the
doors out into the garden...'

'No.' Lucian was looking frowningly at Grace as he
rose abruptly to his feet. 'With your permission, I
believe I will take Grace into the garden for some air.'
He moved to pull her chair back for her at the Duchess's
nod of agreement to the suggestion, and Grace was
grateful for the support of the arm he offered her as she
allowed him to escort her outside.

Grace breathed in the warm summer air, her earlier
discomfort quickly passing as the tightness eased about
her chest and her head cleared of too many thoughts all
clamouring to be heard at once.

Lucian was very aware of the way Grace had looked
at him with such clarity a few minutes ago. As if—as
if she had just found the last piece to a puzzle. Perhaps

she had…? Lucian had noted Grace's intellect on more than one occasion, so there was no reason now why he should be in the least surprised if she had used that intelligence to discover the truth of a situation that had been disturbing her for a few days.

He drew in a deep breath. 'Grace—'

'Could we walk as far as the coach-house, do you suppose?' she prompted brightly.

Lucian was not quite sure of the wisdom of being alone with Grace once they reached the coach-house. 'Perhaps we should just sit here on the terrace?'

She shook her head frowningly. 'I would not like my aunt to overhear any of our conversation.'

'Nevertheless…'

Grace raised teasing eyebrows. 'Surely you are not apprehensive at the thought of being alone with me, My Lord?'

'On my own behalf? No,' he confirmed ruefully.

Grace really did look exceptionally lovely this evening, with her dark curls falling enticingly about her face and nape, the grey of her gown complementing the beauty of her eyes. She was a temptation which, after holding her in his arms this morning, Lucian might find it impossible to resist!

'I am not feeling in the least apprehensive either, Lucian,' she assured him huskily, as she lifted a hand and lightly touched the front of his jacket.

Lucian stepped abruptly away from her. 'Then perhaps you should be!'

Grace studied him quietly, easily noting the clenching of his jaw, the nerve pulsing in his cheek, the glitter of his eyes. She gave a shake of her head. 'I believe I know you well enough now, Lucian, to know you would never do anything to hurt or frighten me.'

He frowned darkly. 'Maybe not intentionally—' He gave an exasperated sigh as he stepped away from her to stare out at the moon-dappled garden, hands tightly clasped together behind his back. 'I believe you have some questions to ask me?'

'Do I?' Her tone was light.

Lucian turned his head to look at her. 'Grace, this is not wise—'

'Oh, Lucian!' She gave a shake of her head, her laugh huskily dismissive. 'I have ceased being wise since that night at the inn when you stumbled into my bedchamber instead of your own!'

The moonlight gave his face a look of hard implacability as he turned his head. 'I was drunk—'

'Admittedly you had taken too much brandy—'

'I was drunk,' Lucian insisted harshly. 'Too damned drunk to have made love to you even if that had been my intention!'

'Which it was not.'

'No.'

Grace looked at him searchingly, noting the bleakness in his eyes now. 'Let us walk, Lucian,' she invited again, very aware of her aunt and Sebastian in the room behind them, and of Lucian's need to talk. Her own earlier concerns were secondary to that. 'Do not look so disgusted by your condition that night, Lucian,' she told him softly, as he fell into step at her side and they strolled towards the coach-house. 'I have noticed that being in Francis's company for any length of time has that effect on most people…'

'Francis's company was not the reason I over-imbibed that evening. Well, not entirely.' His frown darkened in the moonlight as he turned to face her. 'Grace, I am not the man you think I am. The man others think I am,' he clarified harshly.

Her gaze was quizzical as she looked up at him. 'You are Lord Lucian St Claire, are you not…?'

'I am not talking of a title or a name, Grace.' Lucian's movements were restless. 'I am a fake. A charlatan—'

'I do not believe it.' Grace touched the sleeve of his jacket, able to feel the tensed muscle beneath. 'I do not believe it, Lucian,' she repeated huskily, unconditionally.

That nerve pulsed in his cheek. 'Grace, I take too much drink most evenings. In order that I might sleep. Rather, in order that I might fall into a state of unconsciousness—'

'I have not noticed your doing so since being here…'

'These last ten days I have had other things on my mind once I am alone in my bedchamber,' he acknowledged ruefully.

Her? Did Lucian now think of *her* when he was alone in his bedchamber? Dream of her? As Grace thought and dreamt of him…?

'Why?'

Lucian gave her a startled look. 'Why…?'

She gave an encouraging smile. 'Why do you take too much drink in order to fall into unconsciousness?'

Lucian felt a clenching in his gut, a shortness of breath at the empathy he could see in Grace's candid grey gaze. An empathy he knew he did not deserve. 'I have dreams, Grace,' he bit out hardly, knowing that he had to tell her the truth—that she more than anyone had the right to know all that he was.

'What sort of dreams?' Grace prompted quietly.

'Terrible nightmares.' His hands clenched at his sides. 'Of war. And blood. And dying. Of friends whom I will never see again. Of killing—' Lucian drew in a ragged breath. 'At least…I did.' His frown was rueful. 'Since I have met you, those dreams have become— other.'

'You will tell me of those other dreams later,' Grace encouraged huskily. 'Surely the nightmares are perfectly understandable when you have been a soldier? When for years—too many years, perhaps—war and blood and dying were your life?'

Lucian shook his head. 'It is a weakness.'

'It is a strength,' she contradicted softly. 'I would respect you less, like you less, if you had lived through those years without care or reaction to the destruction and death that surrounded you. It is a *strength*, Lucian,' she repeated firmly, as he would have protested. '*You* are a man of strength. You are also a man of compassion. Of caring. A man who could not have lived through such things as you did without some inner scarring of your own.' She smiled encouragingly.

'I do not know of other men who suffer such night-mares—'

'That is because men do not talk to each other of such things. *Because* they consider them to be a weakness,' she continued pointedly. 'It is not,' she said again firmly. 'You are not weak.' She paused, moistening her lips before speaking again. 'Lucian, I was already aware of these—dreams.'

Lucian gave her a sharp look. 'How—? That night at the inn!' He closed his eyes briefly. 'You saw—you have known all this time!' His eyes glittered in the darkness. 'I understand better now your determination not to agree to a betrothal between the two of us!'

She shook her head. 'That was not the reason for my initial reluctance.'

'Then it should have been!' Dear God, all this time she had seen—had witnessed— 'How you must despise me!'

'Never,' Grace assured him with feeling.

'Grace, I killed a man!'

She shook her head. 'I am sure that in the course of your army career you killed many men.'

'This one I killed for the sheer pleasure of doing so,' Lucian told her grimly. 'The memory of that has haunted me. Made my nights a living hell. My days—! Grace, you have witnessed first-hand my need for complete emotional control.'

She had also, Grace noted with satisfaction, several times witnessed his complete *loss* of that control when in her company. 'Tell me why.'

'I have just explained—'

'No, not that, Lucian,' she calmed softly. 'Tell me why you believe you killed this man.'

Lucian drew in a sharp breath, the images of that terrible day more vivid than ever. Could he tell Grace of his behaviour that day? Could he confide his savagery to her and then watch as disgust and horror appeared on her expressive face? Lucian knew he had no choice but to do so if Grace was to know all that he was; if he was not to continue to live a lie in her eyes at least.

He deliberately averted his gaze from the beauty of her face. 'It was at Waterloo. The war with Napoleon was almost over. The whole sorry *mess* was almost ever. We were in a forest, following a particularly bloody skirmish, when we—'

'We?' Grace prompted gently.

'My men, myself and—and another officer.'

'It was my cousin Simon, was it not?' she realized astutely.

Lucian's jaw clenched. 'I— It— Yes,' he grated harshly. 'He had lived through it all, Grace. Had survived every battle. And now—when it was almost over—a French cavalry officer appeared as if out of nowhere. He charged in amongst us, sword raised, swinging to left and right, uncaring if he struck his target or not, simply bent on destruction. Several of the men went down instantly. Amongst them Simon.' A nerve pulsed in his tightly clenched jaw. 'It was too much, Grace. Seeing Simon simply lying there, his eyes wide and looking sightlessly up to the sky, his gaping wound—!' He shook his head. 'I did not even think, Grace. I simply pulled the Frenchman from his horse and began attacking him with my own sword. In front of my men I drove my sword into him again and again, until my fury had abated.'

Grace could not pretend but to be horrified by this account. Shocked and horrified. But those emotions were not directed towards Lucian. Never towards Lucian. He had reacted instinctively, emotionally, and he had paid the price for that excess of feeling when he had returned home by cutting himself off from all emotion.

Until she had entered his life… In these last weeks Grace had seen Lucian display anger. Exasperation. Gentleness. Kindness. Possession. Even a little jealousy, she believed, on the occasion of Lady Humbers's ball, when he had seemed to grind his teeth most of the evening at the attentions paid her by Sir Rupert Enderby and Lord Gideon Grayson. And most especially Grace had seen Lucian's desire for her.

She reached up and laid a gentle hand upon the rigidness of his jaw. 'Lucian, I cannot even pretend to comprehend your feelings on that terrible day. But I do accept them.'

'How can you?' he rasped as he looked down at her broodingly. 'Are you not filled with disgust? With horror at the man that I am?'

Grace gave a shake of her head. 'Lucian, I *know* you to be a man of deep integrity and honour. You are— and always will be—a hero in my eyes, as well as in the eyes of others. In short, Lucian, you are everything that is to be admired. Everything that *I* admire,' she added huskily.

'Grace…!' he groaned achingly, his eyes very dark.

'You are also,' Grace continued firmly, feeling that Lucian had dwelt on death and destruction long enough, 'a man who remains loyal and true to his friends even when all the evidence indicates you should do the opposite—are you not…?'

Lucian grimaced. 'You are referring to Darius.'

Grace gave an inclination of her head. 'I *am* referring to Darius. I was wrong about him, was I not? Completely and utterly wrong.'

Lucian drew in a ragged breath. 'Grace, I have given my word—I am under oath not to discuss certain things with any other person.'

'Very well.' She nodded. 'Then I will tell *you* what I think has happened. You may just listen, if that is what you prefer?'

A nerve pulsed in Lucian's jaw. 'I do not prefer it, Grace, but it is the way that it has to be.'

'Can you first tell me whether or not Francis will ever be returning to Winton Hall?'

'I will not be breaking my word if I acknowledge that he will not.' He gave a terse inclination of his head. 'Francis has decided to go abroad. For his health.' Lucian's smile was grim.

'I see.' Grace gave a slow nod.

'Do you?' Lucian rasped harshly.

'I believe so.' Grace sighed. 'I am not quite sure where this tale begins. Perhaps with my cousin Simon's death…?'

Lucian stiffened. 'Perhaps.'

'It was perhaps the catalyst, for the events that followed…?'

Lucian looked at her admiringly. Grace's intelligence exceeded even what he had come to expect of her. It had taken Lucian some time to draw the conclusions that she had come to in the last few minutes, and even then he had not known of all that had happened until Darius had confided in him.

'As I thought.' Grace's frown was pained as she took Lucian's silence for confirmation. 'And the death of Darius's wife…?'

Lucian's gaze narrowed but he said nothing.

Grace nodded at his silence. 'I recall that Francis was staying with them at the time of Lady Sophie's accident…and with my aunt and uncle at the time of George's death. Something caused his seizure. You have assured me it was not my own altercation with Francis that morning, so it must have been something else…' She considered frowningly. 'Perhaps it was something that Francis either did or said…?'

'I believe Francis and George had been in conversation shortly before your uncle collapsed.'

Grace's eyes widened. 'Then either my uncle had the misfortune to realize what his youngest brother had done and made the mistake of confronting him, or—or Francis, *knowing* of the Duke's heart condition, chose to confide those facts to him and so placed him in a position of inner conflict that resulted in his collapse!' she said accusingly. 'My uncle's integrity would have dictated that Francis could not be allowed to get away with such atrocities, while at the same time he would have known that to expose what he had done would bring shame and scandal upon the whole family!'

She looked at Lucian. His grim silence was enough to tell her that once again she had guessed correctly.

It was unbelievable, incredible, and yet all the evidence now pointed to Francis somehow being responsible for the death of Darius's wife *and* that of the Duke of Carlyne…

'But why would he do such things?' Her expression was pained. 'What could he possibly hope to gain— No!' she gasped, her face pale as final realization came. 'Darius was to be next, was he not? All those hints and insinuations concerning Darius being the one responsible for his wife's death, just like the vindictive ones concerning our own betrothal, will have originated from Francis. My uncle's collapse did not occur until *after* Darius had arrived in London. And once we had all returned to Winton Hall it was Francis who implied— who accused Darius of being cruel and uncaring where the Duchess was concerned, hinting that it was the dukedom Darius had wanted all along. When all the time it was *he* who— He truly *did* inflict that blow upon his head, in another effort to cast doubts upon Darius!' she gasped incredulously.

Grace's conjectures were so close to the truth that Lucian could not hope to deny them. 'Darius believes he was to be found dead in his bed one morning.' He nodded grimly. 'No doubt with a suitable note at his side, explaining that he had taken his own life during the night over the guilt he felt at having killed his wife and his brother.'

'But what had Darius's wife ever done to Francis that she had to be—to be—?'

'This is all conjecture, you understand…?'

'I understand.'

Lucian shrugged. 'Then perhaps it was because Darius's wife might soon have produced another heir and possible rival for the dukedom.'

Grace gave a dazed shake of her head. 'That is what all of this is about, is it not? The dukedom,' she realised weakly. 'Francis becoming the Duke of Carlyne. I wonder how long it took him to realise that Simon dying in that sudden way meant that only two people now stood in his way…?'

'Until Darius's equally sudden marriage and the possible conception of yet another heir, perhaps…?'

'Yes.' Grace gave a shaky sigh. 'That poor, poor woman.'

Lucian grimaced. 'Obviously I can neither deny nor confirm the things you have said—'

'I would not expect you to when you have given your word.'

'But I am breaking no confidence by revealing that Francis has decided to remain abroad for the remainder of his life.' Lucian's mouth twisted with distaste.

'It is better than he deserves!' Grace's eye sparkled with temper.

'The alternative would bring scandal and shame

upon the rest of the family, and it is Darius's belief that the Duchess has already suffered enough.'

Grace looked pained. 'Is my aunt aware of what has happened?'

'Darius does not believe so, no.'

She frowned. 'And it was because Darius feared for my aunt that he instigated her speedy removal to the Dower House?'

'Perhaps. If any of what you have just described actually happened,' Lucian added firmly.

Grace knew that it had! 'But what of Darius? If none of this conjecture is ever to become public knowledge—'

'It will not.'

Grace nodded. 'Then the suspicion concerning the death of Darius's wife, at least, will continue to hang over his head like a dark cloud…'

Lucian's mouth tightened. 'I believe that is a price Darius is willing to pay.'

'That is very noble of him.'

'Yes.' Lucian gave a tight smile. 'He really is not the blackguard you believe him to be, Grace. He is no angel, either,' he added with a hard laugh, 'but certainly no murderer of innocents.'

Neither the devil nor the angel that Arabella had once described Darius as being, but simply a man. A very arrogant man, admittedly, but a man who placed family honour before his own reputation or comfort.

As Lucian was a man who placed honour and loyalty before all else…

Grace regarded him .. 'I have been unfair to you, Lucian, concerning your friendship with Darius.'

He gave a dismissive shrug. 'Until Darius confided certain facts to me I was beginning to have my own doubts,' he admitted ruefully. 'Since that time I have been bound by a promise of silence.'

'It is a promise you have kept, Lucian,' Grace assured him. 'I have merely spoken my thoughts and conjectures out loud. You have remained the soul of discretion.' She gave a slow, enigmatic smile. 'I believe the time has now come for us to discuss your other, more recent bedtime dreams…?'

Lucian's gaze sharpened as he looked at her warily. 'I am not sure—'

'I am.' Grace moved—so close to him now that Lucian could smell her perfume and see the languorous darkness of her eyes as she looked up at him. '*I* am very sure, Lucian.'

Lucian could feel the pounding of his heart, the heightened awareness he experienced whenever Grace was anywhere near, the need to touch her…

'Shall we go inside the coach-house, Lucian?' she prompted huskily at his silence. 'I am curious to see if the effects of being in a stationary carriage will be as satisfying as in a moving one.'

Lucian found himself gritting his teeth once more at the image she provoked. 'Grace, I cannot promise that you will still be chaste if and when I allow you to leave the carriage!'

'My dear, that is my dearest hope…' Grace's laugh

was husky as she gave him one last inviting glance, before moving to open the door of the coach-house herself, stepping inside to be consumed by the darkness within.

Lucian stared after her. Grace knew the truth of him now. The absolutely true self of him. Yet she was not filled with the disgust towards him that he had expected. And dreaded. Instead there had been invitation in her eyes.

It was an invitation Lucian had no power left to resist…

Chapter Seventeen

The coach-house was in darkness when Lucian entered. Only the paleness of Grace's gown was visible to him as she stood a short distance away.

'Grace—?'

'Close the door, Lucian,' she instructed softly.

'Grace—'

'Do you not want to be alone with me, Lucian?'

Not want to be alone with her! Lucian wanted to make love to Grace so badly even his teeth ached with the wanting! Grace knew it, too, and that knowledge was in the soft teasing of her voice.

Lucian wished he could see her, that he could read the expression in her eyes.

'I will light a lamp.'

He moved to do so, hearing the slight rustle of Grace's gown behind him as the coach-house became shadowed in a soft golden hue. Lucian's breath caught in his throat as he turned to find Grace standing behind him, dressed only in her shift, her gown a soft bundle at her slippered feet.

'Grace, there is something I must say—'

'I believe we have talked enough for one evening,' she teased, as she lifted her hands and removed the pins from her hair so that it fell in an ebony cascade about the bareness of her shoulders.

Lucian couldn't think straight with Grace looking so sensually alluring. 'This I *have* to say—' He groaned low in his throat as Grace stepped even closer, her breasts brushing against him. 'Grace, it has never been my intention to fall in love with any woman—'

'I do not recall having asked for your love,' she said.

Lucian reached out to grasp Grace's shoulders and hold her away from him whilst he still had the strength to do so, his eyes glittering in the semi-darkness. 'How could I ever ask for any woman to love me when I knew that to do so might result in her being awoken one night by my shouts of protest at the dreams that haunt me?'

'I consider those dreams to be your wounds of war, Lucian.' Grace put silencing fingertips over his lips. 'The fact that they have wounded your heart rather than your physical person does not make them any less hard to endure. My dear, they are a part of you, are the very reason that you have tried to keep all emotion from your life, are they not…?'

He frowned slightly. 'Yes,' he acknowledged tautly.

Grace nodded. 'Remaining aloof and detached even from the family you love so dearly?'

'Yes!' Lucian drew in a ragged breath. 'I admit I had begun to think of marriage these last few months. But in a detached way. A sedate wife who would make no demands upon me, who would live at my estate in Hampshire, and whom I would visit occasionally when the mood took me.'

'To beget your necessary heirs, no doubt?' Grace drawled derisively.

'Yes,' Lucian acknowledged ruefully, as he easily recalled their conversation that first evening at the inn.

Grace's expression was pained as she gave a sad shake of her head. 'No wonder you have been so disheartened by our betrothal. You *knew* I could never be that sort of wife.'

'I have discovered these last weeks that I want no such wife,' he assured her firmly. 'The only wife I want—the only woman I will ever tolerate for my wife—is you! And the only man I will tolerate as a husband for you is me!' He shook her slightly, his expression darkly frowning as she looked unconvinced. 'I love you, Grace! I love you so much that the thought of any other man—' He broke off, teeth clenched. 'I love you utterly and completely, Grace. I love you until I can see, hear and feel nothing else but you!'

Grace stared up at him wondrously, hardly able to believe what Lucian was telling her. Lucian loved her. He *loved* her! 'I love you, too, Lucian. I believe I have loved you since that first night when you stumbled into my bedchamber and kissed me so passionately.'

He shook his head, a dark frown upon his brow.

'How could you, when that night you witnessed my nightmares first-hand?'

Her hands moved up to cradle each side of his face as she looked up at him. 'I love all of you, Lucian. With every part of me. I see, hear and feel nothing else but *you!*'

His eyes darkened. 'You cannot love a man who may wake in your arms shouting, protesting at the bloodshed and—'

'I love you, Lucian,' she assured firmly. 'Everything about you. Including the scars you bear so valiantly inside.'

Lucian released a shuddering breath. 'Perhaps there will be no more nightmares.' He frowned. 'The only dreams I have now are of you. Of being with you. Of loving you. Of making love with you.'

'I am glad, Lucian.' She rested her head against his chest. 'Tell me of those dreams, Lucian. Share them with me.'

His arms tightened about her. 'First tell me you will marry me, Grace. That you will soon become my wife!'

'Yes, I will marry you, my dearest love!' she assured him joyously. 'Tomorrow, if that is your wish!'

'As soon as ever it can be arranged!' Lucian's arms came about her as his head lowered and his mouth claimed hers.

Hungrily. With a hunger that Grace more than matched. There had been too many occasions between them when their desire had been aroused but not satisfied for either of them to be gentle with the other now.

Lucian threw off his jacket to allow Grace the

freedom to unbutton his shirt and strip it from him, so that her hands might explore the hardness of his chest. The muscles rippled beneath her touch even as his mouth explored the hollows of her throat and the soft curve of her breasts. He drew one of those hardened peaks into the moist heat of his mouth to flick his tongue against the soft material that covered the turgid nipple.

Grace felt the heat between her thighs, hot and damp, as she arched against him, groaning low in her throat as Lucian took her breast deeply into his mouth, before slipping the straps of her shift down her arms to bare her to the waist, so that flesh touched flesh.

'Let me pleasure *you* this time, Lucian!' she groaned achingly, taking one of his hands to lead the way to a closed carriage.

His other hand held the lamp aloft, and Grace waited for Lucian to sit down upon the carriage seat before helping him to remove his boots and strip off his breeches, her gaze darkening hungrily as she gazed down at his thrusting hardness.

Grace felt only awed fascination as she saw how long and thick he was, so beautiful in the lamplight. She moved to her knees in front of him to caress and stroke him, her eyes widening as he grew even larger, his hardness moving against her hand, and she heard Lucian's groan of pleasure as she lowered her head and kissed him there, taking several engorged inches into her mouth, drawing him into her as she licked and sucked the length of him, tasting him on her tongue as his juices began to flow.

Lucian had never seen anything so erotic as Grace as she bent over him, her hair flowing darkly over her shoulders and breasts as she licked and sucked him rhythmically, taking more and more of him into her mouth, until he felt as if he might burst with the pleasure she gave him.

'Not yet, Grace.' He reluctantly drew her away from him. 'A man takes some time to recover after release, my love, and there are still so many things I wish to explore with you, to share with you!'

She looked up at him teasingly. 'I am yours to tutor, my love.'

Lucian groaned low in his throat as he heard his own arrogant words upon her lips. He shook his head. 'I do not believe there is a single thing I can teach you about pleasing me!'

Her gaze held his as she rose gracefully to her feet, moving to place her legs either side of him on the carriage seat, so that she might lower herself and straddle his thighs. The heat of her burned a path along his arousal as she moved slowly, erotically, against him.

'Grace…!' Lucian choked gruffly as he felt the reins of his control snapping.

Her answer was to capture his lips with her own, her breasts pressed against his chest, the fire of her thighs against his driving him wild with need.

'Take me, Lucian,' she pleaded as her lips travelled the column of his throat. 'Take me…!'

Her back arched invitingly, and Lucian was no longer able to resist capturing one of her turgid nipples into his mouth, suckling lightly, then harder, driving Grace to the same wildness as him. Her juices flowed freely against him as she moved even more demandingly against his hardness.

'I do not want to hurt you, Grace—'

'Oh, my love, you could never hurt me by loving me!' she assured him breathlessly. Her gaze once more locked with his, and she was the one to reach down between them and guide him slowly, with agonising sweetness, inside her moist, welcoming sheath.

Fire.

Pure molten fire.

Engulfing Lucian.

Possessing him.

'Now, Lucian!' she groaned achingly. 'Take me *now,* my love!'

Lucian held her tightly to him as with one powerful surge his pulsing hardness impaled her, breathing hard as he rested there, to allow Grace to become accustomed to the invasion. Oh, God, if he had hurt her—!

Grace flung her head back, her eyes glowing with happiness, her expression one of joyful triumph. 'It is beautiful, Lucian. Truly, truly beautiful.' Her voice caught emotionally. 'We are one, my love. There is no you. There is no me. There is only us!'

Lucian's arms tightened about her. 'Always and for ever, my love!'

'Always and for ever,' Grace vowed breathlessly, before Lucian's mouth once more claimed hers and he began to stroke inside her, slowly and then with ever-increasing urgency, until a fire, a pleasure, was building inside Grace unlike anything she had ever known before.

'Lucian…?' She groaned achingly as she felt her release building in intensity.

'I will join you this time, my love,' he encouraged heatedly. 'I promise you I will join you.'

Grace felt the heat of his seed pumping inside her as her own release quivered and shook through the whole of her body, and that release was intensified as Lucian surged fiercely inside her. Their pleasure seemed never-ending.

She would love this man always and for ever, Grace silently vowed minutes, hours later, as her head fell weakly against Lucian's shoulder. And she had no doubt that Lucian would love her in the same way.

Always and for ever.

From now on there would be only joy in Lucian's life. The joy of their deep and abiding love for each other.

* * * * *

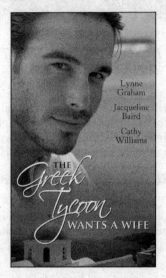

2 FREE BOOKS
AND A SURPRISE GIFT

We would like to take this opportunity to thank you for reading this Mills & Boon® book by offering you the chance to take TWO more specially selected titles from the Historical series absolutely FREE! We're also making this offer to introduce you to the benefits of the Mills & Boon® Book Club™—

- **FREE home delivery**
- **FREE gifts and competitions**
- **FREE monthly Newsletter**
- **Exclusive Mills & Boon Book Club offers**
- **Books available before they're in the shops**

Accepting these FREE books and gift places you under no obligation to buy, you may cancel at any time, even after receiving your free books. Simply complete your details below and return the entire page to the address below. You don't even need a stamp!

YES Please send me 2 free Historical books and a surprise gift. I understand that unless you hear from me, I will receive 4 superb new titles every month for just £3.79 each, postage and packing free. I am under no obligation to purchase any books and may cancel my subscription at any time. The free books and gift will be mine to keep in any case.

Ms/Mrs/Miss/Mr_____ initials _____

Surname _____
address _____
_____
_____ postcode _____

Send this whole page to: Mills & Boon Book Club, Free Book Offer, FREEPOST NAT 10298, Richmond, TW9 1BR